'Look at this!'

Jossie looked at h[...]
You're making an a[...]
thought you'd been [...]

Lord Trenchard, former Captain of Hussars, fresh from Waterloo, and proud of his reputation as a noted and dashing soldier in the field, rose to his full height, ready to give this impertinent brat a piece of his mind. Then as he gazed down at Jossie, still looking like the naughty little boy he had first thought her, he burst into laughter.

'You are...unique, Jossie Morley!' he gasped. 'I can honestly say I have never before met anyone quite like you.'

Jossie flushed painfully. 'Forgive me!'

She gazed at him anxiously and Ivo was touched at her instant contrition. What a curious mixture she was! She was rather like a neglected rose tree—thorny, undisciplined, with little sign of its potential beauty and sweetness... Ivo brought himself up short. What an absurd flight of fancy—his injury must be making him light-headed!

Dear Reader

The Duchess of Richmond's ball in Brussels, on June 15th 1815, was one of the great dramatic occasions in history. But what makes the ball noteworthy isn't the brilliance of the guest list—it is the poignancy of what happened in the three days that followed.

The young men who danced so light-heartedly in their uniforms of scarlet, blue, green and gold on the night of June 15th, dazzling the beau monde with their gaiety and charm, left the ballroom, some of them still in their dress uniforms, to ride straight into one of the hardest-fought battles in European history—the battle of Waterloo. By 18th June the Duke of Wellington had triumphed over Napoleon Bonaparte. But the cost in lives was huge, and many of those young men were never to return.

Firm friends Adam Calthorpe, Ivo Trenchard and their commanding officer Colonel Ancroft do survive the battlefield, to return to London Society's opulent drawing rooms. Three soldiers, skilled at war but not nearly as adept as they think when it comes to the ways of women. How will they fare? *Lord Calthorpe's Promise* introduced these soldier heroes and their exploits are continued in *Lord Trenchard's Choice*. I hope you enjoy reading about them.

Sylvia Andrew

LORD TRENCHARD'S CHOICE

Sylvia Andrew

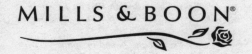

First published in Great Britain 2002
Harlequin Mills & Boon Limited,
Eton House, 18-24 Paradise Road, Richmond, Surrey TW9 1SR

© Sylvia Andrew 2002

ISBN 0 263 83494 8

Set in Times Roman 10½ on 12 pt.
04-0203-80326

Printed and bound in Spain
by Litografia Rosés S.A., Barcelona

Sylvia Andrew taught modern languages for a number of years, ultimately becoming vice-principal of a sixth-form college. She lives in Somerset with two cats, a dog, and a husband who has a very necessary sense of humour and a stern approach to punctuation. Sylvia has one daughter living in London, and they share a lively interest in the theatre. She describes herself as an 'unrepentant romantic'.

Chapter One

Brussels, June 1815

It had been another cloudless day in Brussels, and though the sun was now disappearing behind the Hotel de Ville the air was still warm. There had been more military activity than usual during the day, and rumours were beginning to fly round that the long-awaited confrontation between Napoleon and the Duke of Wellington was not far off. But neither the heat nor the rumours seemed to affect the two officers striding confidently across the Grand' Place in the direction of the Rue de la Blanchisserie.

It was clear to the informed where they were heading. Tonight the Duchess of Richmond was giving what promised to be the most brilliant ball of the season, and, far from being dressed for action in the field, the men crossing the Grand' Place were in full-dress uniform, one in scarlet, one in blue, with much silver and gold lace on their coats. They both wore beautifully fitting pantaloons and carried spotlessly white gloves. The more dashing of the two sported the fur-trimmed pelisse of a Hussar.

Though the good people of Brussels were well used to the sight of the military in their town, this pair attracted many an admiring glance, especially from the female half of the population. They were about the same age, both bronzed, both tall, their close-fitting uniforms revealing lithe, athletic figures, full of grace and power. One, a Major, was not handsome exactly, but there was something very attractive about him in spite of his undoubted air of command. But it was his companion, a Captain in the Hussars, who attracted most interest from the ladies. He was the better looking of the two, with classical features and hair that was so dark a brown as to be almost black. He, too, had an air of confident authority, but there were intriguing lines of laughter round his eyes and mouth, and, as the ladies who caught his eye noticed, he also had a delightful smile and lazily appreciative dark blue eyes.

The two men were talking with the ease of old friendship, and their laughter rang out as they left the square and turned into one of the small side streets which surrounded it.

'So your mind is made up, Adam? This campaign is to be your last?' The Hussar's voice was deep with a touch of a drawl about it. 'I can hardly believe it after all these years.'

Adam Calthorpe spoke quite firmly. 'You may do so, Ivo. I'm needed in England. The Calthorpe estate has been badly neglected for some years, and there's a lot to be done.'

Ivo Trenchard shook his head. 'All the same, it's difficult to imagine Adam Calthorpe of the Fighting Fifty-Second settling down to a quiet life in Somerset.'

'I assure you I shall enjoy it!'

'I suppose you intend to marry, too!' Ivo's voice was so pessimistic that Adam laughed again.

'Why shouldn't I? After all these years of racketing about Europe, what could be better than settling down to a time of quiet with a gentle, home-loving girl? No turmoil, no argument, just a comfortable, orderly life.'

'Well, I wish you luck—if that's what you really want.'

'Why don't you do the same? Once Napoleon's been beaten there's bound to be years of peace. Life in the Army won't be very interesting. What about finding a wife and settling down, too?'

Ivo Trenchard stopped and stared at his friend. 'Adam! Are you quite mad? You know my views on women!'

'I thought you liked them?'

'I do! But not to marry. That's the last thing I want from them!'

'But—'

Ivo ignored the interruption. 'Look, Adam, if you wish to marry, that's your affair. But it wouldn't do for me.'

'Why not?'

'My dear fellow, I hope you are not going to deny that I have some experience of the fair sex?'

'I wouldn't dream of denying it, Ivo,' his friend assured him. 'No one could.'

'Well then, over the years I have come to the sad conclusion that there are only two kinds of women— lively ones with whom one flirts, and boring ones with whom one doesn't. The boring ones make better wives, but they aren't exactly amusing.'

Adam was moved to protest. 'You have to be wrong,

Ivo! My chances of happiness seem pretty small if you're not.'

'I suppose there might be a few exceptions. Let's hope you find one, though it don't seem likely to me!'

'You underestimate me. But what's wrong with a lively wife?'

'Look around you! I'll wager last month's pay that for every beautiful woman happy to be in her husband's company at the ball tonight, there'll be five on the arm of an elderly bore whose only attraction is that he's rich!'

'You're being very harsh!'

'It's true! And Society encourages it. The whole object of a woman's existence is to marry well. The idea is drummed into them from their cradle, and they can be quite ruthless in their quest. Believe me, I know.' For a moment Ivo looked grim. Then he shrugged his shoulders and went on, 'But once a suitable husband is found and the knot safely tied, *then* they look to enjoy themselves. Take it from me, Adam. For most women marriage is a commercial proposition. Loyalty, love, respect play very small parts in it.'

Adam turned a troubled face to his friend. 'I haven't heard you talk like this before. You used not to be so cynical.'

'No? Well, if I am now I have my reasons…which we won't go into at this moment. I intend to enjoy myself tonight. You needn't look so concerned, Adam! I'm not entirely lost—you must have noticed that I leave happily married women severely alone, for example, though I can't say I've noticed many.'

'But the others you regard as fair game? You'll never find a wife that way.'

'You know, I'm really worried about you—you'll

soon be recommending that I turn my attentions to some insipid débutante with a view to matrimony. I swear, I'd rather die. No, I find women such as Arabella Lester, for example, or Heloise Leiken far more to my taste. Charming women, both of them, but I doubt they very often think of their husbands when they are with me.'

'I suppose Madame de Menkelen is another such?' Adam asked.

Ivo looked at him with a grin. 'You don't miss much, do you? Isabelle de Menkelen and I hardly know each other…yet.'

'I'm sure that will change—if Boney gives you time.'

'It doesn't matter if he doesn't,' said Ivo shrugging his shoulders. 'Making love is only one of the two exciting activities in this life. A good campaign is just as much fun.'

'Let's hope I'm more fortunate in my choice of a wife,' said Adam with a smile.

'Choice, choice! What do you mean by choice? Granted that a man is looking for happiness, not wealth, in his marriage, what sensible basis does he have for choosing his partner for life—for the *rest* of his life? No, no, Adam, the only real choice is between marrying or not marrying. Once a man has decided to take a wife, happiness is a matter of chance, not choice!'

'You're making a great deal out of nothing, Ivo. I refuse to believe it will be as hard as you say to find the sort of wife I want. I'm not looking for excitement or passionate love—just a peaceful, unproblematic existence with a reasonable woman.'

'You'll die of boredom within the month!'

'I don't think so.' He looked up at the tall mansion in front of them. 'I believe we're here. The music sounds excellent, but then the Richmonds always provide the best.'

As soon as they went in they were taken straight to a small room on the upper floor. Colonel Ancroft was waiting there for them.

'Good! Tom Payne and the others are already here. The team is complete.'

'Is there any more news, sir?' asked Adam.

'Yes, and it's bad, I'm afraid. The French crossed the Sambre in force early this morning. The Prussians have been under attack all day and it looks as if Charleroi will fall, if it hasn't already done so, indeed. The Army will be in action before dawn. As soon as the Duke and his aides have prepared the orders you'll be required to deliver them.'

'Are we to wait here with you, sir?' Ivo asked.

'On no account! You are to deploy yourselves among the Duchess's guests, doing your best to quell any anxieties. Wellington will arrive before long, and meanwhile he wishes the ball to continue and the guests to be kept reassured. We don't want any panic.' He dismissed them with a nod. 'I'll keep you informed. Off you go, and look as if you are enjoying yourselves!'

'Well, I don't know about you, Adam, but I *shall* enjoy myself!' said Lord Trenchard casting an experienced eye over the gaily dressed company gathered in the Duchess's ballroom. 'And if the ladies need reassuring, I'm the man to do it!'

An hour later Ivo bent over one of the loveliest women in the room and offered her his arm. 'I'm sorry you're feeling the heat, madame. May I suggest we take a turn in the Duchess's garden? It might be cooler outside, though I doubt it. Brussels must be due for a storm quite soon.'

The lady gave him a grateful look from huge brown eyes. 'I should like that, Lord Trenchard.'

As they made their way to the long windows, Ivo could see some of the more stiff-necked guests casting disapproving glances at him. They hadn't yet forgotten the scandal over his recent involvement with the Countess Leiken, but this didn't disturb him. Disapproval usually had the effect of making him behave even more outrageously, and Heloise Leiken had been worth every frown. Beautiful, witty, and enchantingly willing, she had kept him amused for weeks until her husband had appeared on the scene and borne her off to the family estate some miles out of Brussels. He wondered when Menkelen was due to return.

Once outside, Madame de Menkelen smiled up at him. 'I find this most agreeable,' she said.

As Ivo looked down at her his blood stirred. She really was *very* beautiful. 'So it is,' he replied, taking her hand and kissing it. 'Shall we walk to the end of the *allée*?'

The ensuing half-hour spent wandering through the warm, scented air was pleasurable, but Ivo was not unduly disappointed when Madame announced that she wished to return to the ballroom. More exciting things were afoot. He escorted her back, then excused himself and called in on Colonel Ancroft. There was nothing new there. He looked round for Adam, but couldn't see him. With a sigh Ivo joined the throng once again, but, though no one could have guessed it from his demeanour as he danced with one lady, reassured another and laughed a third out of her fears, his heart was not really in what he was doing. After a while he could tolerate it no longer and wandered into the garden again, this time alone. Adam was over on the other side, deep in conversation with Tom Payne, but Ivo avoided them both and stood in the shelter of a tree, smoking one of the small cigarillos he had brought from Spain. He needed to think. For whatever reason he was in a most unaccustomed state of dissatisfaction.

Was it the thought of the coming battle that was unsettling him? Or was it perhaps Adam's talk of marriage, of settling down?

Ivo allowed his mind to wander. For years he had lived life to the full, loving the comradeship, the danger, the exhilaration of fighting the French among the narrow clefts and valleys of the mountains along the Portuguese border, or under a sun beating down on the harsh Spanish landscape. He and Adam Calthorpe had grown close over the years in Spain, sharing the excitements, the narrow escapes, the adventures when the French got too near for comfort. And there had been adventures, too, of a different, more pleasant sort, when he had learned to appreciate the talents, if not the virtues, of the ladies of Spain and Portugal...

It had been much the same here in Belgium, except that the interval of inaction had been longer. Perhaps it had been too long, and now the endless round of concerts, rout parties, fête-champêtres and balls, which had given Brussels the most brilliant season it had ever seen, had suddenly lost its flavour. Even the pursuit of beauties like Isabelle de Menkelen had lost its zest.

Ivo shifted restlessly. Adam had accused him of being too cynical. Was he right? Perhaps. His experience with members of the fair sex had not led him to form a very high opinion of them. After his first youthful escapades he had learned to be cautious in his approach to eligible young ladies. There were one or two mantraps among

them, such as Charlotte Gurney, but most of them were
silly creatures, too easily smitten with a handsome face,
an ability to dance well, a talent for turning a pretty
compliment, especially when they came wrapped in a
uniform! On the whole, he preferred to seek out the company of sophisticated women of the world, who knew
the rules, taking pleasure, as he did, in light-hearted *affaires*, and making no demands other than to be amused.
He had been spoilt, of course, but most of his liaisons
ended amicably. His conscience was seldom troubled.
There were no broken hearts. Indeed, the more he
learned of the ladies of Society, the less inclined he was
to believe they had any hearts to lose. If that was being
cynical, then Adam was right.

But this was not what was causing this feeling of rest-
lessness....

Ivo grimaced. Why was he so reluctant to admit it,
even to himself? The real cause of his unrest was, of
course, the rift with his father. They had had their dif-
ferences in the past, but this would be the first time he
had ever gone into battle while they were still so completely estranged. Five months. Five months since they
had spoken to each other in anything like amity. For all
the distractions of Brussels the memory of that cata-
strophic day in January was still strong. And the prospect
of the battle, the possibility that he might not survive,
had revived his regret, his bitter sense of injustice. Why
had his father not believed him?

A skirl of bagpipes came from the ballroom as men
of the Highland regiments came in to entertain the Duchess's guests. But Ivo didn't hear them. The garden, the
music, the ball, faded away as he re-lived the events of
the past five months, starting with a fateful day at the
beginning of January. Who could have imagined that a

harmless visit to an old servant in the neighbouring village would have such disastrous consequences…?

Sudiham Castle, January 1815

Ivo Trenchard cut down the dead bracken and brambles which were blocking his path and swore. It had seemed a good idea to take the short cut back to Sudiham through the woods, but somewhere or other he had missed the way and now he was having to fight through thick undergrowth to the drive which led to the house. He shouldn't have stayed so long with old Ben, but it had been impossible to get away sooner. Ben was now bedridden and loved to talk of his time as head groom at Sudiham, of teaching Ivo to ride when he was barely big enough to sit on a horse. But now, unless Ivo managed to find his way soon through this damned wood, he would be late for the game of billiards he had promised his father.

He was frowning as he hacked at a particularly vicious branch. It was time he went back to London. Christmas had been enjoyable, but five weeks of Lord Veryan's company was enough. Much as he loved his father, he had forgotten how autocratic the old fellow could be. Their life together had been a succession of arguments ever since Ivo had been old enough to hold an opinion of his own. He had survived a good few battles in his time, culminating in one that lasted for weeks when he insisted on joining the Army. He had never regretted it. The Army had been good to him, and life at home would undoubtedly have become unbearable. He wondered how Peregrine, his younger brother, had stood it for so long. But then Perry was different. Perry hated scenes, and would always give in rather than risk his father's displeasure.

Lord Veryan's latest whim, that Ivo should now sell out of the Army and marry Charlotte Gurney, was absurd, but the notion had been pursued with an insistence which Ivo found irritating. There were undoubtedly advantages in such a match from his father's point of view. Sir George Gurney was his oldest friend, and Charlotte was Gurney's only child. And the closer tie that marriage to Ivo would bring was not the only consideration. Though not exactly wealthy, the Gurneys owned some of the best farmland in the district. The Gurney heiress would bring many rich pastures into Sudiham's domain.

Charlotte was pretty enough, if you liked rosy cheeks and prominent blue eyes, but her manners and behaviour filled Ivo with disgust. A well-developed girl of eighteen, she had already made it embarrassingly plain that she was more than ready to marry him. Ivo had been forced to explain to her, in a very difficult fifteen minutes, that there was no question of his doing what she and his father wished. The ensuing tantrum had revealed a side to Miss Gurney's character which had exceeded his worst expectations. Ivo shuddered now at the memory...

He hacked at one more branch and saw that he had at last reached one of the rides which led through the wood to the back of Sudiham. Ahead of him was a rundown cottage, which he remembered from his earlier days. He would be home in half an hour. But as he drew close he stopped. The cottage had been uninhabited for years, but the flickering light of a fire was coming through the window. A tramp? A gipsy? Ben had said there were a few about. He slowly drew nearer. 'Is anyone there?' he called.

There were sounds of frantic activity inside. Ivo strode up to the door, and gave it a push. It was locked. Now seriously worried, he put his shoulder to it and after a few heaves it gave way. He burst in. The cottage was a primitive affair, with one main room and a small kitchen built out at the back. The windows were filthy, and little daylight penetrated the room. But a fire was burning merrily enough in the hearth, on the floor were several cushions, and, to his amazement, Charlotte Gurney was standing half-hidden in the doorway leading to the kitchen. She must have been startled at his sudden entry, but she was not, as he would have expected, looking frightened... Guilty, perhaps, but not frightened. Her hat was on the floor beside her and she was clutching her cape together. She looked poised for flight.

'Charlotte!' Ivo exclaimed. 'What the devil are you doing here?'

'I...I...' She looked quickly into the kitchen, then shut the door, picked up her hat, and came reluctantly forward. Then she gave him a brilliant smile and heaved an exaggerated sigh of relief. 'Oh, I had such a fright!' she said. 'I thought I heard someone in the kitchen, but there's no one there. And then you burst in... I'm so glad it's you, Ivo. I was sure you were a robber or a thief. I was quite prepared to be murdered!' She gave a nervous little laugh.

'But why are you here? This is no place for you!'

'I know.'

'So what are you doing?'

'Er... The thing is...the thing is, Ivo I...was out for a ride, as a matter of fact, and...and my horse bolted. I managed to land safely, but I didn't know where I was...until I found this cottage. Then it started to rain, so...so I took shelter inside.'

'And you lit a fire?'

'The fire? Oh…yes! Yes! I was cold.'

What a liar Charlotte Gurney was, thought Ivo dispassionately. 'What were you going to do if I hadn't come?'

Her eyes opened wide. 'Once I was warm again I was going to walk to Sudiham, of course! What else could I do?'

'And your groom? Why isn't he here?'

'He…he went after the horse. I expect he's still looking for her.' She drew herself up, and demanded defiantly, 'Ivo, why are you asking me all these questions? Don't you believe me?'

Ivo was quite certain that Charlotte Gurney was lying her pretty head off, but he wasn't prepared to enter into an argument. The sooner he could extricate himself from this potentially dangerous situation the better. However, he had to see that the girl got home safely.

'Put your hat on,' he said. 'And fasten your cape properly. It's cold outside. I'll escort you to Sudiham, and get you taken home in the carriage.'

'Oh, thank you!' she said, as she did as he had told her. 'Whatever would I have done without you?'

Ivo didn't bother to reply to this, but said briefly, 'Sit down there on the window seat while I make certain the fire is out before we leave. You can hold my coat.' He passed his coat to her and started to rake out the hearth.

Before he had finished, however, sounds of a fresh arrival came from outside.

He got up and went to the door, and his heart sank when he saw his father and Sir George Gurney just pulling up their horses outside. They dismounted, then turned and looked at him in astonishment.

'Ivo!' exclaimed his father. 'I thought you'd be at

home. I was sure I was going to be late for our game! What are you doing here? In your shirtsleeves, too! The cottage has been deserted for years—what the devil is going on?'

'Damme, I'll swear he's got a girl in there, Rupert!' said Sir George with a laugh. 'The young dog! Let's have a look at her, Ivo! Is she pretty?'

'No!' said Ivo desperately. 'You're wrong! I...I just...saw firelight through the window, and came to investigate. Some tramp must have spent the night here. I took my coat off because I was working to damp down the fire.'

A crash came from inside the cottage. The two older men shook their heads at Ivo and laughed again. 'Brave try, my boy! Come on! Let's see this beauty!'

Ivo faced the inevitable. He shrugged his shoulders and stood aside as they pushed their way past him into the cottage. He had done his best to protect Charlotte from her father's anger, but he was not going to lie for her. He stood in silence as they stopped short in the doorway. They gazed at Charlotte in horror.

'Charlotte! What the—what's this?' There was a short silence while Sir George gave the room a swift, all-seeing glance, then he turned back to Ivo, his face purple with rage. 'You *damned* scoundrel, sir! You *villain*!'

'What the devil do you mean, Sir George? What have I d—?' Ivo took a step forward, then broke off as Charlotte came into view. When he had last seen her she was putting on her hat and fastening her cape. But now both were on the floor. Her hair was dishevelled, and she was half-turned away from them, apparently buttoning up her dress. He turned to his father.

'Don't believe what you see, sir!' he said angrily. 'I found her here only a few minutes ago. Just before you came she was fully dressed and ready for me to escort her to Sudiham. She's done this deliberately. *Don't let her fool you!*'

'*What?*' roared Sir George. 'Can I believe my ears? You *coward*, sir! You damned ungentlemanly *coward*! Do you hope to defend yourself with a tale like that? To save your own skin at the expense of my daughter? You're a disgrace to your name, sir! A *disgrace*!'

'You'll soon eat those words, Sir George!' Ivo turned to Charlotte and said forcibly, 'Tell them, Charlotte! Tell them the truth! I only came in to look at the fire. I found you here alone less than ten minutes ago!'

The girl had been watching the exchanges between Ivo and her father in silence, but now she gave a cry and clutched the window frame. 'It's no use, Ivo,' she cried. 'Don't you see? We are discovered!'

'Stop talking such theatrical rubbish, you little vixen, and tell the truth!'

'Oh, how could you?' she exclaimed with emotion. 'How could you say such things to me, call me such names! I am telling the truth, you cannot deny it! Oh…oh…oh, I thought you loved me! But I see it all now—you think as little of me as you do the rest of your amours!' She burst into tears and ran to her father. 'Oh, Papa, forgive me!' she cried. 'You must forgive me! I knew I was doing wrong, but I loved him so much! He pressed me so hard to meet him here and in the end I gave in. I've been so wicked, Papa! But I never thought he would cast me aside so quickly… Oh, how cruelly I am being punished! Oh, Papa!' She collapsed into her father's arms.

'She's fainted! The poor child! You see to her, Gurney, while I send one of the grooms for help. Take my coat,' said Lord Veryan.

'Charlotte already has mine,' said Ivo. 'I gave it to her to hold when I tackled the fire.'

Lord Veryan looked disgusted. He went over and handed his own coat to Sir George, who tenderly arranged it over Charlotte on the window seat. Then Lord Veryan picked up Ivo's coat, which had fallen to the floor, and threw it at his son. 'Take it!' he said harshly. 'The poor girl doesn't need your coat. What she needs from you is a little honesty. And amends! Honourable amends!'

Ivo abandoned his attempts to convince anyone, and leant against the wall, arms folded, observing Charlotte's performance with cynical appreciation. She may not be honest, but by God she was quick! And ruthless. She was making a lot of capital out of this little escapade. There might perhaps be a touch of revenge in it for his frank rejection of her a few weeks ago, but there was more to it than that. Charlotte was playing for higher stakes—if she couldn't *tempt* the son of the richest man in the neighbourhood to marry her, then she would try to see that he was *forced* into it. He was damned if he would let her succeed, but he foresaw a highly unpleasant time ahead of him.

Lord Veryan gave his son another basilisk stare, then went out. He called the groom over, told him there had been an accident and sent him to fetch a carriage from Sudiham as quickly as possible. As he came back in, he said to Ivo, 'You needn't think you are getting away with this, sir. We shall discuss your behaviour when that poor girl is safely bestowed. Then will be the time to decide what is to be done.'

'It's clear what is to be done!' shouted Sir George. 'The villain must marry her!'

Ivo was pale, but showed no other signs of disturbance. He ignored Sir George and said steadily to his father, 'I shall be at your service whenever you are ready, Father, but I have nothing to add to what I've already told you.' With that he turned to go.

Charlotte's eyes fluttered open. She tried to struggle to her feet, but fell back with a little cry. Stretching out her hand in a pathetic gesture, she whispered, 'Don't leave me, Ivo! Not like this! Not after all the things you said to me... What we have been to each other...' Her eyes closed again.

Sir George looked over his daughter's head at Ivo. 'I'll horsewhip you for this, Trenchard, by God I will!' he said fiercely. 'You've played your games around the neighbourhood for years, but you're not going to seduce *my* daughter without paying for it!'

'I did not seduce your daughter, Sir George,' Ivo said, somewhat white around the lips, but still steady.

Lord Veryan erupted into rage. 'That's *enough*, sir!' he shouted. 'I refuse to listen to any more of your lies! It's clear what has been going on, and I'll make you marry the girl, if it's the last thing I do!'

It had been impossible for Ivo to stay at Sudiham after the scene in the cottage. Though he swore he was innocent he was simply not believed. His past reputation in the neighbourhood for success with the ladies now served him ill. When Charlotte 'recovered' enough to talk, she stuck to her story, swearing that Ivo had persuaded her to meet him by promising to marry her. The two fathers ignored the fact that Ivo's light-hearted flirtations in the past had been conducted largely in the open, and never with the young daughters of decent families. They preferred instead to believe every syllable uttered by a sobbing Charlotte.

However, in spite of the fierce pressure put on him, Ivo categorically refused to marry the girl. He repeated his story and swore it was the truth—he had visited Ben, lost his way, and had ended up investigating the light of a fire inside the empty cottage. But he had to agree that there had been no sign of anyone else. He could not blame them for refusing to believe the tale of a bolting horse and a search for shelter from the rain. He hadn't believed it himself—especially after the horse was found neatly tethered in the trees behind the house. No drop of rain had fallen that morning, either. And who had lit the fire? Not Charlotte.

Charlotte Gurney had obviously arranged to meet someone at that cottage, and both fathers were convinced that this was Ivo. He was tried and condemned by the two of them as a dishonourable liar who had shamelessly seduced the daughter of his father's oldest friend, and then disowned her.

So Lord Veryan lost both his old friend and his elder son on the same day. In the face of Ivo's refusal to 'do the right thing', Sir George rode away from Sudiham, swearing he would never enter its gates again. If he hadn't been desperate to save his daughter's reputation, he would have denounced Ivo as a villain to the world at large.

As soon as he had gone, Lord Veryan, nearly speechless with rage and humiliation, banished Ivo from Sudiham, forbidding him to return until he was prepared to confess the truth, and make suitable amends.

Ivo was not surprised at Charlotte Gurney's behaviour. He had known that women, even a girl as young as Charlotte, could be unscrupulous in their pursuit of profitable marriages, and he would have said himself that her manipulation of the evidence against him was nothing less than brilliant.

But he was deeply, bitterly, resentful that his father, whom he loved, who had brought him up to be honourable and truthful, who in spite of their many disagreements had apparently always admired and respected his son, had so easily believed her lies. He had left Sudiham immediately, suffering from a severe attack of injured pride and outrage at his father's lack of faith.

Then in March news came of Napoleon's escape from Elba, and war seemed inevitable. Ivo knew that he would soon be recalled for duty. He had swallowed resentment and pride, and decided to seek reconciliation with his father. But when he arrived, far from giving him an opportunity to make his peace, Lord Veryan still refused to see him, not even allowing him to set foot in his home.

Shocked, sick and angry, Ivo had decided to seek temporary lodging with his aunt, Lady Frances Danby, who lived some fifteen miles from Sudiham in a village called Lyne St Michael. On the way he spent a miserable night at an inn, eating little and attempting to drown his sorrows in particularly vile brandy. He woke up the next morning with a massive hangover, almost wishing he had died in the night. The inn was no place to linger, so he set off doggedly, every movement a penance, on the road to Lyne. At some point he must have left the high road by mistake, and was forced to follow a bridle path that seemed to lead in the right direction. The path was unfrequented and for a while Ivo rode along peacefully enough, almost grateful that he had left the noise of the high road behind him. But then misfortune struck again.

His horse cast a shoe about three-quarters of the way along the path.

Ivo cursed the day he was born, dismounted gingerly and tied the animal to a tree while he considered the situation. The bridle path followed the contour of a fairly steep slope, and below him he could hear the sound of running water. The wish to cool his aching head was overpowering and step by step, with frequent pauses for recuperation, he slowly made his way down...

Chapter Two

Lyne St Michael, March 1815

The stream splashed and sparkled in the spring sunshine, and as Ivo approached the dancing light dazzled him. He could hardly believe his eyes when he saw a superb horse standing on a patch of grass nearby, a bay, with glossy coat and powerful flanks. A thoroughbred if ever he saw one. Amazed, he slowly drew near. It was saddled, but there was no sign of a rider. Had he been thrown? The horse seemed calm enough, but looked as if it would have plenty of spirit if roused. He stretched out a hand…

'You leave him alone, do you hear? Move away from my horse!'

The voice rang out, high and clear. Ivo winced as the sound sent his head throbbing again, and slowly turned. The next moment headache, heartache, everything was forgotten as he stared into the muzzle of a pistol, which was pointing directly at his head, not ten paces away. It was in the hands of a boy who couldn't be more than eleven or twelve. Ivo shuddered as a chill ran down his spine. Guns in the hands of children could be fatal, and this boy looked angry enough to shoot him.

'You scum!' the boy went on, without moving. 'I suppose you meant to sell Star at Taunton, along with all the others you've stolen.'

Ivo found his voice. 'You're making a mistake,' he said, taking a step to the side. The pistol followed him inexorably. He swallowed. 'I'm no horse thief.'

'What were you doing, then?' asked the boy, clearly not believing him.

'I…I saw the horse. I wondered if its rider was…was lost,' Ivo said. This sounded feeble, even to him. What the devil was wrong with him? He cleared his throat and tried a charming smile. 'Forgive me for asking,' he said, 'but… are you used to guns? They're chancy things—especially your sort. You realise that if you fired it you might well injure Star? As well as me.'

Unimpressed by the charm, the boy nodded. 'You're right!' he said. 'Move over!'

'Well, no, I won't do that,' said Ivo apologetically. 'Staying put seems to be my best chance of survival at the moment. Why don't you put that thing down? I'm not a thief, I assure you. You could even consider me respectable, though I know I don't look it at the moment. My name is Trenchard, and I'm on my way to visit Lady Frances Danby. I'm her nephew.'

'Lady Frances!' Disconcerted, the boy took a step back, caught his heel in the root of one of the trees and stumbled. As he struggled to keep his balance the gun went off. For a moment all was confusion as the horse reared and bolted, and the boy staggered, then fell. Ivo, relieved to find himself unharmed, leapt forward. He snatched up the pistol and threw it out of reach. Then he knelt down by the boy.

'Are you all right?' he asked.

'Of all the stupid, bone-headed things to do…' said the boy in disgust as he sat up. 'Yes, I'm all right. I never really meant to shoot, you know. I just wanted to frighten you.'

'Believe me, you did, young man,' said Ivo grimly. 'You frightened me half to death. And now I'm going to give you your just deserts.' He rose, took hold of the boy's collar and hauled him up. 'Bend over!'

'No! You can't! You mustn't!' In a panic the boy broke loose, and took off. Incensed, Ivo forgot his bad head and gave chase. He caught the young imp before he had gone very far and brought him down, but even then the boy didn't give up, wriggling like an eel and kicking hard in a frantic effort to escape. They rolled over the ground, the boy locked in Ivo's arms until he was held firmly down with Ivo sprawled on top of him. There was a moment's shocked silence, then the struggle was suddenly cut short. Ivo released his prisoner and leapt to his feet.

'You're a girl!' he exclaimed in horror.

The girl scrambled up and, hastily tucking in her shirt and fastening her jacket, she snapped out, 'What if I am? What does it matter whether I'm a boy or a girl?' She fastened the last button and then looked up at Ivo defiantly. 'Whatever *I* am, *you*, sir, are a bully and no gentleman, to take your temper out on someone so much smaller than yourself.'

'Of all the cool customers…!' Ivo was practically speechless with shock and anger. 'You deserve worse than anything I could do to you! What the hell do you think you're doing, masquerading as a boy? It's bad enough that anyone of your size carries a pistol at all, but a *girl*!'

'Don't you talk like that! I can handle a gun better than any boy!' the girl flashed back.

'Oh, yes, I could see that,' said Ivo with heavy sarcasm. 'You're a real expert, a proper nonpareil! You do realise, I suppose, that you damned near killed one of us? Not to mention your horse.'

'Star! Oh goodness, Star!' The girl looked round frantically and then gave a piercing whistle, which did nothing to improve Ivo's pounding head. He watched in grim silence as the horse came slowly back into the clearing, and the girl wheedled it into coming to her. She tethered it to the tree nearby, then went over to pick up the pistol. Ivo pulled himself together and was there before her. He held it away from her.

'Oh, no! You can't have this again before I've checked it.'

'Give it to me!' She made a grab for it.

'I can see I'll have to do something about you, you little madam!' Ivo hauled her without ceremony over to the tree and used the remaining length of the tether to tie her to it. 'Stay there till I've finished!'

Ignoring her shouts of rage, he examined the gun. It was a beautifully made duelling pistol, slightly old-fashioned, but by no means a toy. Ivo wondered what on earth the child had been doing with it. He made sure it was safe, and then went back to the tree and released both girl and horse.

'Here!' He presented her with the gun.

She looked at him in surprise. 'I thought you were going to keep it!' she said.

'I was tempted. But I don't steal guns any more than I steal horses. You'd better take it back. I expect it's quite valuable. Your father might well want to know where his best pistol has gone.'

'It's not my father's. It's mine.'

'Really?'

'You needn't sound so sceptical. It *is* mine. And I do know how to use it. It's just that I was surprised. You're Lady Frances's nephew?'

'As I said, yes.'

'Danby Lodge is three miles from here. What are you doing off the road, roaming over our land?'

Ivo realised with amazement that this impertinent chit was actually cross-examining him! But he replied equably, 'My horse has cast a shoe. I left him up on the bridle path. Where's the nearest smithy?'

'Follow the path for another mile or so. It will bring you into the village. The smithy is at the near end of it. Hold Star while I mount, will you! He's still nervous.'

Ivo's sense of humour began to take hold. Amused at her imperious tone, he helped her to mount. Then as she clicked her tongue at the horse, and prepared to leave, he realised that he didn't know anything about her.

'Wait!' he called. 'Who are you? What are you doing carrying that pistol? Does your family know what you get up to?'

'You'll have to find that out for yourself, won't you? Bye!' She dug her heels in, and horse and girl disappeared at a fast trot.

Ivo watched her go. In spite of his condition he had a strong inclination to laugh. For years he had faced Napoleon's armies without a qualm. He had had some close shaves in his time, but never before had he been so afraid as he had been just a few minutes before. It had taken a chit less than half his age and much less than half his weight to put a genuine fear of death into him! And all in a quiet English valley within twenty miles of his home! What would the rest of the regiment say if they knew? He could hardly put forward a hang-over as a valid excuse.

When he told his aunt about the incident, she said amid much laughter, 'You've just met my goddaughter, Jossie. What a girl she is! Poor thing.'

'What do you mean? She looked happy enough to me.'

'Oh, she's happy enough. For the moment. But you're surely not suggesting that it's normal for a grown girl to be racketing about the countryside, dressed as a boy, threatening strangers with a gun, are you?'

'Well, no, not really. How has it come about?'

'She's the only child of a monstrously selfish father. When Gerard Morley didn't have the boy he wanted, he decided to bring Jossie up as a substitute son. It is a most unnatural life for a girl, but she adores him and spends most of her time and energy trying to be the boy he desired. I've done my best to help the girl, but there's not much I can do! Major Morley allows no one to interfere.'

'What about her mother? Has she nothing to say?'

Lady Frances shook her head. 'Lucinda Morley died not long after I left London and came to live here. I had known her parents for years, and was delighted when I was asked to be Jossie's godmother, but I can't claim to have done much for her. Her father and I have never liked one another. He believes I tried to put Lucinda off from marrying him, and he's right. I did. It's a pity I wasn't more successful. Now, of course, Jossie is growing up, but she has no idea how to behave. What sort of wife she'll make for Peter Radstock I cannot imagine.'

'Wife? She's just a child!'

'She is very nearly sixteen.'

'I would have thought her about twelve!'

'No, she's almost sixteen, and it won't be long before she is married. It's been known for years that she and Peter would be wed as soon as he is of age. The two estates neighbour one another.'

'Ah, I see!'

'You needn't talk in that odiously cynical tone, Ivo. It don't become you! And there isn't the slightest need for it. If it had been a marriage of convenience I would have done more to stop it. But Jossie and Peter have been inseparable ever since she could escape from her nurses to play with him. They would have no eyes for anyone else, I assure you. And marriage to Peter Radstock would at least mean that Jossie would be free of her father.'

She gave him a piercing look. 'But that's enough about Jossie for the moment. Tell me why you are so out of sorts. Is that pig-headed brother of mine the reason? I take it that you wouldn't be here if Rupert had seen sense at last?'

'What do you mean, Aunt Frances?'

She shook her head at him. 'You needn't try to keep me in the dark. I already knew about the quarrel with your father, but I've now learned the reason behind it.'

Ivo frowned. 'Who told you? Not my father.'

'He won't even hear your name mentioned! No, it was Perry.'

'Perry!' Ivo frowned. 'I am surprised. He ought not to have done it. The aim was to keep it—'

'In the family? Am I not family? But you needn't think ill of your brother—he didn't volunteer the information.'

'I don't suppose he did,' said Ivo with a slight smile.

'I could never keep anything from you myself, once you had made up your mind to know it.'

'Well, then, I guessed some of it and he told me the rest. As you know, I have never liked Charlotte Gurney. A sly little minx, if ever I saw one. So what has your father said or done now to make you so down-hearted?'

'Nothing. He still won't see me.'

She shook her head again. 'I can't account for it. I know that the evidence against you was pretty damning—'

'I didn't seduce Charlotte Gurney, Aunt Frances,' Ivo said in an even tone.

'Oh, I know that, my boy. You always had an eye for a pretty face, but you were never a liar. But why can't *Rupert* see that? He has always been obstinate, but this passes my understanding. *Why* won't he listen to you?' She shook her head in puzzlement. After a moment's reflection she asked, 'What about Perry? Can't *he* do anything? Did you manage to see *him*?'

'Perry met me at the door. He advised me to wait until he could have a word with my father. Then he came back to tell me that it was no use. Father refused even to see me.' Ivo got up, and his aunt eyed him anxiously as he got up and walked restlessly round the room. 'It's no use asking Perry to do anything, Aunt Frances. He would never tackle my father about any controversial matter, especially not one as explosive as this. No, his advice is to carry on playing a waiting game, to give my father more time.' Ivo uttered a harsh laugh. 'I told him that the way things were going in Europe there might not *be* any more time.'

'You think there'll be a fight?'

'Of course there will. The Allies can't let Boney escape from Elba and march around Europe, without doing something about it. They'll have to attack him. And it will be a fight to remember, Aunt Frances. Wellington against Napoleon.'

'We're not talking about a boxing match, Ivo!' Lady Frances said tartly. 'You might well get yourself killed!'

'Do you think my father would mind? Perry would make just as good a successor.'

'You know you don't mean that!' said Lady Frances severely. 'Rupert thinks the world of you. He just won't admit it at the moment. Perry is clever enough, but he hasn't half your character! You take care of yourself, Ivo! And when you come back—I say *when*, you notice—we must put a stop to this ridiculous matter...'

Brussels, June 1815

Sounds of cheering and loud applause brought Ivo back to the present and the garden of the Richmonds' house in Brussels. The Highlanders had finished their reels and strathspeys and were now marching out of the ballroom. Dancing would soon begin again.

Ivo threw away his cigarillo with a gesture of impatience. Nothing was more useless than regretting the past! He looked round. Adam and Tom Payne had vanished. They had probably gone inside to join the Colonel, and it was time he did the same. Unless he was very much mistaken, the present situation was about to change dramatically. This ball was likely to prove the last Brussels would see for some time. From what the Colonel had said, the French had already begun their attack just a few miles to the south.

But one thing was certain. If he survived the battle that would surely follow, he must make an even more determined effort to heal the breach with his father.

* * *

Not much more than twenty-four hours after Adam and Ivo had crossed the Grand' Place on their way to the Duchess of Richmond's ball, the French had taken the Allies by surprise and the Hussars had been required to cover Wellington's retreat from Quatre Bras. And the day after that, the final battle had been fought near the village of Waterloo. It had been fierce, long and bitter and in it Ivo had lost some of his best friends, including Tom Payne. Colonel Ancroft had been wounded, but survived and stayed with his men to the end. Adam and Ivo had escaped unscathed, apart from a number of cuts and scratches, but, along with most of their comrades, they had been left with a desire never to fight another such battle. Victory, when it had come, was welcome, but the cost had been almost too high.

Wellington had lost so many of his most experienced Staff Officers in the battle that those who had been left were expected to accompany their Commander-in-Chief to Paris. It would be almost three-quarters of a year before Ivo could get back to Somerset.

In the meantime he had written both to his father and to Lady Frances. There had been no response from Sudiham, but his aunt had kept him posted of events there.

'I have noticed before,' she wrote in one of her letters, *'that elderly gentlemen can get some kind of fixed maggot in their brain, and no one can persuade them that they are wrong. I have never known your father so immovable. He still absolutely refuses even to mention your name, and Perry tells me that any efforts he makes on your behalf only meet with what amounts to an apoplectic fit. But do not despair. Rupert will have to see reason sooner or later. It will not do for his heir to be so totally excluded from the estates. Perry does what he can, but he is, when all is said and done, merely a*

younger son. He always looks so miserable nowadays. I thought at one time he was interested in Charlotte Gurney, but she never visits Sudiham now, of course.

'*Jossie Morley's exploits continue to arouse disapproval, delight and pity in equal measure in the neighbourhood. It all depends on who is talking of her...*'

The letter continued, but it was the first paragraph that gave Ivo food for thought. His aunt might have a somewhat cavalier manner, but he would trust her judgement before that of many others. If she thought his brother had at one time been interested in Charlotte, then the probability was that it was true. Could the man Charlotte had gone to the cottage to meet have been *Perry*?

Ivo had never given the question of Charlotte's real lover much thought. For months he had deliberately put Sudiham and all its affairs out of his mind, and he was really not very interested in her amours once he had successfully fended off her father's demands to marry her. What had hurt was his own father's attitude. The rest of the world could have believed Charlotte Gurney's every word, condemned him to perdition and back, and he would not have given a damn...if only his father had trusted him. That was the pain he had attempted to forget in Brussels.

But now the excitements of the war and the consequent negotiations in Paris were finished with, and Ivo was back in London with time and leisure to think. His father's silence since he had been turned away from Sudiham the previous March, the fact that he had not written, even after Waterloo, was proof that the rift between them was too deep to be mended easily. Perhaps a straightforward reconciliation would never be possible? Hurtful though it was, Ivo's word was not enough. In the end Lord Veryan might have to be convinced of the truth by some other means.

Could Perry have been Charlotte's lover? The fact that he had run away would be in character. Peregrine had always run away when danger threatened. But he surely *couldn't* have stood by without saying a word when Ivo was so unjustly accused and punished... Perry was weak, but not vicious. On the other hand, unless Charlotte was enjoying an affair with a groom or a stable boy, who else could it have been?

Ivo at first dismissed his suspicions as unworthy. Though Perry was nearly six years younger, and first school, then Ivo's service abroad, had kept the brothers apart, they had got on as well as most. And in their childhood he had done quite a lot to protect Perry from the worst of their father's rages. Ivo reminded himself that Perry had certainly tried to help since his banishment from Sudiham... But the small, suspicious voice inside him pointed out that Perry's help had not been very effective. Indeed, if his aunt's letter was anything to go by, the situation was as bad now as it had been in the beginning—if not worse.

The small voice gradually got louder. In between returning to England, conducting his affairs in London, signing off from his regiment and enjoying life in the capital again, he found himself debating how to establish the truth. He was quite certain on one point. He would never again announce himself at Sudiham without preparing the ground beforehand. His aunt's house in Lyne St Michael was only fifteen miles from there. When he next went down to Somerset, he would stay with her at Danby Lodge, and take time to assess the situation before trying once again to see his father.

* * *

Ivo put away his unpleasant preoccupations for a while when Adam Calthorpe came to London for a few weeks in March. They spent a good many hours enjoying the clubs and amusements of the capital, and frequently visited Colonel Ancroft, who was convalescing with some Army friends. They talked of Adam's plans for Calthorpe, and at one point Ivo asked his friend whether he had yet found a suitable lady to be his 'pretty little wife'.

'Not yet, but it's early days,' said Adam.

'Er…did Tom Payne's sister like the silks you asked me to bring from Paris for her? Weren't you going to give them to her for Christmas?' asked Ivo casually.

'You needn't look like that, my dear fellow. Tom Payne's sister is as far from my ideal as it is possible to be!'

'I see. Didn't I hear that she and your mother had been in London with you just a week or two ago? And that she's at present living with your mother at Bridge House?'

'Yes, dammit! But you can blame my mother for that. She thinks Kate a wonderful girl. In fact, she has this ridiculous notion that Kate would make me an excellent wife. She's quite mad, of course!'

'Really?'

'Yes, really!' said Adam emphatically. 'The sooner I can see Kate Payne safely married to someone else the better. Look, why don't you spend a night with us in Bridge House on your way to Somerset? You can meet Kate and see for yourself what I mean. In fact, we could travel to Dorking together. I want to take a mare down with me…' Adam paused.

'Well?'

Looking slightly embarrassed Adam said, 'Well…it's

for Kate.' Then, as Ivo burst into laughter, he went on, 'Ivo! I've told you! Kate Payne is a headstrong termagant. She insists on riding a hulking great horse that belonged to Tom, and one day she will kill herself on it. I've been forced to look out for a more suitable mount for her, just to save her neck. And my conscience. After all, I did promise Tom I'd see she was safe. But there is no, *absolutely no*, significance in it! I tell you, all you have to do is to meet the girl—you'll soon see what I mean!'

They left London together and Ivo spent the night at Dorking with the Calthorpes as Adam had suggested. He found Kate Payne enchanting, a delightful exception to his view of women in general. In other circumstances he might have been tempted to seek a closer acquaintance with her. But he decided against it. For one thing he was not in the market for marriage, and Kate was not the sort of girl one would offer anything else. For another, he found himself in complete agreement with Mrs Calthorpe. Kate Payne would make the perfect wife for his friend, though perhaps not exactly the 'pretty little thing' that Adam had planned for!

Ivo set off for Somerset after his night at Bridge House with some reluctance. For the past few months he had managed to put the situation at Sudiham to the back of his mind, but now he must face it. He desperately hoped that his suspicions of Perry were unjust. If Charlotte Gurney's lover did turn out to be his younger brother, then the problem was even trickier than he had ever imagined.

Chapter Three

Somerset, 1816

Lady Frances gave Ivo a warm welcome, but she had little to offer him by way of comfort. She had been making a few enquiries of her own, but, though her circle of acquaintances in the county was vast and her gift for gathering information considerable, she had not learned anything to help him. Lord Veryan, who had disowned his own son on Charlotte Gurney's behalf, would have been astonished at what his neighbours thought of her. More than a few were privately of the opinion that the girl was sly, if not downright deceitful. But even so there was no hint of any lover. Charlotte's name was not even speculatively coupled with any young man in the district.

It was no surprise to Ivo when, with her usual bluntness, Lady Frances said, 'It's Perry, isn't it? It has to be. There isn't anyone else.'

Ivo nodded. 'I'm afraid so,' he said with a sigh.

'So what are you going to do about it?'

'I wish I knew!'

'I should have thought it was obvious. You must tax

Peregrine with it, and if he is the man, then Rupert should know!'

'I'm not the one to tell my father, Aunt Frances. And nor are you.'

'But, Ivo—'

'Peregrine will probably tell me the truth if I challenge him, but I can't see him confessing it to my father. He's too frightened of him.'

'He's a grown man!'

'You think that makes a difference?' Ivo got up and walked restlessly round the room. 'Perry suffered a lot when he was younger. He was such a delicate, nervous child—'

'Your mama's baby. I know. And she was always far too protective of him.'

'Perhaps she was. That was certainly my father's view. He wanted both his sons to be robust young versions of himself. And when Mama died he was determined to toughen Perry up. He went about it in quite the wrong way, of course. Perry got so frightened of him that he would do anything, even lie and cheat, to avoid his displeasure! I often felt very sorry for my younger brother, Aunt Frances, and so would you have. I even sometimes took the blame for something Perry had done just to protect him. Father's wrath didn't frighten me— my shoulders were broad enough to take it. But I'm not sure now that I did Perry a service.'

'You didn't! Perry should have been made to face things long ago, before he caused any real harm. Now look what has happened!' She sat in silence for a moment, then she said, 'Ivo, if Perry was so in fear of Rupert, why did he never leave home?'

'I did once suggest to him that he should get away, as I did. The Army would never have done for him, but my father might have agreed to let him take over the management of our estate in Derbyshire. But Perry wouldn't even consider it, and now I think I know why.'

'Charlotte,' his aunt said.

'Yes. I believe he's been fond of her for a long time.' Ivo stopped and shook his head. 'He's a fool! Why didn't he make an offer for her? Sir George is...*was* one of my father's oldest friends. There was no need for the secrecy.'

'My dear boy, do be realistic! Perry is a younger son. Sir George is as hardheaded as the next man, and from what I've heard his daughter is just like him. I doubt very much that either of them would have considered your brother a suitable match—not for one moment. Certainly not while you were alive, and Perry unlikely to succeed to the title. And now that you have left the army and are back safe and sound, it's even less likely.'

Ivo thought for a moment. Then he said with determination, 'I can't betray Perry to my father. I won't!'

'Then what *are* you going to do? Remain an exile?'

Ivo looked at his aunt sombrely. There was another silence, then he said, 'You'll have to excuse me, I'm going out for a ride. I need to think.'

Lady Frances nodded sympathetically. Then she called after him, 'See if you can find Jossie Morley!'

'Jossie Morley? The girl with the gun? Why on earth should I do that?'

'She's a fascinating child, and I'd like you to know her better. This would be a good opportunity. Peter Radstock and his parents are spending several days in Bath, so Jossie will be on her own. Bring her back with you.'

'I hope she's improved since we last met.'

'She may have grown a little.' His aunt twinkled at him. 'Though I doubt enough in the right places. You

might still not be able to tell her at sight from a boy.
And she's as madcap as ever.'

Ivo sighed. 'Where shall I find her? At home?'

'Good Lord, no! Jossie is never in when she can be
out.'

'I rather wanted to be alone myself…'

'Try to see Jossie,' his aunt urged. 'I have a suspicion
that that child is going to need a friend or two soon.'

'What does that mean?'

'I just have a feeling… Never mind. Do your thinking,
then go and find Jossie.'

Ivo went back to the valley where he had encountered
Jossie Morley the year before. There was no sign of her
there, but he went down once again to the stream and
sat on a rock beside it. He could think here as well as
anywhere. It was a sheltered spot, and the spring sunshine was warm on his back. The burbling of the stream
provided a pleasant background to his musing…

But his thoughts were not agreeable. He couldn't see
Perry confessing anything at all to his father. Ivo sighed.
He would not betray Perry, whatever his aunt said. And,
in that case, his only hope, a forlorn one, was that Lord
Veryan should eventually see Charlotte in her true col-
ours for himself. How long would that take?

He sat for a few minutes longer, but then gradually
became aware of a dog's excited barking and the sound
of voices. His curiosity was aroused, and he went further
down the valley to investigate. As he had half-expected,
he found Jossie Morley. She was on her horse, swearing
at a villainous-looking gipsy who was standing just a
few feet away, holding a cudgel high in the air. At Jossie's side was a large hound, snarling and growling, its
lips drawn back to show wicked fangs. Even as Ivo

looked, Jossie gave the word and the dog leapt forward to attack. The gipsy hesitated, then dropped the cudgel and fled for his life into the woods behind him. The dog would have given enthusiastic chase, but when Jossie gave a short imperative whistle, he came back to sit down beside her, staring into the wood, every nerve alert. She jumped off the horse, then knelt down a few paces away. She didn't hear her dog's low growl, as Ivo approached. All her attention was on a fox which lay panting in front of her, its leg caught in the jaws of a cruel trap. She stretched out her hand…

'Don't do that!' exclaimed Ivo. 'Don't go near it!'

Jossie gave a startled cry, snatched up the cudgel and turned round, ready to defend herself. The dog stood up, bristling, but to Ivo's relief she recognised him.

'Oh! It's only you!' she said, dropping the cudgel and ordering the dog to lie down. She turned back to the fox again. 'I'll be careful,' she said. 'But I can't just leave him here. He'll die.'

'It'll die anyway,' said Ivo. 'Look at that leg. The kindest thing would be to put the animal out of its misery.'

'No! Some of them do survive, I've seen them. Besides, it's surely better for him to die in his own place, not cruelly held here.' She stretched out her hand to the trap.

Ivo took a stride forward and pushed the girl out of the way, not particularly gently. 'I said don't touch that animal!' he said sharply. 'It's mad with pain and fright, and quite certain to bite you. Here, let me see!'

Holding Jossie back with one hand he examined the trap, keeping well clear of the animal's frantically snapping jaws. The trap was a simple one, and the leg was not as severely damaged as he had first thought. He took

out his pocket knife, a dangerous-looking thing he had
acquired in Spain, and stretched out to release the fox.
Jossie leapt forward.

'Leave it alone! I've told you, you mustn't kill it!' she
cried and jerked his arm back. Ivo lost his balance and,
though he managed to spring the trap, he couldn't keep
his hand out of reach of the fox. The animal sank its
teeth into him, and then, as he shook it off with a curse,
it leapt away into the trees more nimbly than one would
have thought possible.

Ivo looked down at his hand, then regarded his companion. 'You don't give up, do you?' he said grimly. 'If
you can't shoot me, or bludgeon me, you'll poison me
instead. God knows what diseases that fox is carrying!'

'Pooh! That's not much! It's hardly broken the skin!
Go and bathe it in the stream and it'll be fine.'

'Only if you promise not to try to drown me,' said
Ivo sourly. He went to the stream and squatted beside
it. Holding out his hand, he went on, 'Look at this!
Hardly broken the skin, you say? I'm covered in blood,
dammit!' He dipped his hand in the water and gave a
gasp at its unexpected iciness. Jossie regarded him disparagingly.

'You're making an awful fuss about nothing. I thought
you'd been in the Army?'

Lord Trenchard, former Captain of Hussars, survivor
of so many campaigns that he had given up counting,
fresh from Waterloo, and proud of his reputation as a
noted and dashing soldier in the field, rose to his full
height, ready to give this impertinent brat a piece of his
mind. Then, as he gazed down at the scornful figure
before him, still looking like the naughty little boy he
had first thought her, the absurdity of the situation struck
him, and he burst into laughter.

'You are…unique, Jossie Morley,' he gasped. 'I can honestly say I have never before met anyone quite like you.' He wrapped his handkerchief round his hand and added, 'I still think I had better get this hand cleaned up properly, however. Are you coming?'

'Who told you my name?' she asked, not moving.

'My aunt. She likes you, I cannot imagine why. She asked me to bring you back to visit her. Can you come?'

'Yes, I'd like to. Peter's gone to Bath with his family and I'm on my own. I've nothing else to do.'

'And that might have been better put,' said Ivo. 'Has no one ever taught you any manners?' The pain in his hand was now intense, and he perhaps spoke more sharply than he intended. She flushed painfully and bit her lip.

'Oh, I didn't mean… Yes, it must have sounded very rude. Forgive me! I'm very pleased your aunt has asked me.' She gazed at him anxiously, and Ivo nodded, touched at her instant contrition. What a curious mixture the girl was! One minute an ill-mannered brat, dressed in boy's clothes and behaving like one, the next a sensitive young girl, ashamed of her clumsiness. It was obvious that no one who was interested in her future position in society had ever paid Jossie Morley much attention. She was entirely without artifice, completely untrained, rather like a neglected rose tree—thorny, undisciplined, with little sign of its potential beauty and sweetness… Ivo brought himself up short. What an absurd flight of fancy! The bite from the fox must be making him light-headed. 'Good,' he said. 'My horse is on the bridle path. Come on.'

She collected her horse and they walked up the hill together. She went on, 'I'm sorry about what I said. I *like* Lady Frances, I really do! It's just…well, I was a bit miserable. I suppose I'd hoped the Radstocks would take me with them to Bath. After all, I'll be one of the family once Peter comes of age, and that's only just over a year away. They ought to have taken me, I think. Don't you?'

Ivo imagined the effect Jossie Morley would have on the staid citizens of Bath and fully sympathised with Lady Radstock's failure to invite her. However, Jossie looked so cast down that he said, 'You would have liked to go? I'm surprised—you don't strike me as a girl who is interested in town life.'

'I'm not! But Lady Radstock is always saying that she wished I was…more ladylike. And how can I learn if I never go anywhere?'

Ivo didn't reply. They had reached the bridle path and, after helping Jossie up, he concentrated on mounting his own horse without revealing the trouble his hand was giving him. He was damned if he would expose himself to any more accusations of weakness!

They rode in silence for a while. Then, when Ivo had got his breath back, he said, 'So it's all fixed, is it? You're to marry this Radstock fellow and live happily ever after?'

'Oh, yes!' said Jossie, completely unconscious of any irony in Ivo's voice. 'That's what we've always said we would do. I can't imagine a future without Peter—and he feels exactly the same.' She turned to him, her face full of animation. 'I'm so lucky, Lord Trenchard. I've had the best of fathers, and later I shall have the best of husbands.'

'I shall look forward to meeting this Peter of yours,' said Ivo.

'Oh, you'd like him!' said Jossie. 'Everyone does. It's funny—we get into all the same scrapes together, but people just laugh at Peter, whereas they look prune-faced at me. It's because I'm really a girl, I suppose.'

'Yet you do your best not to look like one?'

'That's because of Papa. I'm his only child and he wanted a boy. I was a great disappointment to him. I still am, I suppose, though I do my best to behave the way he wants. Don't tell him about that fox, will you? He regards them as pests—and they are! He'd have killed it. He would be very annoyed with me for being so weak.' She sighed. 'There are some things I just cannot bring myself to do, even to please Papa!'

Ivo found he was beginning to dislike the girl's 'best of fathers', but he didn't comment. Instead he said, 'Tell me why you're called Jossie. It's a curious name for a girl.'

'Why do you go on so about my being a girl? I wish you would not—I don't like it! Jossie is short for Joscelin, and yes, it's a boy's name. It belonged to one of Papa's ancestors, Joscelin de Morlaix. The boys in Papa's family have been called after him for hundreds of years. And I'm the last of the Morleys. That's…that's why I'm such a disappointment. And now I'd like not to say any more about it, if you don't mind.'

She spoke with determination, and they rode on in silence. Ivo looked at her. She must have grown a little in the year since they had last met, but it was still difficult to imagine her as a girl, and even more difficult to think of her as nearly seventeen. She still had the straight gaze of a child, and her voice remained uncompromisingly direct. At the moment her face was half-hidden from him by a tousle of short dark curls, rather like those of the gipsy she had chased away a short while before. Indeed, altogether she had something of the air of a gipsy, though the breeches and jacket she wore were of

excellent cut and quality. Her horse too was a very handsome creature, but though he obviously had plenty of
spirit she had him well under control. There must be
more strength than Ivo would have thought in those slender wrists.

What sort of father was it who called his only daughter by a boy's name, dressed her in boy's clothing, had
apparently brought her up to be as like a boy as possible,
giving her a pistol, a powerful thoroughbred to ride and
a fearsome dog for company? What sort of father demanded that she disregard the gentler side of her nature
and was angry with her when she failed?

Ivo studied the girl. What he could see of her face
was as contradictory as the rest of her. There was a hint
of severity in her profile, with its straight nose, short,
disciplined upper lip and firm chin. But the line of her
jaw was delicately drawn and her lower lip full and vulnerable. The potential was there for great beauty. He
wondered what colour her eyes were…

'You're staring!' Jossie said. 'What's wrong?'

'Er…nothing,' said Ivo, most unusually at a loss for
words. 'I'm sorry. Shall we move a little faster? My aunt
will be expecting us.'

'Well, I don't see how she can be,' said Jossie. 'She
couldn't be sure you would find me as easily as you
did.'

Ivo drew a deep breath. 'No,' he said firmly. 'Are you
always as logical? But perhaps you should know that
she always has tea at four o'clock. Don't you want some
tea?'

'With muffins? Rather!' Jossie dug her heels in and
the bay moved into a trot. Ivo followed suit. He would
rather have died than mention that the jolting movement
was doing no good at all to his injured hand.

* * *

Lady Frances was delighted to see them both, but exclaimed when she saw Ivo's hand. As he removed the handkerchief they could see it was an angry red and very swollen.

'I shall send for Dr Hargreaves immediately!' she said. 'Jossie, go and tidy yourself up while I see to Lord Trenchard. How on earth did you do this, Ivo?'

Ivo's eyes met those of Jossie. He winked. 'A fox was quicker than I was,' he said. 'But it's nothing, really.'

'It looks awful,' said Jossie, gazing in horror at the mess of his hand. 'I'm sorry. I didn't realise…'

'Don't say another word! I'm near to tears as it is, and any sympathy from you would completely overset me!' said Ivo solemnly. 'We Hussars are babies at heart, you know.'

'Ivo! What on earth are you talking about?' said his aunt, looking bewildered. 'I think you must be delirious. Go and bathe that hand, while I send John Coachman for the surgeon.'

In the days that followed Ivo was hard put to it to maintain his sense of humour. The hand was badly infected and the fox's teeth had crushed two of the bones. It took all of Dr Hargreaves's skill to put it right. Fortunately Ivo's splendid physique served him well. The infection did not spread, and after a week the only serious cause of dissatisfaction was that he still had to keep it held up in a sling, unable to use it for anything strenuous. Boredom would have been his chief enemy but for the fact that Jossie was apparently suffering from a severe fit of conscience. That, combined with the Radstocks' decision to stay longer in Bath, meant that she spent a great deal of her time at Danby Lodge, doing her best to keep Ivo entertained during his convalescence. She demanded to hear about his campaigns in Spain and Portugal, and was eager to learn everything about Wellington. She made him draw out a plan of the field at Waterloo, and was scornful when he couldn't remember every detail.

'I thought it was the Ninety-Fifth who were in the sandpit by La Haye Sainte?' she said once. 'And how could Grouchy have been over there? He was well to the east. You mean Ney, don't you? Really Ivo, I'd have thought you'd know that!'

'I do, I do! I simply got confused. After all, I was just fighting in the damned battle, not designing it for posterity! And who gave you leave to call me Ivo?'

'Well, I can't keep on calling you Lord Trenchard. It's too stuffy. Especially when you owe me so much money.'

Ivo had seldom found himself laughing more often. Jossie was a constant source of amusement, sharp as a pin, full of fun and imagination and always ready with her own particular, original point of view. Her father, probably for his own amusement, had taught her to play piquet and several other games of chance and she was a surprisingly accomplished gamester. They played by the hour. Ivo himself was no mean player, but, at the moment, he was in her debt to the tune of four thousand three hundred and twenty-three guineas. Imaginary stakes, of course, but he still found it galling, and was as eager as any addict to win them back.

They played chess, too, and here Ivo came into his own. She had only played before with Peter Radstock, and was apparently unused to an opponent who thought more than a few moves ahead. Ivo enjoyed watching her as she hung over the board, a frown of concentration on her mobile face, biting her lower lip or touching the upper one with the tip of her tongue. He began to wait for the gleam in her eye when she thought she had him, the expression of disgust when she was caught out, or the crow of triumph when she succeeded. One thing was clear. Jossie Morley was keenly competitive, and a fast learner. The more they played, the greater the effort required to beat her. Ivo made the effort. In chess at least he was not going to be beaten by a mere child, however bright!

A child was how he thought of her. She was so unlike any female he had ever known, so direct, so without artifice, that he simply could not think of her as a young woman. She had a closer resemblance to some of the junior ensigns he had known in the army, except that she was quicker and bolder than any of them. And much, much more impudent. His wider experience, the fact that he was more than ten years older than she was, counted for nothing with Jossie Morley. She very quickly saw through any attempt to cozen or charm her and treated it with laughter or scorn. The way to win her respect was to out-think her at chess, or beat her at piquet, and the secret of holding her serious attention was not to pay compliments but to talk of his life in the Army. She listened eagerly to this, obviously storing up snippets of information with which to amuse her father.

This, of course, was why Jossie remained so immune to the charm which had made Ivo famous all over Europe. She had two idols, her father and Peter Radstock, and the rest of the world hardly existed except in relation to them. The contradictions in her nature were more evident in this than anywhere else, and Ivo found it almost incredible that a girl who was otherwise so sceptical should be so blindly, so uncritically partisan. Her chief aim in life seemed to be to earn her father's approval, to make up to him for the regrettable fact that she was a girl. Her chief happiness was to roam the countryside with Peter Radstock, behaving like the boy Major Morley had wanted. If her father was pleased with their escapades the rest of the county could disapprove to its heart's content, Jossie didn't care.

She was as insouciant about the future. She knew what it was to be, had known for as long as she could remember. She would marry Peter Radstock and live with him in the countryside they both knew so well. Ivo came to see that Jossie had a deep love and understanding of the land, its people, its wild life, its trees and plants. She had no desire to live anywhere else, to see anything of the world outside.

'London?' she replied in answer to a question he put to her. 'Of course I haven't seen London! Nor have I any desire to. I think I would suffocate in a great city such as that—no fresh air, no greenery, all those restrictions and artificialities. And what should I find to amuse me in London?'

'Jossie Morley, how can you possibly dismiss one of the great cities of the world with all its treasures, its beauties, in such a cavalier fashion? I never thought to find you such a narrow-minded little country bumpkin!'

Jossie jumped up, scattering the chess pieces over the floor. 'I'd rather be a country bumpkin than a…a pasteboard fashion plate, talking with a plum in its mouth, and thinking of nothing but the tying of a cravat, or the set of a sleeve! At least Peter and I are *real*, and we shall lead *real* lives!'

'Is that how you think of me?' asked Ivo in some amusement. 'A pasteboard fashion plate?'

'Oh, you're all right. I suppose it's because you've been in the Army. But you should see the young *gentle-*

men round here when they've spent a few weeks acquiring town bronze in the ''Village'' as they call it! Five minutes in their company and Peter and I can hardly speak for laughing! They are ridiculous with their huge collars and elaborate cravats. And the girls are worse, fluttering their fans and their eyelashes, mincing along in silly sandals and frilled skirts. Do you know, Ivo, some of the girls think themselves *failures* because they haven't acquired a Viscount or a Duke, or even just a rich man, in their first season? It wouldn't have mattered what he was like or how old he was—the important thing was to have captured someone eligible. How can they *bring* themselves to take part in such a cold-hearted arrangement? How can they contemplate sharing their lives with a man they have only met three or four times, someone whose only virtue is that he has a title, or wealth?'

Ivo nodded. Jossie's words were an uncanny echo of what he had often thought himself. She swept on, 'Perhaps I am a country bumpkin. If those are London values, then I prefer country ones. When I marry Peter I shall marry someone I have known all my life. I know him as well as I know myself. He and I are friends! We always have been and we always will be.'

'Do you...*love* him?' Ivo asked.

'Well, of course I do! Haven't I just been saying so?'

Ivo didn't answer. He wasn't sure what to say. Jossie's feelings for Peter were obviously deep, a part of her passionate love for her home, her land. They might well be enough for a long and happy marriage, and he sincerely hoped they would. But, though it might not seem so to her, friendship was far from being the whole story in matters of the heart. There was another, potentially more problematic, side to love, and he doubted that she was even aware it existed. What would happen when she encountered physical attraction, desire, the reality of marriage? How would that affect her feelings for Peter Radstock? Ivo took himself in hand. It was none of his business. In any case, how the devil could he even mention such matters to this unawakened child? It was out of the question.

Nevertheless, as time went on, he grew more concerned for her. Her vision of her future seemed to him to be dangerously unrealistic, more a child's view of life, a storybook world in which none of the characters changed or matured like real human beings, but carried on exactly the same forever. He knew neither of her idols as yet, except through what he had heard from his aunt and Jossie herself, but he doubted that any man in the world was worthy of such complete, such unquestioning admiration and devotion.

He saw no reason to change his mind when he did eventually make the acquaintance of the two men in Jossie's life.

Chapter Four

Jossie arrived one day at Danby Lodge in a gig. 'I must just take a piece of harness to the smith,' she said, 'and then I'll come back to fetch you.'

'To fetch us? Where?'

'Papa wishes to meet you.'

Ivo looked at the gig. 'There isn't room for all of us in that thing,' he said.

Jossie looked uncomfortable. 'Just the two of us. Papa didn't mention Lady Frances.'

Ivo frowned and began, 'In that case, I'm afraid—'

'Do go, Ivo!' urged his aunt. She turned to Jossie. 'Don't look so worried, Jossie. Lord Trenchard will come. You take whatever it is to the smith and call back here. I'll make sure he's ready.'

As soon as Jossie had driven off Ivo turned to his aunt, ready to argue. She laughed at him. 'You needn't say a word! I'm not at all offended, and I want you to go. Major Morley would never willingly invite me to see him. I've told you before, he and I are not exactly the best of friends.'

'Then why should I accept his somewhat peremptory summons?'

'For Jossie's sake. And because it would be an interesting experience. I find him a most unpleasant man, but
I suppose he has some excuse for it. He was a very able
soldier, until his career was cut short. Since then, his life
has held nothing but disappointments—in his own eyes,
at least.'

'What happened?'

'He was badly wounded years ago, and has been
something of an invalid ever since. Lucinda was expecting a baby at the time, and he hoped desperately that
it would be a boy. There…there wouldn't be any more
children. That's why it was such a bitter disappointment
when the child turned out to be a girl. He has a great
sense of family pride, and she is the last of the line.'

'I see. When did Mrs Morley die?'

'When Jossie was three. But if you're thinking that
she might have had a restraining effect on the Major,
then you're wrong. She would never have denied him
anything, and he is a self-indulgent autocrat. There, I've
been most unkind about one of my neighbours, and I
don't regret it a bit. I may be sorry for the man, but I
cannot forgive what he has done to Jossie…'

'The child seems happy enough.'

'She's not a child any more!' his aunt said impatiently. 'That's what worries me. The signs are that before very long she will turn into an intelligent and beautiful woman. She's bright enough already. How will she
feel when she wakes up to the fact that her two idols
have feet of clay?'

'I had already decided that they couldn't possibly be
as perfect as she thinks them—but feet of clay, Aunt
Frances? Aren't you being a touch harsh?'

'I shan't say any more. I've wrecked enough reputations for one day. Go and visit Major Morley and draw your own conclusions.'

When Ivo first met Jossie's father he was favourably surprised. The Major was sitting in a study furnished for comfort rather than style. Though he was surrounded by books and dogs, there was a sense of severe discipline and order in the room. A large fire was burning in the open fireplace, and on a table close to the Major's chair were a chess set, and a tray of drinks and glasses. The Major got up as Ivo approached and limped towards him.

'There you are, Trenchard! Come in, come in and sit down. I'm delighted to meet you. What'll you have? Jossie, give Lord Trenchard something to drink, there's a good fellow. Then lose yourself. Come back in half an hour.'

Jossie obediently, and expertly, poured out wine for Ivo and brandy for her father, then quietly withdrew, leaving the two men to themselves.

They surveyed each other. Major Morley was in his early fifties, but he was still a handsome man with carefully brushed iron-grey hair and spruce moustaches. His linen was spotlessly white, his coat of a military cut, and he wore pale buff breeches with boots polished to a high gloss. The hand holding the glass of brandy was well formed and well cared for. The Major was obviously a man who took pains with his appearance—unlike his daughter.

'So, Trenchard! Jossie tells me you fought at Waterloo? Cavalry. What was your regiment?'

'The Seventh Hussars, Major.'

'*Hussars!* What sort of soldier is that? New-fangled nonsense! There weren't any...*Hussars* in my day. We were happy to be called Dragoons, none of your fancy foreign names.'

'I fancy we both *fought* much the same, sir' said Ivo mildly. 'Cavalry tactics haven't changed all that much...'

'Tactics! I could tell you a thing or two about tactics. Why, in '97...'

Over the next twenty minutes Ivo changed his mind about Major Morley. His manner was civilised enough, but what he said proved him an opinionated bore, vain, unwilling to give credit to anyone else but himself. He had read the accounts of the battle of Waterloo, and had formed his own opinion of how it should have been fought. Ivo's version of the action was of no interest to him and he gave only grudging admiration to Wellington's performance.

'Arthur Wellesley made his name in India, of course. It was easy enough out there. And once you've got a reputation, those idiots at the Horse Guards think you can't go wrong!'

Ivo reminded his host of Wellington's many battles with the Horse Guards, not all of them ending in victory, and finished by saying firmly, 'He's a very great soldier, sir. His tactics against the French in the Peninsula were brilliant—and I doubt anyone else could have carried the day at Waterloo.'

He didn't convince the Major, who shook his head and said sourly, 'Well, I have my own view on that, but I won't argue with you. It's natural you would be prejudiced in his favour. What d'y think of Jossie?'

The sudden change of subject took Ivo by surprise. 'I...I like her.'

'Not after her y'self, are you?'

Ivo's voice was cold as he said, 'I regard Jossie as a delightful child. No more.'

'Don't stiffen up on me. You have a bit of a reputation, Trenchard. Just wanted to make sure it don't affect my family.'

Ivo suppressed a spurt of fury and said calmly, 'I am surprised you should think that possible, Major. Jossie might well one day be a very beautiful woman, but at the moment you have seen to it that she is too much of a boy to be in danger.'

In a voice of suppressed anger his host said, 'A boy! Ay, that's what she should have been, not a damned girl!'

Then, perhaps sensing Ivo's disapproval of this outburst, he added more calmly, 'Jossie's a splendid chap, a first-rate shot and up to as many tricks as any lad. But that's just what she ain't, dammit!'

'I think you could be proud of her, all the same,' Ivo said somewhat coolly.

'I am, I am! As far as I can be. And if she marries Peter Radstock, that's the next best thing, I suppose. He isn't the son I'd have chosen for myself either, but Jossie and I between us will soon lick him into shape.'

Ivo wondered what Sir Thomas Radstock would make of this, but he merely smiled politely. He reminded himself once more that it was none of his business.

To his relief, Jossie came back as ordered after half an hour and sat cross-legged on the floor by her father's chair. During the conversation which followed Ivo learned a lot about the Morleys. He became aware that Major Morley not only dressed his daughter like a boy, he treated her as one, forcing her to live under a Spartan regime with no concessions to her femininity. He saw that Jossie, who was by no means a mindless puppet, accepted her father's dictates without argument or question, and began to understand the origin of some of the contradictions in her character. The child was courageous and spirited enough to play the boy, loving her father so much that, to please him, she suppressed any signs of the girlishness which he so despised. She was even ashamed of it herself. Jossie Morley would continue to be the son as long as she could.

As they drove back to Danby Lodge, Ivo was unusually silent. He now understood his aunt's comments on the situation in the Morley household, and he didn't know which he felt more—anger, admiration or pity. Jossie Morley's blind acceptance of her father's decrees angered him, her courage in obeying them aroused his admiration, but perhaps most of all he was sorry for her. Whatever she did, however hard she tried, Jossie Morley was intelligent enough to know that nothing would ever make up for the fact that she could never really be the son her adored father had wanted.

Fortunately Jossie hardly noticed his preoccupation. As they came into the village they saw the housekeeper from the Hall. When Jossie stopped to speak to her she told them that Sir Thomas and his family were due back in Lyne St Michael the next day. For the rest of the journey Jossie was bubbling over with excitement and plans for outings with Peter.

Ivo found himself hoping that the other man in Jossie's life would be more worthy of her devotion than the one he had just met, and two days later he was able to judge for himself. He and his aunt were invited to tea by Lady Radstock.

* * *

The Radstocks lived in a substantial house built about forty years before. It lay among lush acres of pastures and farmland, and the house itself was surrounded by a handsomely laid-out park and garden. Evidence of prosperity and good husbandry was all around. The rooms inside the Hall were furnished with quiet good taste, and the drawing room where they were received was a spaciously elegant apartment with long windows leading on to a terrace which overlooked the garden.

Sir Thomas Radstock was a bluff country gentleman, typical of his class and breeding. He was well informed and talked sensibly of the recent wars, but his chief interest clearly lay within his own county. Bath and town life in general did not appeal to him. His wife was a gentle, delicate-looking lady with exquisite manners. She and Lady Frances were obviously old friends, and Ivo was made to feel very welcome.

'So you fought at Waterloo, Trenchard? Was that where you injured your hand? Is it permanent?' asked Sir Thomas, looking at Ivo's hand, which was now free of a sling but strapped up.

'This? No, this is nothing, Sir Thomas. I did it down here just a few days ago.'

'He was out with Jossie Morley, Sir Thomas,' said Lady Frances.

'In that case I'm willing to wager that Jossie had something to do with that,' said Sir Thomas, nodding his head at Ivo's hand.

'It was a stupid piece of carelessness on my own part,' said Ivo affably but quite firmly.

'We've seen quite a lot of her while you were away,' Lady Frances went on. 'She has been keeping Ivo entertained after he injured his hand. The poor child missed you all so much.'

'So you know Jossie, do you?' said Sir Thomas. He eyed Ivo carefully. 'What a girl she is! She leads our Peter a pretty dance, I can tell you! Still, that'll all change once they're wed. She'll settle down then.' Having made the situation clear, he sat back with a smile and accepted a cup of tea from his wife.

Ivo was amused. First Jossie's father and now Sir Thomas, each warning him off! They could both rest easy. He still found it impossible to take the idea of Jossie Morley as anyone's bride very seriously, and would never be in contention himself. What was more, their fears were quite unnecessary. It would be a brave man indeed who would interfere with Jossie's own fixed determination to marry Peter Radstock!

'I know better than to ask Sir Thomas whether he enjoyed his stay in Bath, but were you pleased with your visit, Lady Radstock?' asked Ivo's aunt.

'Very much so. And Sir Thomas took the waters, you know, so he had some benefit. We made some very pleasant acquaintances. In fact, one of them, a Mrs Cherton, may well come to stay here in Lyne St Michael when she has completed the course of treatment in Bath. She is looking for a small house in the country and I recommended our village to her. I think she and her daughter would be a welcome addition to our little society.'

'I take it she is a widow?'

'Yes, she lost her husband some years ago. We felt quite sorry for her, and took them with us once or twice to the Assembly Rooms.'

'Sir Thomas dancing? I can hardly believe it!'

'Well, you need not. Sir Thomas stayed at home, and Peter escorted all three of us ladies to the Rooms. Mrs Cherton was most touched, and her daughter was delighted. Poor child, she has had little enough amusement in her life. I think she was quite taken with Peter. But where is he now?' Lady Radstock got up to look out of the window. 'It's too bad of him. He promised to be back for tea.'

'They went to Heversham Beacon,' said Sir Thomas.

'But that is miles away! He's with Jossie, I suppose?'

'Aye, she was here before the lad was rightly up. I'm sure they'll be back soon, my dear—they set off quite early.'

Lady Radstock pursed her lips. 'He shouldn't have gone so far,' she said.

Sir Thomas gave a laugh. 'I don't suppose he had a say in it! Not when Jossie's in charge! What a girl!'

This was obviously not the most tactful of responses. Lady Frances saw that her friend was quite upset and intervened. 'Please don't be disturbed on our account—' But she came to a stop as Jossie erupted into the drawing room, followed by the errant son of the house.

Jossie gazed round and began to look guilty. Lady Radstock looked at two sets of muddy boots and wind-blown hair, gave a slight sigh, then said gently, 'Jossie, Peter, pray go and get yourselves tidied up. You know where Mrs Marston will be, Jossie. Ask her to help you. Then you can come back and join in our tea party. I am sure Lord Trenchard will be happy to wait a little longer to meet you, Peter.'

After they had left the room, she turned to Ivo. 'Lord Trenchard, I hope you'll forgive my son. Peter isn't usually—'

'Please, Lady Radstock! What is there to forgive?' Ivo exerted himself to put his hostess at ease. Underneath her calmly elegant manner he sensed that she was seriously annoyed, and he wondered whether she was as enthusiastic as Sir Thomas about the proposed match between Jossie and her son. As the visit went on he could see why she might not be.

Peter Radstock was a handsome lad. He had inherited his colouring from his father—dark reddish-gold hair, paling to blond where the sun had caught it, frank blue eyes, and a tanned complexion. His manners were good, and he had an attractively diffident smile. But the character and strength so evident in Sir Thomas's face were lacking in that of his son. Though the boy was two or three years older than Jossie, it was clear to Ivo that Peter followed where Jossie led. Knowing as he did the girl's strength of personality, Ivo would be willing to wager a considerable sum on which of the two would rule the roost once they were married. No wonder Lady Radstock was worried!

All of which was none of his business, of course. He liked Jossie Morley, but he was not her keeper. There was no conceivable reason for him to interfere, nor did he wish to. All the evidence was that her future was fixed, and any doubts on his part about the couple's chance of happiness were simply impertinent.

But when the Radstocks produced their next bit of gossip, he forgot his conjectures on the subject of Jossie, Peter and all the rest. Unaware of the shock she was about to give her guests, Lady Radstock began, 'We met another family in Bath who might interest you, Lady Frances. Sir George Gurney was an old friend of your brother's, was he not? Well, it seems that he and his daughter have been living in Bath for over a year. Did you know that Charlotte Gurney is now married?'

'I beg your pardon?'

'Married to a man old enough to be her grandfather!' said Sir Thomas disapprovingly. 'Courtney Malcot.'

'Lord Malcot?' said Lady Frances, astonished. 'But he has been twice widowed already! Are you sure?'

'Quite sure.'

'I can hardly believe it!' said Lady Frances. 'He has *children* who are years older than Charlotte! What can Sir George have been thinking of to allow such a thing! His only daughter!'

'I dare say it's not what he would have chosen, but the girl had apparently set her heart on it. They were saying in Bath that she was ready to run off with Malcot, and her father caught them just in time. I'm surprised at Malcot—he should know better. But at the risk of shocking you, Lady Frances, it's my opinion that the girl cozened him into it. She's a sly little minx.'

'Sir Thomas, you are too severe!' exclaimed Lady Radstock. 'That poor girl! She cannot be more than twenty and he nearly fifty! Why would she do such a thing?'

'Money, my dear! Money! Malcot's as rich as a nabob. The world may look sideways at the pair, but Charlotte now has a position in Society and enough carriages and servants to satisfy the most ambitious of girls.'

'Well, well,' said Lady Frances, casting a quick glance at Ivo. 'This is a surprising bit of news. I wonder if it has reached Sudiham.'

'Surely!' said Sir Thomas.

'Oh! Er…yes, of course. Though if Sir George has been in Bath for over a year, my brother may not have heard yet. Ivo, I think you should go over to Sudiham tomorrow. This is no occasion to be bearing old grudges. Your father has had time to recover from his anger at your insistence on staying in the Army.'

'Ah! Was that what it was?' said Sir Thomas. 'We had wondered…'

* * *

Ivo wasted no time. He thanked his aunt for her help and hospitality during the past weeks, and set off for Sudiham the next day. He approached the house with some misgivings, but this time the doors were open and his father was waiting in the library to receive him.

'So! You've come to your senses, have you?' Lord Veryan asked gruffly. 'Come to beg pardon?'

Ivo knew his father. 'I've come to beg pardon for allowing my temper to get the better of me, Father. I should have stayed to argue my case instead of storming off as I did, and I'm sorry for it. But I have nothing else to apologise for.' There was a slightly awkward silence. Then Ivo added, 'We've been at odds for too long. I should prefer us to be friends.'

'Would you? You don't sound as if you would! Still, since you've come... Sit down, sit down! Are you staying?'

'If you will have me.'

'Of course I will! And I may as well tell you right away, before we start—' Lord Veryan shifted restlessly in his chair. 'I've decided to forgive you.'

'For what, Father?' said Ivo evenly.

'Don't look at me like that!' roared his father. 'I'm not one of your men, dammit!' He glared at his son. After a moment he said abruptly, 'I've had time, plenty of time, to think. You don't tell lies, never have, not to me. I should have accepted your word. The trouble last year was that I was too angry to think straight. It was such a shock finding you and Charlotte Gurney alone in the cottage like that! George Gurney was so sure you were guilty, and you have to admit, Ivo, the evidence was pretty damning. Then, afterwards, the arguments... losing one of my oldest friends... And then you stormed off—'

'You told me to go.'

'I know I did! But you shouldn't have gone, confound it!' Another glare. 'You ought to have known I didn't mean it.'

'I don't see how! Your words were, I believe, that you wished never to set eyes on such a villainous, un-natural monster again.'

'Yes, well, there's no need to go on about it! I dare say I was a touch out of line.' He paused. 'Oh, very well! Totally out of line. But you shouldn't have gone, all the same. It didn't take long for me to come to my senses. I still don't know who was with Charlotte Gurney that day, but I do know it can't have been you.'

Ivo was puzzled. 'But if that is the case, why didn't you tell this to me sooner?'

'I wanted to. I wanted to send for you. But Perry said you were so angry that you would probably refuse to come. I wasn't ready to risk that. He was right, wasn't he? I was sure you would come down here before you went to Belgium, but you didn't. So I tried to put you out of my mind...'

Surprise and anger kept Ivo silent. He *had* come down to Sudiham, but Perry had fended him off, had told him that his father's orders were not to admit him to the house. Any doubts Ivo might still have cherished about Perry's guilt now vanished. His anger grew as he real-ised that he and his father had been kept apart for all these months solely because of his brother's lies. Why had Perry done it? Had he been afraid that the truth about his affair with Charlotte would come out after all? But that was ridiculous! He *must* have realised that he couldn't keep the two of them apart forever—Ivo would surely see his father again, sooner or later! Or...Ivo grew cold. With the threat of war so close, had Perry hoped that his problems would be solved if his brother died in battle? He shook his head. No! Perry might have behaved badly, but that was something Ivo refused to believe.

Lord Veryan said, 'You're very quiet. Was I mistaken? Did Perry misrepresent you? Did Perry lie to me, Ivo?'

Ivo didn't reply, but instead asked, 'Where is Perry now?'

'He's in Derbyshire, at Arneston. He hasn't been himself for some time, so I thought a change of scene would do him good.'

Ivo made an effort to sound calm as he said, 'I'm glad to hear that. He should have gone up there years back, when you first suggested it. Does he intend to stay?'

'I don't know. He might. He seems happier away from Sudiham, and me. But then, he and I never did agree.' There was a pause, then Lord Veryan added bitterly, 'Changing the subject won't help, Ivo. I've noticed that you still haven't answered my question. But perhaps you needn't bother. It's clear enough what happened. Perry deliberately kept us apart, God knows why.'

There was a silence which Ivo found impossible to break. His father went on slowly, 'And yet…and yet, perhaps I do. Perry was afraid you would convince me of your innocence. And if that happened I would look elsewhere for the guilty party. Gurney was right, wasn't he? Someone in my family was to blame for that poor girl's seduction. But it wasn't you, it was Perry! And he was afraid you would betray him.'

Ignoring this last sentence, Ivo said scornfully. '*Poor girl?* So you haven't heard? That "poor girl", as you call her, has just married a very rich man. And Thomas Radstock believes she arranged the whole thing.'

'What's this? Who is the man?'

Ivo went on to give his father the news from Bath.

This was the last time Charlotte Gurney was mentioned between them, and by mutual consent they also avoided any further painful discussion of Perry's manipulations. It was easy enough to ignore them. Now that Charlotte was lost to him, Perry no longer found Somerset so attractive, and, to Ivo's relief, he accepted his father's suggestion that he should continue to look after the Arneston estate indefinitely.

During that year Ivo and his father lived in comparative harmony. Lord Veryan was much changed. The old fire still occasionally flashed out, but he was visibly frailer. The two were both anxious to build bridges over their separation and over the next months Ivo gradually took over a great deal of the older man's responsibilities. But he found time to visit his friends occasionally, and in May he spent a few weeks in London. He saw Adam again, and for a short while there was a danger that he might lose his heart to Kate Payne. She was so unlike any woman he had ever known before, so straightforward, so courageous, that he was strongly attracted. Kate liked him, it was clear. But fortunately, long before any serious damage was done, it became just as clear to him that she was in love with Adam Calthorpe. And it amused him to observe that Adam quickly became jealous of any undue attention paid to Kate by others, including Ivo himself. Though Kate was far from being the tame little housewife he had planned to marry, Adam Calthorpe was rapidly falling in love with the girl! Much as he would have liked to watch the progress of this intriguing love affair, Ivo decided it would be wiser to withdraw from the scene and look forward to an easy friendship in the future with Adam and his wife. And later in the year his discretion was rewarded when he was invited to their wedding.

Between Ivo's visits to London and the great deal of work he found otherwise at Sudiham, he had not had time to go back to Lyne St Michael. He occasionally thought of Jossie with a smile and wondered what tricks she had been up to since they had last met, but the girl's affairs were no longer at the forefront of his mind. When his Aunt Frances came to Sudiham for Christmas she gave him scraps of news—little seemed to have changed, though the Radstocks had begun to plan for the celebration of Peter Radstock's coming of age.

'When is that?' Ivo asked.

'Next July.'

'But that's over six months away!'

'This is a major event, I assure you. Half the county will be at the ball, to say nothing of all the feasts and so on for lesser folk. Lady Radstock is already drawing up the lists. You may assume your name will be on it, Ivo. I hope you will come.'

'I wouldn't miss it for the world! Isn't this the final culmination of Jossie's plans? The moment she and young Radstock become officially engaged?'

'Yes. I have to say the whole idea of those two getting married still seems absurd. They show no signs of settling down. I sometimes wonder if Jossie will walk up the aisle in breeches and that old coat of hers!'

'Lady Radstock would never permit it.'

There was more news of the families in Lyne St Michael at Easter. Jossie had a chaperon! Major Morley had finally given in to pressure, and a distant relative of his, a female of uncertain years, had been installed in the Morley home. What was more, Jossie was being made to wear skirts as often as the chaperon could catch her.

'I feel sorry for the poor woman, Ivo,' said Lady Frances, 'though she is something of a misery. She does her best to instil her charge with some elements of lady-like behaviour, but Jossie spends most of her time carrying on exactly as before. She ignores her chaperon's pleas not to spend so much time running wild with Peter Radstock, and as for the skirts... Halfway down the drive that wretched girl has changed, and is once more in breeches. The two of them—for Peter is as bad as Jossie—just make fun of her! They are a graceless pair, but one cannot help laughing.'

Lady Frances also told them that à Mrs Cherton had arrived in Lyne St Michael and had taken up residence in a modest house in the High Street.

'This is the lady the Radstocks met in Bath, is it not?' asked Ivo. 'Is she as much of an asset to the village as Lady Radstock seemed to think?'

Lady Frances pursed her lips. 'A very elegant lady. A beauty in her day, I imagine... She has been ill, of course, but I find her air of delicate suffering very irritating. I have frequently observed that she is seldom too ill to accept an invitation...as long as it's from the right people.' She paused, then said firmly, 'It is early days yet. I prefer to wait before giving an opinion.'

'You've just given one!' said Ivo, laughing. 'What about the daughter? Is she pretty, too?'

'Ye-es. In a quiet, ladylike way. Blonde hair, lightish blue eyes, plump cheeks, and what I believe is called a rosebud mouth. She is very much in her mother's shadow, and seldom speaks unless spoken to. She blushes a lot.'

Ivo gave another shout of laughter. 'Oh, Aunt Frances, Aunt Frances! Pray don't let your enthusiasm for the Chertons run away with you!'

'Oh, the girl is well enough. I suppose. I hardly know either of them. But Lady Radstock has been very kind to them both, particularly the girl, Rosalind.'

'Indeed?'

'She has made a great effort to introduce them to the other families in the district. Lyne St Michael has become a hive of social activity recently. You would hardly recognise it.'

'How is Jossie faring in all this social activity?'

'I think you can imagine. She hates it, and avoids it whenever she can. She is never at her best in society, Ivo.' Lady Frances started to laugh. 'But her father more than makes up for her.'

'The Major?'

'There's been the most surprising change there! He was seldom seen in public before, but now I think he is at last beginning to take his duties as Jossie's father more seriously. He accompanies her to the Radstocks, and one or two other very select neighbours. He even comes to me! I have to say his company manners are excellent. He can be most charming to the ladies, particularly the pretty ones.'

'So the Major has turned out to be a ladies' man, eh? Does it make him kinder to Jossie?'

'I do think he is trying to face the fact that he can't pretend she's a boy for much longer...' Lady Frances paused, then said, 'He has done that girl such a lot of harm! She has so many talents, so much natural vivacity that she ought to be the star of the neighbourhood. But she is completely out of her element in polite company. She hasn't the slightest idea of how to behave. If I didn't know her as well as I do, Ivo, I'd think her a true country bumpkin!'

'That is exactly what she said she wanted to be.'

'Well, it won't do!' his aunt said tartly. 'Not when there are other pretty girls in the neighbourhood, all apparently better fitted to marry the heir to the second-largest estate in this part of the county!'

'There's no danger there, Aunt Frances! Jossie would see any one of them off.'

'You may say so, Ivo, but it's time she grew up! If she is serious about marriage to Peter Radstock, then it's time she started to treat him like a lover, not a companion for pranks.'

'I'm quite certain she is serious about Peter Radstock. She talked of nothing else when I stayed with you.'

'I know. I wish…'

'What? Really, Aunt Frances, these stops and starts are most unlike you! What's wrong?'

'I had hoped you would have some influence on Jossie. Perhaps even take her mind off Peter a little. But it didn't work.'

Ivo looked at her and laughed. 'Oh, come! You must have known it wouldn't!'

'It might if you had put your mind to it… You have a great deal of address, Ivo.'

'Nothing that could compete in Jossie's eyes with Peter Radstock's perfections.'

'I was afraid it was so,' said his aunt gloomily. 'Poor Jossie!'

Chapter Five

Jossie herself would have echoed Lady Frances's sentiments. She had escaped with difficulty from her chaperon's vigilance and had ridden over to the valley where she had arranged to meet Peter, only to find that he wasn't there. It had been a morning of vexations and this was just one more of them. She shivered. Spring had come late. The track was still covered with dead leaves and on either side the muddy ground was thick with withered fronds of bracken and untidy trails of bramble. The landscape seemed to echo her own feelings of gloom.

Such a short time ago she would have laughed at herself, found something to amuse her while waiting for Peter—would have burrowed under the leaves for signs of the spring flowers, searched a hole in a tree in the hope of finding a sleepy squirrel still in residence. But now she was unable to shake off a vague but growing feeling of apprehension. Life was changing and she was changing with it, little though she liked it.

Jossie let her horse wander along the track as she considered the situation. Why had things begun to change? It could hardly have been the arrival of Cousin Martha—

her chaperon was a nonentity, not to be taken seriously by anyone. For a time, frustrating Cousin Martha's attempts to make her into a lady had even added spice to life. And while her skirts were a nuisance, she usually managed to wear her breeches when she went out with Peter. She didn't *feel* any more like a girl.

So what was wrong? Her father hadn't wanted change. True, he was mixing more in Society, but that was because he loved her and wanted to give her his support. He knew she often felt lost among the fine ladies and gentlemen and their elegant offspring at the parties that seemed to be mushrooming all over the neighbourhood. And her father wouldn't have invited Cousin Martha to come to live with them if Lady Radstock hadn't been so persistent…Lady Radstock and Mrs Cherton.

Jossie frowned as she thought of Mrs Cherton. Everyone else in Lyne St Michael, with the possible exception of Lady Frances, who had not expressed an opinion, approved of her. Lady Radstock was firmly in her favour, and Peter had said only the other day that he thought her very pleasant. Was she, Jossie, the only person in the village who was not charmed by Mrs Cherton? Even her father…

Jossie's apprehension suddenly crystallised. Her father, too, approved of Mrs Cherton. It was after an afternoon spent at the Radstocks in Mrs Cherton's company that he had seemed to change. Since then he had stopped laughing at Jossie's exploits…

Her musings were interrupted by a call from behind. 'Jossie! Jossie, old chap, wait!' It was Peter.

She turned with relief, her doubts and worries forgotten. 'Where've you been?' she asked. 'I thought we were to meet half an hour ago.'

'I'm sorry, Mama got hold of me just as I was leaving, and I couldn't get away. She had Mrs Marston in tow—'

'Your housekeeper? What on earth did your mama wish to talk about?'

'Arrangements for my party. Don't look so blank! My coming of age.'

'But that's months ahead!'

'That's what I said. But apparently there's so much to be done that it all has to be considered now. It'll be a big affair, Jossie. There's the feast for the estate workers, and the party for the children, and then there's the ball in the evening. Half the county will be invited…' He went on giving her details, taking it for granted that she would be as excited as he was.

Jossie stopped listening halfway through, boredom and resentment taking over in her mind. That damned birthday party! That was the root cause of all this desire for her to be proper, to wear skirts, to behave like a lady! For years she and Peter had planned for the day when he would come of age, what they would do after they were married, but it hadn't entered her head that there would be all this fuss, the ball, the feast, the dancing. She hadn't really ever thought about the event as a public celebration, only what it would mean to Peter and herself. She interrupted him impatiently. 'For heaven's sake, let's not talk about it any more, Peter!'

'Why ever not?'

'Parties and fêtes are boring! Anyway, it's a long time ahead, and there are other things to think about! We haven't been to Heversham Beacon since last year.'

'Heversham Beacon! That's much too far, Jossie. We'll never get back before dark.'

'Don't be such an old woman! We can do it as long as we don't waste time talking about it. Come on!'

She dug her heels into her horse and, paying little heed to the dangerous state of the path, started off up towards the high road.

'Jossie, wait! Slow down! Why are you angry? Have I said something wrong?'

Jossie ignored him. She felt a desperate need for fresh air, the wind, the feeling of freedom that a hard ride to the top of the hills would provide. Peter would follow— he always did.

As they rode swiftly over the hills the weather improved and so did her temper. The sun came out, the wind got up, and patterns of cloud and sunshine raced over the hills and valleys. Jossie laughed with relief and delight.

'This is what I want!' she cried. 'Isn't it glorious? The space, the freedom, the air! There's nothing to compare with it. Certainly not making stupid conversation with stupid people in stuffy rooms. Let's stay up here forever!'

'You don't really mean that, Jossie. You know we can't do it. Besides, I quite enjoy meeting new people, talking to them. They can be very interesting. In Bath—'

'Oh, Bath! You're surely not about to say that you *enjoyed* Bath, are you, Peter? I can't imagine any town being enjoyable. I'll race you to the top of the Beacon! Come on!'

'No!' For once Peter spoke so decisively that Jossie stopped in surprise. He went on, 'No, Jossie. I want to talk to you. Let's walk for a bit.'

The expression on his good-natured face was unusually solemn. Jossie grimaced as she felt again that shiver of apprehension, but she dismounted and they tied up the horses and set off along the path to the top.

'I know you don't like parties and such, Jossie,' he

began. 'Though I think you would enjoy them more as time went on and you got used to them. But they don't matter all that much. This coming of age—no, don't turn away! Listen to me.' He stopped and made her face him. 'I've been thinking a lot about our future and you must let me say what I have to say. This coming of age isn't just an excuse for a series of parties. It's more serious than that. It's the threshold of a new life.'

'Is that what your father said? Or was it your mother?' asked Jossie impatiently. When she saw the look of hurt on Peter's face she shook her head at herself and held out a hand. 'I'm sorry,' she said. 'That was rude of me.'

Peter took her hand and held on to it. 'You're forgiven. My mother did say something of the sort. But I agree with her, it is! And...and...these parties and things... Well, we can't go chasing round the countryside forever as if the real world doesn't exist! We have to start taking up our roles in society, Joss. I'll be one of the biggest landowners in the county when our two estates are joined, and that gives me obligations.'

'Your mother again?'

'No, my father. But I'm still in agreement. And you should be, too. We have to start growing up.'

'Of course we do! But that needn't mean we have to become part of the social scene. I hate the social scene, Peter!'

'But you can't avoid it forever! We can't bury ourselves in Lyne St Michael, it wouldn't be right. I hope we might even spend some time in London, do the season, perhaps. I'd like to see something of the great world... And Mama agrees. She thought it would—'

'In *London*! Are you mad? I'd *die* in London! Why do we need London, when there's so much here? Look round you, Peter! This is what matters—the land. *Our* land.' When he was silent, she took his other hand and made him look at her. 'I know you really feel the same as I do,' she said persuasively. 'This sudden desire to visit London isn't the real Peter Radstock. No, we shall do what we've always planned. We shall live in our own home country together… I thought you loved the land, Peter?'

'I do! But I'd still like to see a bit of life—'

'Life!' she exclaimed. '*This* is life *here*! Real life! Oh, I know your mama has always wanted you to be a gentleman of fashion, but look at you! You're handsome enough, but you're hardly a pink of the *ton*! You would be as uncomfortable as I would be in London Society, I know you would. You may tell your mama that I won't hear of our going to London.'

Peter gave in, as he always did when Jossie sounded so fierce, but he was unusually quiet for a while, refusing to respond to Jossie's attempts to amuse him. Finally she gave up and said sadly, 'You're like the rest. You're changing.'

'Oh, no! No, never that! You know I love you, Joss! I always have. But now that…now that we're older, and thinking of marrying, things must change—'

'But I don't want them to!' Jossie's cry came from the heart. 'I want things to stay as they are! Forever!'

'That's nonsense! You can't mean it!' He looked at her mutinous expression and his voice softened. 'Look, it needn't be for the worse. We can carry on much as we always have, if that's what you want. Cheer up, Jossie! What is worrying you now?'

She said bitterly, 'Your mother will try to make me into a proper housewife, I know she will.'

Peter burst into laughter. 'Is that all? What a clunch you are! We needn't listen to her!' When Jossie didn't react he grew sober and went on anxiously, 'You…you still want to marry me, don't you?'

This time her response was instant. 'Of course I do! I can't imagine life without you, you know that. But—'

'But what?'

'I've looked forward to your coming of age for so many years. It's absurd to say that I feel I need more time. But there's *something* wrong. All this talk of celebrations…Cousin Martha's attempts to make a lady out of me…things your mother has been saying…' She looked at Peter's puzzled face and said desperately, 'Marriage makes people so…so serious! And suddenly…I don't feel ready.'

The colour in the boy's face deepened. 'Is it because you're afraid? Do you want us to…to get to know each other better? I know I would like to.'

She said in astonishment. 'Of course it's not that! What on earth are you talking about? We know each other as well as anyone could expect!'

'Not…not in the way I mean.' His flush grew even deeper as he took her hand. 'You've been the best friend a fellow could ask for, Jossie. But there's more to it than that. Will you…will you let me kiss you?'

She stared at him. 'Kiss me? What a strange notion! You've never wanted to kiss me before.'

'It was different before. We were children and I…I didn't think of you in that way. But now…I feel differently. Let me kiss you, Jossie!'

'Well, if that's what you want… Very well.' She shrugged and held up her cheek.

'No, not like that. Like this!' Peter put his arms round her and kissed her firmly on the lips. 'Oh, Jossie!' he murmured and kissed her again hard, holding her so tightly that she could scarcely move. No one had ever held her so closely, so intimately, before, and for a moment she was in a panic. She felt stifled, wanted to push him away, to escape from that suffocating embrace... But then she remembered who was kissing her. This was Peter, the man she was going to marry, and marriage, she knew, entailed closeness of body as well as of mind. If she rejected his first approach as a lover, he would be so hurt... So she willed herself to remain still, to stay passive in his arms. The kiss seemed to last forever, and the sense of relief when he released her was enormous. She looked at him apprehensively. How would he react to her lack of response...? He smiled and gave a sigh of contentment.

'Oh, Jossie! You see? Wasn't that wonderful? Things will be better than ever, don't you agree?'

Jossie bit back an exclamation. He hadn't even noticed! He thought the embrace had given her pleasure! How *could* he be so mistaken?

'Yes, yes,' she murmured. 'Of course.' Then she straightened her jacket and turned away, surreptitiously wiping her mouth on her sleeve. She found herself desperately hoping that she would learn to like such demonstrations. Or at least to accept them with more warmth.

But things did not get better, and after a while it was inevitable that Peter began to notice her reluctance. They started to quarrel, especially when Peter tried to kiss her more often.

'Why can't we enjoy each other's company without all that sentimental rubbish?' she cried one day.

Peter was hurt and angry. 'Because I love you! And you ought to *want* my kisses, Jossie!'

'Oh, fustian! All this kissing and cuddling is boring!'

'Not everyone thinks so! I could tell you of some who would welcome it!'

'Well, go and play with them, then. I'm off to Holcroft's farm.'

Of course he came with her, but there was a restraint between them that had never been there before, though they both tried to bridge it.

Jossie said pleadingly, 'I'm sorry, Peter. Don't let's quarrel any more! I hate it when we quarrel. I'll try to be...to be more like the other girls.'

His response was immediate and generous. 'I'm sorry, too. It's my fault, I'm too impatient. I forget what a strange life you've led. I can't treat you like a boy for so many years, then expect you to turn overnight into a girl, Joss. Perhaps we both need more time.'

They left it there and for the rest of that day he treated her very much as he had in the past.

The next day a message came from the Hall to say that Peter wouldn't be able to see her for a while. His mother had asked him to escort her to Bath. Apparently she needed a number of items connected with the celebrations in the summer which only Bath could provide, and Sir Thomas was busy with matters on the estate. Since one of the requirements was a new ball dress, it would be ten days to a fortnight before she and Peter would return. The note was affectionate, and full of concern. *'I wish we did not have to be apart at this time, Joss,'* he wrote. *'We used to be such good friends before my stupid lack of patience upset you. But I cannot imagine a future without you. I will wait as long as it takes, Joss. I would do anything for you, you know that!'*

Jossie was touched, but she was ashamed to admit to herself that she felt relief rather than disappointment.

This would at least give her a breathing space, time to adjust to the fact that she could no longer be Peter's 'capital fellow' and his best friend. Peter wanted something more. And since she genuinely could not imagine life without him, she must do her best to change.

The drawback was that she could not imagine how she should begin.

She spent long hours roaming about the countryside pondering this question, and after a while came to the conclusion that Peter was right. She had lived as a boy, been treated as a boy for so long, that she had forgotten how to be a girl. She must learn. Judging by some of the things he had said recently, her father would no longer object to seeing her in skirts, so she would stop resisting Cousin Martha and do as she asked. There would be no more breeches, she would wear the riding habit lying in the wardrobe, look out her mother's side saddle, and do her best to behave like a lady. Perhaps that would do the trick. It would at least be a beginning.

She occasionally sighed at the loss of the freedom her breeches had given her, but once she had made her decision she resolutely followed this plan. If Peter wanted a girl, then he would find one when he returned! But whether skirts and elegant behaviour would be enough remained to be seen. The delicate matter of her response to his embraces hovered at the back of her mind, colouring everything she did. If only there was someone who could offer her advice or help! She had never before felt so isolated. Consulting her father was obviously out of the question. The idea of Cousin Martha as a confidante was laughable! Lady Frances? Possibly. Jossie had a suspicion that the older woman was not altogether in favour of a match between Peter and herself. She might not be all that sympathetic a listener.

* * *

At this point Ivo arrived in Lyne St Michael. He had arranged to be in London for the season, but had decided to spend a few days with his aunt on the way. The situation she had described during her Easter visit had aroused his interest. He was curious about the charming widow who had come to live in Lyne St Michael, together with her nondescript daughter. And he found the idea of Jossie in skirts even more intriguing!

He was disappointed on his arrival in Lyne St Michael, therefore, to learn from his aunt that Mrs Cherton and her daughter had just left to spend a few days with friends, though no one was quite sure where.

'Lady Radstock is away, too, though we do know where she has gone. It appears that Bath is the only place outside London that can provide a dress suitable for the ball.'

'So I am not to see the Radstocks either? That's a pity.'

'Sir Thomas is here. Peter volunteered to escort his mother.'

'What about Jossie? Has she gone with them to buy a dress, too?'

'No, Jossie is with us here in Lyne. But I haven't seen her at all since Peter and his mother left. She has been more elusive than ever. She's not happy, Ivo.'

'I would have thought she would be full of plans for the summer?'

'I suspect that's half the trouble. Jossie doesn't like the idea of all the fuss, and Peter is relishing it. I've tried to talk to her, but she's too loyal to Peter to confide in me. I've tried not to show it, but she knows I don't think he's good enough for her.' She paused. 'I don't suppose that you could do something while you're here, could you, Ivo? She always seemed ready to talk to you.'

'I doubt very much that I could succeed where you've failed. Still, I like the child. If you think I could do something…'

'Good! The next problem is where to find her!'

'Oh, I'll find her,' said Ivo confidently. 'I know where to look.'

Jossie was where he had expected, down in the valley by the little stream. She was sitting on a rock, moodily throwing stones into the water.

'Good morning!' called Ivo, keeping his distance. He had no wish to startle Jossie when she had stones in her hand. The accident rate at their meetings had so far been too high. But all she did when he called was to look up, then turn back to the stream.

'What do you want?' she asked moodily.

Ivo came down the path and joined her. 'That's no way to talk to a man who owes you money!'

She gave him a fleeting grin. 'You never did win it all back, did you?'

'I will, one day.'

'I doubt you'll have the chance. I'm becoming respectable. A lady.'

Ivo looked at the discarded boots and stockings, the hat lying on the ground beside her, the skirts turned back to reveal bare legs and feet dangling in the water. 'I can see that,' he said.

She laughed, jumped up, and shook out her skirts. 'I have lapses,' she said. 'Sometimes it all seems too much. How are you, Ivo, and why haven't you been to Lyne St Michael before this?'

He had forgotten how direct she was, how natural her manner, how she wrinkled her nose when she laughed. She had grown, too. He liked the way her severely cut riding habit outlined her figure. One could never mistake her for a boy now...

'You're staring!' she said. 'Turn your back while I put my boots and stockings on.'

'I left my horse at the top. I'll fetch him down. Let me know when you've finished.'

He waited on the bridle path until she whistled, then led his horse down to join her. 'You've a long way to go, Jossie Morley. Ladies don't whistle! And they don't know how to dress without a maid to help them.'

'I've told you. I have lapses. Besides, I doubt you would make a very good ladies' maid. And there's no one else here.'

'Don't be so dismissive. I've had my moments—' Ivo stopped short. He had spoken without thinking. This was not the sort of thing one said to an innocent young lady! The trouble was he still half-thought of Jossie as a boy. He shook his head and said frankly, 'I'm sorry, Jossie. That slipped out, I'm afraid. Can you forget I said it?'

She regarded him speculatively. Then she said, 'So you've "had your moments", have you? I should have remembered. Everybody says you're a man of experience, though I must say I've never noticed it.'

'It's not the sort of thing I've ever wished to discuss with you,' said Ivo solemnly. He was finding it difficult not to laugh at this unexpected reply! His reputation had evoked a variety of reactions from disapproval to admiration, but never one as coolly objective as this. What was Jossie up to now?

She was still eyeing him with a look of assessment. 'I wonder if you'd do,' she said slowly. 'I know I could trust you. And if anyone could show me, you could. But would you be willing to do it?'

'I'm not sure I understand what you're talking about,

Jossie, but I don't like the sound of it. Explain, please. I'll help you if I can—without loss of limb, that is.'

'You do go on about that fox… Your hand is quite recovered, isn't it?'

'What do you want?'

Jossie looked at him, took a breath, was silent, then took another breath and began. 'I need help,' she said. 'If there was anyone else, I would speak to them about it, believe me. Lady Frances would have done, but she doesn't want me to marry Peter, so she wouldn't be very sympathetic. Besides, she's a woman.'

'I'm still waiting.'

'I would never have thought of you, before you came today. But I always felt I could talk to you about anything. And you could be perfect. I hope you don't find me unbelievably impertinent?'

'I can't find you anything until I know what the devil you're talking about!'

Ivo's impatience spurred her. 'It involves Peter. Peter and me. And I have to talk to someone!'

'Now wait! I'm not sure—'

'Oh, please, Ivo! Listen! I'm not asking you to be a mother or anything. I know about the…the processes of nature. You can't associate with farms all your life and *not* know.'

'Well, that's a relief!'

'This is more complicated.' She walked a step or two away from him and spoke without turning. 'I suppose it's natural that Peter wants…wants to kiss me, now that our marriage is not so far off. And because we've always had more freedom than many other young people, the opportunity is often there. But…but…' She put her face in her hands and her next words were muffled. 'I don't know how to say this…I dislike it!'

Ivo smiled and came over to her. 'Is that all? That's the most natural reaction in the world. Of course you're afraid. It's a new and disconcerting world you're about to enter. But if you love Peter—'

She turned round. 'I do! But it isn't *fear* that I feel. That's what he thinks, but he's wrong! I'm not afraid when he kisses me, I'm bored, impatient... I'm not nervous, I feel *stifled*. But I *am* afraid of something else.' He waited. She threw him a quick look then turned away again. 'I'm so afraid that I shall always feel like that.'

Ivo said calmly, 'I'm quite sure you won't.'

'How can you be sure? My father wanted me to be a boy and that's what I've tried to be. Perhaps all those years pretending to be a boy have...damaged me? I shall never enjoy being kissed.'

Ivo gave a shout of laughter, pulled her round and hugged her. 'My sweet, darling Jossie! No one with as kissable a mouth as yours could possibly not enjoy being kissed sooner or later.'

Her eyes shining, Jossie looked at him. 'Well, that's what I wanted to ask you, Ivo. I wondered if you could teach me how to respond.'

Chapter Six

Shock kept Ivo quiet for several seconds. In all the wide world, he thought, only Jossie Morley could have made a request such as that. So naturally, so unselfconsciously. Could he do as she asked? With almost anyone else he would have refused unhesitatingly, suspecting some sort of trap. But not with Jossie. For no one else would he have broken his cardinal rule never to become involved with an unmarried girl, but Jossie was different. She didn't want involvement, she wanted help. She had asked him as a friend, someone she could trust. Ivo did not allow himself to speculate what the request revealed of the situation between Jossie and Peter Radstock, the so-called lovers. That was none of his business. He must think only of helping Jossie.

But first he must clear the ground.

'Are you sure you're being sensible?' he said at last. 'You must have heard what they say of me.'

'Lady Frances said once you were the worst flirt in the county before you went into the Army, and she didn't suppose you had changed.'

'How very kind of her! Doesn't that put you off?'

'Of course not—it's what I want! It's no use asking

someone who doesn't know what they're doing to help me in this. I need an expert. That's what they say you are. Please, Ivo!'

If the situation had been less sensitive Ivo would have laughed. Of the many bizarre assignments given him in his career, this one must surely take the prize. But it *was* sensitive and he must do his best. Jossie's absurd fears mustn't be allowed to grow. He made up his mind.

'Let's walk a little way along the valley,' he said. 'The horses will be safe enough here.'

'I thought you were going to kiss me!'

'I am. But not yet. It's no use kissing you when you're standing like an ornamental statue waiting to have its face washed.'

Jossie burst into laughter. 'Did I really look like that?'

'The essence of an enjoyable kiss is its romance—in the beginning, at least. Come, walk with me. I'm not sure I've ever looked properly at this valley. It's quite pretty.'

As they wandered down by the side of the stream, they soon fell into their old companionship, Ivo asking questions and Jossie eagerly showing him the beauties of the place. It was obviously very special to her. Finally they came to a small waterfall. Here they paused, and after a moment Jossie fell silent. The only sounds were the wind rustling in the trees and the plashing of the water. Ivo turned her gently to face him.

'Let me look at you,' he said. 'You've changed quite a lot in the past year.' Then he smiled as she stared up at him trustingly. 'You know, I've never been sure about your eyes,' he said. 'When I first met you I thought they were blue. But sometimes they look turquoise, and sometimes they are truly green. I never know what I shall find.' He smoothed her hair back from her fore-head. 'This is longer than it was.'

'I...I've been letting it g-grow. C-Cousin Martha said l-long hair was...was more s-suitable for a lady.'

'I don't know that I agree. Those short curls were very appealing.'

Jossie wasn't quite sure what was happening to her. Why was she stammering? Why, when she had not been walking at all energetically, did she feel so short of breath? The touch of Ivo's fingers was feather light, but it was burning a trail over her face, down her cheek, over her lips, under her chin....

He bent his head and kissed her. There was no feeling of compulsion, he was hardly holding her at all, just his hand under her chin... But the warmth in her face was spreading along her veins and through the rest of her body, a delicious languor was melting her bones so that she had to clutch his arms to steady herself...

He raised his head and gazed down into her eyes. 'They're purest sapphire,' he said softly. 'And so lovely.' Then he put his arms right round her, holding her close. 'Jossie!' he murmured and kissed her again. This time the kiss was more passionate, more demand-ing... These were altogether deeper, more dangerous wa-ters, and Jossie felt a momentary panic, a brief wish to escape. But her trust in Ivo held. She forgot her fears and let him gather her to him. Soon she had forgotten everything but the delight of the moment. She had never before felt so gloriously exhilarated, not even on the highest hilltop. It was so easy to respond, to seek even closer contact with this body that was giving her such pleasure. She laughed in astonished joy, put her arms round his neck and pressed herself against him, her lips soft and yielding under his... With a muffled groan Ivo locked her even more closely in his arms...

Suddenly he pulled himself away. He was breathing fast. After a moment he swallowed and said, 'I think we've proved something, don't you?'

She took his hand and held it against her cheek. 'Oh, Ivo, that was...was *wonderful*! I didn't know anything could be as exciting. Is it always like that?'

He was staring at her as if she was someone he had never seen before. Then he took his hand away and Jossie felt unaccountably bereft. 'Not always,' he said. 'In fact—' He stopped and said brusquely, 'I have to get back. I'm really on my way to London. Aunt Frances will be looking for me...'

'Ivo! Have I done something wrong? Is there something else I need to learn?'

'No!' He looked at her anxious face and made a visible effort to speak naturally. 'My dear girl, you have no need to learn anything. Peter Radstock is a very fortunate man, and I wish you all the joy in the world with him.'

'But you'll be there at the ball? You'll come back from London in time? I want you there, Ivo.'

He hesitated, then, as her smile began to fade, he said, somewhat grimly, 'I'll be there.'

'Good!' They walked up to the horses, then led them on to the bridle path and mounted. When they came to the village Jossie asked him if he would like to see her father.

'Thank you, but no. I'm afraid I must hurry back. Aunt Frances is expecting me. Goodbye, Jossie.' He held out his hand.

She took it and said, 'I shall never forget what you've done for me, Ivo. For us both, Peter and me. I was so afraid that there was something lacking in me, that I would never be able to behave as Peter wishes. But now I know what pleasure there can be in a kiss…' She paused, smiling, remembering, and said softly, 'What *delight*…'

Ivo made a sudden gesture, and she came down to earth. 'I'm keeping you,' she said apologetically. 'I do realise you have to go, though I wish you didn't. I owe you so much, Ivo. Thank you.' She turned up the drive to her home.

Ivo watched Jossie go, and then started off back to his aunt's. According to Jossie he ought to have been basking in a glow of virtue, but in fact his mood was blacker than it had been for a long time. He must have been mad! What had started out as a piece of kindly indulgence had turned into a nightmare. He hoped to heaven that Jossie Morley would never know how close she had come to being seduced that afternoon. Though…now he came to think of it, the reverse would be nearer the truth. She had all but seduced him! Her reaction to his first kiss had been sweet beyond measure. But the second! Ivo felt the sweat breaking out on his brow as he remembered the Herculean effort he had needed to keep them both under control, the intensity of his regret when they had parted. His body ached again at the thought. She had been so innocently abandoned, so desirable… He pulled himself together with an effort. This would not do! The sooner he escaped to London and away from the temptation to take over Peter Radstock's part in teaching Jossie Morley to be a woman, the better!

He left for London the next day, resolving not to return to Somerset before July, and hoping that he would by then have recovered his sanity. To that end he threw himself into the pleasures of the London season, and soon Ivo Trenchard was his normal self again—essential to the success of any function, a charming companion to the many ladies who sought him out, and the despair of Society's mamas. He never quite forgot the scene by the waterfall, and Jossie's eyes just occasionally haunted his sleep, but in the end he could look forward with equanimity to Peter Radstock's coming of age and Jossie's engagement.

Meanwhile in Lyne St Michael the preparations for the summer celebrations increased in intensity. Peter and his mother returned from Bath in very good humour after what had obviously been a highly successful excursion. Lady Radstock showed Jossie not one but several new dresses, and urged her to make her mind up very soon what she herself was going to wear at the ball. Jossie had not given it a thought.

'I have any number of dresses that will do,' she said carelessly. 'Most of them new. Since we've had all these dances and parties in the neighbourhood Papa has seen to it that I am always suitably dressed.'

'But Jossie, this is a very special occasion,' Lady Radstock protested.

'You mean our engagement?'

There was a little silence. 'Not quite,' said Lady Radstock. 'I think it would be better to celebrate one thing at a time, Jossie dear. And the ball in July is meant for Peter's coming of age. Let's not be hasty about anything else.' Her face was troubled. 'Has Peter spoken to you about the ball...or...or anything?'

Jossie was aware that Lady Radstock had always had reservations about her as a suitable bride for her only son. She found this completely understandable. Peter's mother placed a high value on perfect manners and an elegant appearance, and Jossie failed these two tests abysmally. But she had never been afraid that Lady Radstock's doubts would affect the outcome. Peter's mother was fond of her, in spite of her faults. Moreover, she would never refuse Peter anything he wanted. And Sir Thomas, Peter's father, was all in favour of a match between his son and the Calverton heiress. He wouldn't allow himself to be influenced by any objection Lady Radstock might raise. So she answered cheerfully enough, 'Not yet. You've been keeping him very busy since he got back, I've hardly seen him. But I expect he will soon. I need to talk to him myself.'

'See that you have a new dress, Jossie,' said Lady Radstock with unwonted urgency. 'Things seem easier when one feels one is looking one's best.'

Somewhat surprised, Jossie agreed to talk to her Cousin Martha that very day, but that was as far as her interest in the matter went. She categorically refused to go to Bath, and indeed there was hardly enough time to do so. So Cousin Martha took her to a draper's shop in the nearest small town, an establishment which was well known in the district for making clothes for the wives and daughters of prosperous farmers. The dressmaker and Cousin Martha between them decided that as Jossie had not yet formally 'come out', absolute simplicity was most suitable. The dress they produced was certainly simple, of plain white muslin and several years out of date in style. It would have suited a young girl at her confirmation. As the ball gown for the daughter of one of the richest families in the neighbourhood it was woefully inadequate. And as Jossie would never stay still long enough to have it fitted, it was not even flattering.

But no one close to Jossie either knew or cared—certainly not Jossie herself.

Jossie had other things to occupy her mind. She had looked forward to Peter's return from Bath, had wanted to show him how she had changed, to prove that she was now ready to respond to more ardent embraces. But the first attempt was hardly a success. Peter seemed unsure of himself, and her own response was at the most lukewarm. A disastrous second attempt ended in stammered apologies from Peter and tears of disappointment from Jossie. After that Peter held back from further close contact. At first Jossie was puzzled, then she decided that he was trying to display the patience he had promised before he had gone to Bath, and was touched at his restraint. She told herself that things would change once they were officially engaged. They would feel easier with each other again, and she would be able to demonstrate then how much she loved him.

She saw him much less often than before. As the date of his coming of age approached, his days seem to be filled with business, interviews with the lawyers, discussions with the land agents, consultations with both his parents and all the other duties arising from his new status. The moments they spent together were often cut short by some urgent appointment which demanded Peter's presence.

Jossie found herself increasingly alone, without even the companionship of her father. Major Morley seemed to have acquired a new lease of life. Whereas in the past he had seldom left the house, and was usually prepared to play a game of piquet or whist, he was now more often out visiting in the neighbourhood. Jossie had no wish to attend dull tea parties or other social gatherings, but she was slightly hurt that he did not seem to want her to go with him.

Finally Peter's birthday arrived. It was a beautiful July morning, and Jossie got up early. The tedious months of waiting were over at last, and she was filled with excited anticipation. She dressed more carefully than usual in the prettiest of her new dresses and made her way to the little valley, surrounded by the scents and colours of high summer: dog daisies, meadow sweet, campanulas. As she walked, she gazed around her in contentment. This was the day, and this the place! Years ago she and Peter had agreed that early in the day on the morning of his twenty-first birthday they would meet by the stream. Here in this special place, this loved, familiar valley, they would make their own vows to each other, put a seal on all their plans, everything they had lived for.

Jossie sat on the bank lost in dreams. This was all she had ever wanted, and it was so soon to be hers. Life with Peter, the love and companionship they would share through the coming years, children... She and Peter had always been true friends, and they would be true and faithful partners in marriage. That was what was important. Their recent difficulties faded into insignificance when compared with all those years of loyalty and friendship.

She sat like this for some time, until she became aware that the sun had got much higher. Where was Peter? Surely he wouldn't let his mother stop him for any reason from keeping such an important tryst? She sat for a few minutes longer, then got up and looked around. There was no sign of him. She hesitated for another few minutes, then made up her mind to go to meet him—he was sure to come along the bridle path.

But Jossie had reached the gates of the Hall before she finally met him. He was on horseback.

'There you are at last,' she cried. 'What on earth kept you?'

Peter looked startled. 'Jossie!' he exclaimed. 'What are you doing here?'

'I got tired of waiting by the stream, so I thought I'd come to meet you. Did your mother delay you?'

'Oh, my lord!' A slow tide of red mounted in Peter's cheeks. 'I...I... Jossie, I...'

'What on earth is wrong with you, Peter? You can't have forgotten. That's impossible. What happened?'

'I...I didn't forget exactly! Of course I didn't! It's just that I—' Peter stopped and slowly dismounted. Then he turned and said, 'Were you waiting long, Joss?'

'Long enough. But that doesn't matter now. You're here. Shall we go back to the valley?'

'There...there isn't time. I shall soon have to be back. I'm sorry.' Peter spoke jerkily, as if under some strain. 'Joss, I have to talk to you...Mama said...'

At the sight of Peter's discomfort Jossie forgot her own disappointment. Concerned, she asked, 'Has Lady Radstock been upsetting you? Is it because she doesn't want us to make any announcement today? That's all right, Peter! Please don't worry, she has already told me so, and I don't mind a bit. Don't fall out with your mother because of that. We can easily leave any official announcement to another time.' He appeared to be unconvinced. She went on gently, 'Dear Peter! You shouldn't worry so much! As long as we know our own minds, what can your mother do? Your father is wholly on our side. Your mother is reasonable. She'll come round in time.'

'But, Jossie, there's something else—'

Wanting only to reassure him, she said, 'Nonsense! There can't be anything else, Peter. This is your special day. You mustn't let anything spoil that! Congratulations, my dearest fellow.' She came over to him, held out her hand and after a slight hesitation offered her cheek. Peter bent forward to kiss her. 'I'm sorry, Jossie!' he said. 'I'm really sorry! I wish…' He gazed miserably at her, then turned away. 'I…I…I have to go!' He got on his horse and prepared to ride off.

'Wait!' Peter stopped a few paces away. Jossie ran up to him. 'When shall I see you?'

Without looking at her Peter said, 'I…I don't know. I shall be busy all day, Joss. We…we have so many aunts and uncles staying with us and they all want to talk to me…Mama insisted…' He looked ashamed.

'That's all right. Truly!' Jossie tried to speak cheerfully for Peter's sake. 'Till this evening, then.'

Peter nodded and rode off. Jossie watched him go. She had never before seen Peter so distressed. He was clearly suffering from conflicting loyalties. What had Lady Radstock been saying to him to upset him so on this day of all days? He had always been devoted to his mother, and on the rare occasions when she had been seriously displeased he had always been eager to make amends as soon as possible. But why was she making difficulties today? Jossie frowned. Peter's mother must disapprove of her more than she had realised.

Hurt and bewildered, trying not to feel angry, Jossie went home, changed into her breeches, collected some food from the kitchen and set off on a long ride. The day she had looked forward to for so long was rapidly turning into a disaster. If she was to rescue it, she would have to ride some of this resentment out of her system before meeting the Radstocks this evening.

*   *   *

She arrived back refreshed, her natural optimism and courage restored. During the ride she had faced the situation and decided that it was not incurable. It was unfortunate that Lady Radstock apparently disapproved of her so strongly. Jossie would never have guessed it from her manner. But when she saw how hard Jossie was trying to be more like the daughter-in-law she desired, she would relent, and they would all be happy again together.

Jossie had little time for further reflection. Her father seemed to think that she should have spent the day preparing for the ball, and was angry that she hadn't.

'Look at your hair!' he said. 'And your nails are a disgrace! You stink of the stables, girl!'

'I'm sorry, Papa. I know I should have been back sooner, but I was feeling rather down, and had to ride it out of my system. But I shall take pains now to make you proud of me. Wait till you see me in my new dress!'

He said impatiently, 'You haven't left much time!'

Jossie took a breath and said pleadingly, 'Please don't be cross with me, Papa! I'll do my best.' She added with a nervous little laugh, 'Isn't it strange? I've been waiting for this evening for years, and now I feel quite nervous about it! I expect it's because everyone suddenly wishes me to stop acting like a boy, and to be more like a girl instead. It's all so new! You must give me a little time to get used to it, Papa.'

Jossie took more trouble with her appearance than she had in her whole life before, and came downstairs rather pleased with herself. But when her father saw her he was not encouraging.

'I wonder if I should have consulted Madeleine Cherton on that dress? It doesn't do much for you. Why the devil didn't you take more trouble to find a decent dress-maker?'

Jossie faltered, 'Cousin Martha thought the dress was very suitable. I'm sorry you don't like it, Papa.'

'My cousin has no more taste than a scarecrow, which is what she looks like most of the time. I wish I had thought to consult Mrs Cherton. Her taste is excellent. She and her daughter always look a picture of elegance. But then they take trouble, Jossie. They know how to present themselves to advantage. That's something you'll have to learn.'

Jossie looked down. Not for the world would she show how much his words hurt her. 'I...I don't suppose anyone will look at me very much,' she said quietly. 'Lady Radstock doesn't wish any announcement about Peter and me to be made tonight.'

'What? No official betrothal? But everyone is expecting it! It's been understood for years that it would be announced on young Radstock's twenty-first! You must have done something to upset her!'

'I don't know what, Papa. I thought she liked me.'

'This is a pretty state of affairs, I must say! What will people say? I'm surprised at Lady Radstock...' He regarded his daughter and frowned. 'She probably wants to wait until you are more of a credit to Peter. It was a mistake letting you run wild for so long, wearing breeches and the rest. I should have insisted sooner that you learned how to handle skirts. Well, it's too late for this evening, but once this ball is over we shall have to see about making you into something like a lady. If Lady Radstock won't help you, Mrs Cherton might give you advice.'

'I don't think I know Mrs Cherton well enough to ask her, Papa.'

'You may not, but I believe I do. She would be an excellent mentor, and I flatter myself that she would be willing to do it as a favour to me. You should cultivate her, Jossie. She's a damned fine woman.' He looked at his daughter and frowned again. 'Now, go back upstairs and get the maid to do your hair properly. Half the pins are coming out. And that rose looks ridiculous.'

Jossie did as he asked, then came down and waited patiently in the hall while he regarded her critically and told her to give her bodice a pull here, and her skirt a twitch there. Finally, still sounding dissatisfied, he said, 'I can't do any more, we should have left a quarter of an hour ago. You know how I dislike unpunctuality, Jossie. I regard it as discourteous. Come along!'

Jossie didn't argue. Papa was not usually so critical. He must be as nervous as she was. She followed him dispiritedly into the carriage. It looked as if she would have something to prove to her father as well as to Lady Radstock at the ball tonight.

They sat in silence in the carriage, but his displeasure was patent. Jossie sighed and wondered if Ivo would keep his word and be there. He at least had seemed to approve of her. He had even found her worth kissing... Her spirits lifted a little as she thought of Ivo's kiss. He had been so kind. He had shown her a new world, a magic world, one she had badly wanted to share with Peter. Why hadn't they managed it? After all, Peter was the one she loved. It was a pity he had been so busy, they had hardly had any time at all together. But after this fuss was all over and they were back on the old footing... Jossie grew more cheerful. She knew, and Peter knew, the strength of their attachment. Nothing could break that. As the carriage bowled along to the Hall, she hugged to herself the thought of her future with Peter. It did something to dispel the chill caused by her father's words.

Chapter Seven

The ball had already started when they arrived, which was another cause for a show of displeasure from her father. He gave her no time to arrange her clothes or hair, but himself gave her cloak to the servant and ushered her in.

The rooms on the south side of the house all ran into one another, and tonight the doors between them were folded back. The evening was warm and the long windows on to the terrace were open. An orchestra was playing on a dais at one end of the room, and a set of country dances was in progress. Jossie and her father were announced and made their way to Sir Thomas and Lady Radstock, who were waiting near the door to welcome new arrivals. Most of the guests were already inside, and they were standing quite alone. Peter was nowhere to be seen.

'Major! Jossie! How nice to see you!' Lady Radstock's greeting was warm, her smile kind. No one would have guessed that Jossie was at all out of favour. She went on, 'You…you look charming, my dear. Very…very fresh, especially on such a hot night.' They exchanged a few more words, then their hostess said,

'Except for a few distant cousins of Sir Thomas, I am sure everyone here is known to you. Lady Frances has brought her nephew, Lord Trenchard. I believe you know him quite well, Jossie?' She paused.

'Yes, I do. I'd like to talk to him later.' Jossie looked round. 'But where's Peter?'

Lady Radstock's smile faltered, and she hesitated. Sir Thomas said with a laugh, 'Oh, he's dancing some-where, but he'll be back. I dare swear he'll come looking for you as soon as he's free.' He took Jossie's hand and said with mock gravity, 'You must promise me not to play any of your tricks tonight, Jossie! It's a solemn occasion. A coming of age *and* an engagement.'

Lady Radstock said quickly, 'But, Sir Thomas, I thought we had agreed. No announcement tonight. A coming of age is quite enough.'

'So we did, so we did! But I can't claim to understand why. The sooner it's all signed and sealed the better, that's what! It's not as if the two of them don't know their own mind. Why, they've been talking about it for years! And I still think it ought to be made official to-night.'

Lady Radstock gave her husband a look. He said re-luctantly, 'Whatever you say, my dear...'

It was as well, thought Jossie, that her father had wan-dered ahead and had not heard this exchange. He would have been more annoyed than ever. She gave the Rad-stocks a tentative smile and followed her father into the ballroom. He was already in conversation with a small group which included Mrs Cherton, Ivo Trenchard and one or two others.

The sight of Ivo's tall figure, a smile on his lips, his dark head bent to hear what one of the other ladies was saying, had a surprising effect on Jossie. For a moment she was filled with confusion as the memory of his kisses returned in full force. Nothing before or since could compare with the feeling of sublime happiness she had experienced in his arms... Her face burned and she moved away. She mustn't think of it. She must look for Peter.

'Aren't you going to say good evening to me, Jossie?'

From behind her came Ivo's voice, deep, drawling, with a hint of irony about it that was totally characteristic. She turned round. 'Ivo!' she exclaimed. 'I...I didn't see you!'

He raised an eyebrow. 'No?'

Jossie was too honest to persist in the lie. 'Well, I did,' she confessed. 'But I wasn't sure what to say to you.'

'That's a little unkind. I thought you were a friend. You could say perhaps, "How are you?" or, "How nice to see you again!" or, "What have you been doing since we last met?"'

This reminder of their last meeting caused Jossie to blush more deeply than ever. Ivo smiled. 'You look very pretty when you're confused, Jossie, but there's no need. Did it work?' She hesitated and he said quickly, 'No, don't tell me. It has nothing to do with me. Are you happy tonight?'

'Not...not yet. But I expect I will be.' She added nervously, 'I just have to find Peter.'

'He's dancing with Rosalind Cherton. He'll bring her back here when the music stops.'

Jossie allowed him to lead her back to the group. Ivo seemed preoccupied, but she was quite happy to stand and observe the others. Her father was in animated conversation with Mrs Cherton. What he had said was true, she thought with a pang. Mrs Cherton was perfectly groomed, from the exquisite creation on her head to the glittering buckles on her shoes. Her slender figure dressed in lilac crêpe, with pearls in her ears and a collar of pearls and diamonds round her throat, she was easily the most elegant woman in the room. It was clear that Major Morley was very taken with her. The lady was less demonstrative, but seemed quite content to accept his admiration with a smile.

The music stopped and Peter came towards the group with Miss Cherton on his arm. She was more animated than usual and smiled enchantingly at Peter as he relinquished her with a bow to her mother. The two women were remarkably alike, both slender, both beautifully groomed, both exquisitely feminine in appearance. Rosalind was slightly shorter than her mother, and more simply dressed, as befitted a young lady. But what exquisite simplicity! A plain slip of white silk, a few rosebuds sewn here and there on a net overlay, tiny cap sleeves caught up with rosebuds. A small string of pearls round a smooth white throat. Pale gold curls dressed high except for one lock which fell gracefully over her shoulder. Jossie looked down at her muslin and felt like a clumsy rustic.

'She has no wit to speak of,' said a voice in her ear. 'Playing piquet with her would be like taking candy from a child.'

Jossie looked round. Ivo was regarding her with amusement and something else in his eyes. She was not quite sure what it was, but it made her uneasy. She shook her head at him, and moved over to stand between her father and Peter who, having delivered Miss Cherton to her mother, had remained to talk. Ivo looked rueful, shrugged his shoulders and wandered through the windows on to the terrace, where Lady Frances was enjoying the fresh air.

Major Morley barely spared a glance as Jossie joined him, but Mrs Cherton turned and gave her a sweet smile.

'Have you been hurrying, Jossie? You look quite flushed, my dear,' she said, her eyes taking in every detail of the white muslin dress.

'Jossie was out all day and arrived home late,' said Major Morley with a little frown.

'Roaming the countryside again? What a girl you are for the outdoors! But there's something I've been meaning to ask for ages, my dear. Tell me, where does the name Jossie come from? It's almost like a boy's!'

'It's a family name, Mrs Cherton,' said Jossie stiffly. 'Joscelin. And it is a boy's name.'

'How odd! Have you no other, child?'

'I was christened Helena Joscelin.'

'Helena! Oh dear,' exclaimed Mrs Cherton laughing merrily. 'How unsuitable! I can quite understand why you prefer Jossie!' She ran her eye over the muslin dress once more, then turned to Jossie's father. 'I see what you mean, Major, and I'm sure I could do something. Jossie is tall, of course. But that can be an advantage, if one is taught to carry oneself well.' She turned back to Jossie. 'You poor girl, I dare swear you have sadly missed the influence of a mother.'

'Not at all, ma'am,' said Jossie stiffly. 'I have always been perfectly happy with my father.'

'Indeed, who would not be?' said Mrs Cherton. Then, raising a playfully admonitory finger, she went on, 'But I'm afraid he deserves just a little scold, all the same.'

'Mrs Cherton! What have I done? Only tell me and I shall put it right immediately!' said Major Morley gallantly.

'I am sure Jossie's upbringing has been delightfully natural, but from what I hear you have been neglecting her education, Major!'

'Oh, come, Mrs Cherton, you are being too harsh with poor Morley!' said Sir Thomas. 'Jossie is better educated than most young people round here. She rides as well as any boy, she knows more about the land than even Peter here, and she knows as much about the natural history in the neighbourhood as any professor! What's more, she can outdo me any day at reckoning.'

He smiled kindly at Jossie, who, deeply embarrassed, was trying to make herself invisible.

Mrs Cherton shook her head. With a charming smile she said, 'Forgive me, but men, of course, do not always understand what a young girl needs to learn! I am sure Jossie is enormously clever, unlike my poor Rosalind, who can hardly count! Such a dear muddlehead, she is! But I was astonished to learn from Lady Radstock that Jossie has never had proper music or dancing lessons! Not one! Now Rosalind here started before she was twelve.'

'And to wonderful effect,' said Peter, gazing in admiration at Miss Cherton. 'A perfect dancing partner.'

Sir Thomas, who had come up just in time to hear this last remark, looked disapprovingly at his son. 'I hope you're going to dance with Jossie before the evening is much older,' he said sternly. 'You haven't even said good evening to her yet.'

'I haven't had time,' Peter somewhat sulkily replied. 'She wasn't here when the ball began.'

'Well, you can put it right now, my boy. Here she is.'

'Sir Thomas!' protested Lady Radstock. 'Let the young people decide for themselves what they will do. Jossie may not wish to dance at the moment.'

'I don't expect she does,' said Peter. 'She doesn't like that sort of thing. She never has.'

'Then you can take her away and give her an ice or something,' said Sir Thomas decisively. 'Dammit, Peter, you're supposed to be marrying the girl before long. You can at least talk to her!'

'Please, Sir Thomas—' Jossie was scarlet with embarrassment, and Lady Radstock looked as annoyed as good manners allowed.

Sir Thomas seldom interfered with his wife's arrangements. He was a man who liked his comfort, and though he was not sure how she did it, Lady Radstock could make life quite uncomfortable for those who disagreed with her. But he was not stupid. He had seen the way Peter had looked at Rosalind Cherton, and hadn't liked it a bit. And now he decided to risk his wife's displeasure. The sooner Peter was officially committed to Jossie Morley the better. The two were not only ideally suited, but Jossie would bring with her a substantial dowry, to say nothing of her large future inheritance. This Cherton girl was pretty enough, and had pretty manners, too, but there was little else to recommend her. No visible fortune. Lady Radstock may say what she wished, but a prudent father would not let a prize like the Calverton Manor estate slip through his fingers just because of some scruples on the part of his wife!

So he now turned to Lady Radstock, said, 'I'm sorry, my dear, but I've changed my mind. Peter's future must be settled tonight.' He marched off purposefully towards the dais. After an anguished look at his mother, who had turned very pale, Peter hurried after him. They reached the dais together, and Peter clutched his father's arm in a desperate effort to hold him back. Sir Thomas said sternly, 'No, sir! I forbid you to say a word! My mind

is quite made up—this matter must be settled tonight.'
Then he got up on the dais, asked for a chord from the
orchestra and looked benevolently at the assembled company.

'My friends,' he began, 'we are here tonight to celebrate my son's coming of age....' He talked for some
minutes, quite amusingly, about Peter's exploits in the
past. Jossie's name quite frequently cropped up. Most of
his audience was very appreciative, and when he went
on to talk of the future, and mentioned a long-awaited
piece of news a murmur of anticipation went round the
room. It was not difficult to guess what Sir Thomas was
about to tell them. But Lady Frances, standing next to
Ivo in the window, whispered, 'Look at Peter! What's
wrong with him? And why isn't Jossie up there beside
him?'

Ivo stiffened. Peter was gazing at his father in horror,
seemingly rooted to the spot. Ivo said urgently, 'He
doesn't want to marry her! My God, Peter Radstock
doesn't want to marry her! But why the devil doesn't he
do something? Why doesn't he stop his father before it
is too late?'

But it was too late already. Sir Thomas was in full
spate. 'And now,' he said, 'it is my great pleasure to
announce that my son is to marry someone we all know
very well. It will hardly be a surprise to you that he has
asked Miss Helena Joscelin Calverton Morley to be his
wi—'

Peter found his voice at last. 'I haven't,' he cried. 'I'm
not going to marry Jossie. I know you want me to, but
I can't! I don't love her, I love Rosalind Cherton. And
she has already agreed to marry me.'

For a moment there was dead silence. Then it was
broken by a loud, shocked *'No!'* Jossie tore herself out

of Lady Radstock's restraining arms and ran up to the
dais. 'No, Peter, no! That's wrong! It must be! You don't
know what you're saying!'

'I'm sorry, Joss…' he said awkwardly. 'I wanted to
tell you, but—'

'You can't have anything to tell me. We've already
made our plans, we've known them for years! I won't
let you throw them away like that. I won't let you!' She
was whiter than her dress, frantically clutching Peter,
fighting to hold on as he tried to disengage himself.

The Radstocks' guests murmured in shocked disapproval at the scene unfolding before them. Peter Radstock had obviously behaved abominably, but this public
exposure of such raw feeling was not the way to behave!
But then Jossie Morley had never known how to conduct
herself.

Major Morley came up to them. 'Jossie! Pull yourself
together!' He turned to Peter, who was now standing
shamefacedly by his father. 'I'll see you later, sir!' he
said. 'Meanwhile—Jossie, come with me!'

'No,' she cried. 'How can you ask such a thing? It's
my life I'm fighting for! I must stay here and talk to
him. He doesn't understand. I can't let him make such
a mistake.' She turned to Sir Thomas, who was stiff with
anger and embarrassment. 'You tell him, Sir Thomas.
Peter loves *me*. I'm his friend. I've been his friend for
years. How can he love that girl? She's nothing! A nonentity. He doesn't even know her!'

Peter turned on her. 'You be quiet, Jossie!' he said
angrily. 'I do know Rosalind. We got to know each other
in Bath. She means a great deal to me.'

'She can't mean more to you than I do!'

'Well, she does! She's a proper girl! More of a girl

than you'll ever be. I want a woman for my wife, Jossie Morley, not a *friend*. I love her, I tell you!'

Jossie shook her head frantically. 'No, no! That can't be so! It can't! It's because I disappointed you. But I can make love now, Peter. I know how to kiss. Try me!' She tried to cling to him once again.

Scarlet with embarrassment, Peter dragged her arms down and pushed her away. 'Stop it! This won't do you any good! It's too late. My mind is made up.'

Major Morley looked at the crowd which had gathered round them and grew purple with rage. 'Jossie!' he said sharply. 'Come with me, I say! You're making an unforgivably disgusting exhibition of yourself!'

Lady Frances gave an involuntary exclamation at these heartless words, and came hurrying up. But the Major waved her back impatiently. 'Leave Jossie alone, ma'am! Allow me to deal with this in my own way, I know what I'm doing.' He barked, 'Jossie, I *order* you to come with me! This minute!' He took Jossie's arm and hauled her roughly away.

Jossie was distraught. She looked wildly at Peter, who was now engaged in an altercation with his father, stared at the circle of shocked faces which surrounded them, then wrenched herself out of her father's grip, and ran unseeingly past Ivo down into the garden. Ivo took a step after her, but Lady Frances held him back. 'Wait,' she said. 'You can't go yet. Her father's following her, and he's made it clear he doesn't want anyone else to interfere. We must wait. Oh, Ivo, I wish I knew what to do! That cold-hearted man doesn't know how to treat her properly. I'm very worried.'

'Damn Morley! He isn't fit to handle a dog!' Ivo looked into the room behind them. 'The Radstocks have disappeared, but they've started the music again. No one would notice if we were to leave. I'll go down into the garden and look for Jossie. She might have calmed down by now, but she can't stay here. Shall I try to talk to Morley? Offer to take Jossie back to the Lodge? You're surely the best person to look after her at the moment.'

'Do!'

Ivo moved quietly down the garden, almost as if he was in enemy country. He wanted if possible to see what was going on between the Morleys before he approached them. Persuading Jossie's father to let her go to Lady Frances might not be easy. But, far from comforting or calming his daughter, Jossie's father was still berating her, his voice trembling with rage.

'And what people must think I cannot imagine!' he was saying.

Ivo stopped in shock and listened unashamedly as the Major went on, 'You have behaved disgracefully to-night!' His voice rose. 'Disgracefully! I am utterly ashamed of you!'

Jossie's voice, full of anguish. 'But, Father…what was I to do? Peter—'

'There can be no excuse for the manner in which Peter Radstock jilted you. I was never so humiliated in my life, and I intend to have it out with him at the earliest opportunity. But I am forced to say that I cannot blame him in the slightest for preferring to marry Rosalind Cherton! She's a girl who would make any man proud to call his wife! And look at you! What man of taste would want to be tied to such a badly dressed, untidy, ungraceful hoyden? A girl who hasn't the smallest idea how to conduct herself! Believe me, my girl, not all your fortune could recommend you to any man of feeling.'

Ivo winced at the passionate entreaty in Jossie's voice as she said, 'I'll be better, Father! I'll try!'

'It's too late now! Peter Radstock's gone. He wasn't much of a fellow, but he was the best catch in the neighbourhood.' His voice rose in temper. 'Why does this have to happen to me? What have I ever done to deserve such a burden! You were never the boy I wanted, God knows, but you can't even make a decent *girl*!'

There was a cry of agony followed by a moment's shocked silence. Then Jossie's voice was almost unrecognisable as she said harshly, 'You have made me what I am, Father. And now you and Peter Radstock between you have destroyed me!'

Then Ivo saw a slim white figure speeding down the garden towards the drive, and heard the Major shouting, 'Jossie! Come back this instant! Come back, I say!'

Jossie didn't stop. Her father swore and turned back towards the house. He saw Ivo. 'That *damned* daughter of mine,' he said, shaking with fury. 'She's nothing but trouble.'

Ivo was tempted to knock the man down, or at least tell him what he thought of him, but there was no time. It was more important to find Jossie. 'I'll go after her,' he said.

'Do what you like! I've washed my hands of her. She'll come home when she's ready. Excuse me, Trenchard. I must do what I can to reassure Mrs Cherton and her daughter. This business must have distressed them very badly. I can hardly bear to think what they must be feeling. They need my support.' And Jossie's father marched up the steps and into the house.

Ivo thought briefly, then went back to Lady Frances. 'Jossie has fled. I think…I hope I know where. I'll borrow a horse and go in search of her. Can you go back to the Lodge by yourself?'

'Of course. I'll wait for you there. Take my shawl!
She may be cold.'

Ivo saddled one of the horses and set off straight
away. There was a full moon and it wasn't difficult to
see his way. He pushed the horse as hard as he dared.

He found Jossie as he had expected in the little valley.
She was sitting on the bank of the stream much as he
had found her once before, slippers discarded, feet dangling in the water. There were signs that she had come
over the fields, pushing her way unheeding through trees
and bushes. Her dress was torn and dirty, her hair in
wild disarray.

'Jossie?' he said softly. When there was no reaction
he came and squatted down beside her. He took her
hand. It was cold and lay limp in his grasp. 'Jossie, look
at me.' Still nothing. He put out his other hand and
turned her head towards him. There was no resistance,
she was quite passive. But her eyes were blank. Her face
was covered in streaks of blood and dirt. Though it was
a warm night, she was shivering.

'Come, I'll help you out of the water. Lady Frances
has sent her shawl for you. Put it on.'

Again she made no effort to resist as he lifted her up
and wrapped the shawl round her. Ivo grew worried. He
had come across this kind of reaction before, in men who
had had some severe physical injury. This injury was to
the spirit, not to the body, but the result was the same—
Jossie was in a state of acute shock. She urgently needed
warmth and care. He sat her down again, took off his
coat, added it to the shawl and carried her, swaddled like
this, up the slope to his horse. With a prayer of gratitude
that he had chosen a sturdy mount, he put Jossie up,
then clambered on behind. They slowly made their way

to the Lodge. Jossie occasionally gave a convulsive shudder, but neither raised her eyes nor spoke.

During the next few days there were serious worries in Lady Frances's household for Jossie's state of mind. There were no tears, no outbursts of emotion. She lay perfectly passive in the bed that had been prepared for her on the night of the ball. But she never spoke. Nor did she eat anything, accepting only the occasional sip of water. After a day or two Lady Frances brought her downstairs, hoping that a change of scene might make a difference. Jossie lay on a daybed gazing out of the window, but not even Ivo could rouse her.

Ivo went back to Sudiham soon after. Lady Frances pointed out to him that it was necessary.

'This is a small village, Ivo, and there has been enough gossip already. Jossie is in no state at the moment to protect herself from further scandal, so we must do it for her. The world knows by now that you found her and brought her here on the night of the ball. It might wonder why she is not with her father.'

'With her father! I wouldn't leave a dog with that cold-hearted villain!'

'Yes, yes. We both know why Jossie is better with me. Indeed, she would be better with practically anyone other than Gerard Morley. Between them Peter Radstock and her father have very nearly destroyed that poor girl. But though the world was present when Peter Radstock treated her so cruelly, it doesn't know what happened afterwards. Indeed, I doubt anyone would believe you if you told them how inhuman her father was to her.'

'I can still hardly believe it myself.'

'I can. Just. When Gerard Morley's self-esteem is injured he is capable of anything. Jossie had let him down.'

'Let him down? But he is entirely to blame!'

'You will never convince him of that. Let us not waste our time talking of it. I mean what I said, Ivo. It is natural you feel protective towards Jossie, but you must take care. We want no excuse for speculation on the part *you* might have played in this dreadful affair.'

'What the devil do you mean by that?'

'Our neighbours are aware that Jossie frequently visited you when you were here last year. Yes, yes, I know that this was entirely innocent, and at the time I think everyone agreed. But if you spend any length of time here now, they might wonder whether Peter Radstock has some other grounds for jilting Jossie, and that is the last thing we want. Go back to Sudiham for now. It would be reasonable, I think, for you to come to enquire after her later.'

Ivo accepted her advice, though all his instincts were against it. He had been outraged by the treatment Jossie had suffered on the night of the ball from the two men she trusted most in the world. If he had had the slightest right to act on her behalf he would have seen both of them before now to demand an explanation. But he had none, and his aunt was right. To intervene would only create more scandal. But he had no intention of abandoning Jossie. He would take care not to cause gossip, but he *would* see that, from now on, she would have someone to look after her interests—even from a distance.

He found himself wondering what his friends from earlier days would have thought of this desire to protect Jossie. They might well have been astonished. Ivo Trenchard, it was well known, avoided young girls like the plague. His interest in the opposite sex was for his own pleasure, not for any altruistic motives. And it was true that in the past he had had many affairs, not all of them ending by mutual consent. But most of his amours had been ladies who had little enough heart to wound. Not one of them had been anything like as vulnerable as Jossie. Even so, he had always tried to manage the parting with grace, to minimise the hurt to their feelings or, more often, the damage to their pride. The scenes on the night of the Radstock ball, the cruelty to a girl whom he admired for her loyalty, her lack of guile, her innocent directness, had shocked him beyond measure. He did not think himself in love with Jossie. But he badly wanted to be her champion.

Chapter Eight

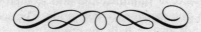

Ivo waited two weeks before he came back to Danby Lodge. Lady Frances met him at the door. 'Come this way, Ivo,' she said. 'I want to talk to you before you see Jossie.'

Ivo followed her into her own small sitting room, but when she gestured to him to sit down he shook his head. 'Tell me how she is,' he said.

His aunt frowned. 'She has started to eat a little—perhaps enough to keep a sparrow alive. But she still says nothing at all. I do so hope you can do something—she never stopped talking when you were here last year.'

'I'll do what I can. Is that what you wanted to say?'

'No. I want to bring you up to date on what has been happening in Lyne during the last fortnight.'

'Well?'

'The Radstocks have been doing their best to repair the damage. There's a great deal of feeling in the village about Peter's treatment of Jossie, you know.'

'You amaze me! But don't tell me that Peter has changed his mind again!'

'On no account. He is as determined as I have ever known him to marry the Cherton girl. The Radstocks are having to put a brave face on it. Sir Thomas was bitterly disappointed, and for a while we thought there would very likely be a rift between father and son. But Lady Radstock has managed to smooth that over. To tell the truth, Ivo, it is my opinion that she is pleased rather than sorry about Peter's rejection of Jossie. She was shocked at the manner in which it was done—indeed, who could possibly approve? But Rosalind Cherton is exactly the sort of daughter-in-law she would have chosen.'

'A pretty trinket, compared with a diamond!'

'Peter and his mother may prefer trinkets. Diamonds can be very demanding to live with. Peter would always have been the weaker partner if he had married Jossie.'

'What about that wretch of a father? Has he visited his daughter?'

'He tried once, about a week ago. But Jossie refused to see him. He hasn't been near her since.' She paused. 'Major Morley has had other preoccupations.'

'Indeed?'

'He is to marry Mrs Cherton. After a suitable interval, of course.'

'Really?' said Ivo, his lip curling in scorn. 'So Peter Radstock is to marry the daughter and Major Morley the mother. How neat!'

'Neat indeed! Nor did it come about by chance! Do you know what that woman did, Ivo? I was never so shocked in my life.'

'I've met quite a few Mrs Chertons in my time,' said Ivo sardonically. 'I doubt I'll be shocked. But tell me.'

'We all knew that Lady Radstock and Peter had gone to Bath. And I for one thought nothing of it when Mrs Cherton announced that she and Rosalind had decided to visit friends for a few days. What neither I nor anyone else here knew was that they went to Bath, too. These friends of Mrs Cherton apparently reside there. Quite a coincidence, wouldn't you say?'

Ivo said cynically, 'In my experience a mother with a marriageable daughter deals in such coincidences. I can assume what happened next, I suppose?'

'She and Lady Radstock met, naturally. So did Peter and Miss Cherton. And while Lady Radstock was busy acquiring new dresses for the ball, Mrs Cherton was equally busy acquiring a rich husband for her daughter— at Jossie's expense. Those two young people were absolutely thrown together. Poor Peter hardly stood a chance.'

'One has to admire Mrs Cherton's singlemindedness, if not her ethics. From what I've seen of Radstock, I can quite believe that he found it impossible to resist both the girl and her mother!' He smiled contemptuously. 'My own opinion is that Jossie is better off without him. He's a weakling.'

'I agree with you. If it weren't for Jossie's distress, I would say that Rosalind Cherton is welcome to him. But Mrs Cherton's activities did not end there. She has now caught a husband for herself, too!'

Ivo shrugged. 'A few months ago I would have said that all women were like the Chertons. Quite ruthless in pursuit of a successful marriage—by which, of course, they mean a rich marriage. Charlotte Gurney is another such.'

'Well, Miss Cherton will be rich enough, but her mother may find she is less fortunate.'

'What do you mean?'

'Not many know what I am about to tell you, Ivo, so you will keep it to yourself, if you please.' Lady Frances smiled with malicious pleasure. 'Major Morley comes from an old family, but he has very little persona wealth. I dare say he thought he would remedy that when he married the Calverton heiress. But Sir Robert didn't altogether approve of his daughter's choice of husband, any more than I did.'

'How right you both were!'

'If Lucinda had lived longer she might have come to agree with us! But at the time she was desperately in love with Gerard Morley. Sir Robert gave in to her, as he usually did, but he was determined not to let Morley profit from the marriage. So he set up in a trust in favour of Lucinda's children. Jossie is the only child of the marriage, and she is the sole heiress. The Major has a life interest in the house and can draw a suitable income from the estate, but nothing more. On his death it will all be Jossie's.' She paused, then said delicately, 'I am not sure that Mrs Cherton is aware of this…'

Ivo started to laugh. 'Will he tell her before they marry, do you think? She would be well served if he didn't!' He stood up. 'Have you told Jossie about her father's intention to marry Mrs Cherton?'

'No. I don't want to add to her unhappiness. How can she possibly live at home with that woman as a stepmother?'

'It remains to be seen whether she can live in Lyne St Michael at all! Has she no other relatives?'

'None.'

'Can you do something? After all, you're her godmother.'

'I would love to give Jossie a home with me. So far her father has blocked anything I have tried to do for her, but I have a feeling that the situation may well have altered… I have been making great plans for her, Ivo.'

'Good! What are they?'

'When she is better I shall take her away for change

of scene. I am fairly certain that her father will now be only too glad to have her off his hands. After that, I want to fulfil a long-held ambition, one I had thought impossible before the events of last month.'

'What is it?'

'When Lucinda died and Jossie was left without a mother, I said that, when the time came, I would prepare Jossie for presentation to society. Unless Gerard Morley married again there would be no one else to do it. But then as Jossie grew older it became evident that she would marry Peter Radstock before she came out. The girl wouldn't hear of going to London. I couldn't fight Jossie as well as her father, so I had to give up the idea. But my way is now clear!'

'You would still have Jossie to fight. She would hate it! She has never wanted to live in a town, particularly not London.'

'Aha! That was before July. She may have changed her mind about living in the country now. All her ambitions for country life were focussed on Peter and her father, and that dream is at an end.' Lady Frances paused, then said briskly, 'Besides, I think she should be persuaded. She is wasted down here.'

Ivo nodded his head. 'I agree with you there. But aren't we running a little ahead of ourselves? From what you tell me, Jossie has a long way to go before she could face the world.'

'She is a *little* better, but far from herself. Come and see what you can do.' Lady Frances led the way to a sunny room at the back of the house. Jossie was by the window, gazing out as usual.

'I've brought you a visitor, Jossie.'

Ivo didn't wait for a reaction but went over to the daybed and drew up a chair to sit beside it. He sat waiting for a moment. Then he began, 'I remember you were once very scornful of me, Jossie. I believe you thought I was making a great deal of fuss about nothing. A fox bite, if you remember. Do you?'

Jossie turned her head and looked at him. Her eyes were haunted pools of dark in her thin face.

Ivo hid his shock and went on calmly, 'You didn't think much of my military knowledge, either. You couldn't imagine how anyone, least of all a serving soldier, could confuse the names of Grouchy and Ney. And as for my skill at cards…'

'You were good at cards.' Jossie's voice was low, but clear.

'You beat me too often for my own self-esteem, all the same. How much do I still owe you?'

Her interest had died. 'I don't remember…,' she said listlessly.

Ivo nodded. 'You obviously don't care, and I can't blame you for that.' He regarded her for a moment. Then he said in a different tone, 'But tell me, what has happened to all that fighting spirit you prized in yourself and others? All that wit, all that will to win? I'd like to know.' She turned her head away again, but Ivo could tell she was listening.

He went on with a touch of irony in his voice, 'I suppose the answer is that it had always been too easy for you. You had never really been tested before. You knew about Grouchy and Ney, but that was all in the mind, you had never had to fight, as I have, in a real battle. You've never had to watch while men you have known for years, some of them your best friends, are cut down in front of you. You haven't had to outwit your opponent, not to win money, but to save your life. You've never had to pick yourself up from a body blow and begin again. Not before now.' He waited. Jossie turned again to look at him.

'You're saying I'm a coward.'

'Not *yet*. You've been wounded. Badly wounded. But if you were one of my men I wouldn't let you linger many more days before you came back on duty. It's time to sit up properly and come back to life, my young soldier.'

She sat up with a jerk. 'Don't! Don't speak to me as if I was one your men! I don't want to hear about fighting and killing and battles. I'm not a soldier, or a fellow, or a good chap. And you needn't call me Jossie, either! That's a boy's name. It's an ugly name. A name for a *son*, not a daughter! From now on I'm going to be a girl, and I'll use the name my mother gave me. Helena Calverton Morley.'

Ivo smiled in relief at this return to life. He got up and bowed. 'My dear Miss Calverton Morley, I am delighted to make your acquaintance!' Then he took her hand and held it to his lips. Jossie's cure had begun.

The village of Lyne St Michael at first found it strange that Jossie Morley should stay so long with her godmother. But when it became known that Major Morley was to marry Rosalind Cherton's mother they all thought it perfectly understandable, a very good solution in fact. Indeed some of them wondered whether Jossie would ever go back to live at the Manor.

Jossie herself was faced with the same question. Till Ivo's visit she had been in a kind of limbo, hiding behind an invisible curtain that she had drawn between herself and the world in order to keep out the unbearable pain and humiliation of what had happened. She tried to be nothing, to feel nothing, to respond to nothing. The two people she had loved most in the world had rejected her. Nothing was left. At that stage she had no will to survive, so the future simply did not concern her.

But Ivo's visit had roused her from the comparative peace of that state. His deep voice, with its characteristic drawl, reminded her of the person she had been, reminded her that she had always scorned weakness or cowardice, reminded her of the uncomplicated pleasure she had had in his company, and it brought back, as perhaps no one else could have, her interest in life. From the day of his visit she started to take a more active part in the world around her, to eat with more enjoyment, to respond to Lady Frances more willingly. She was young, and she recovered her physical strength quickly enough. She was soon walking round the garden, helping Lady Frances in the stillroom, playing with the dogs. But she would not go out of the grounds. And she refused to see anyone from the village or the neighbourhood, though there were plenty who came, out of sympathy, or pity, or simple curiosity.

But with returning life came the questions. The pain, the sense of betrayal, were buried deep inside her, but the practical problems could not be ignored. What was she to do? Where was she to live? When Lady Frances told her somewhat apprehensively of Major Morley's plan to marry Mrs Cherton, Jossie showed little reaction.

'You seem to think that will distress me,' she said. 'But why should it? I cannot imagine living with my father ever again… Or that he would ever want me to.'

This was the moment Lady Frances had been waiting for. 'In that case I should like to make a suggestion,' she said. 'If your father would agree, I should like to take you away from Lyne as soon as possible. People mean well, but they will never leave you alone long enough to forget, quite apart from any…any unhappy associations of place. And next year I would hope to take you to London. I think you should be presented.'

'I have never wanted to go to London.'

'Not till now,' said Lady Frances comfortably. 'But I am hoping you will change your mind after you have had time to consider. I should love you to see London. And London to see you.' Taking a look at Jossie's face, she went on, 'However, there's time enough before we have to make any decision about that. For the present I should like to take you on a visit to my brother. Sudiham is large enough for us both to lose ourselves in if we wish! On the other hand, you may enjoy making Ivo's father's acquaintance. He is eccentric, but interesting.'

Jossie said slowly, 'I should like that. But, forgive me—I don't quite understand why you are doing this. I have no real claim on you.'

'You have a very real claim, Jossie! You are my god-daughter. I loved your mother, and have always regretted that I could not do more for her daughter. Now I can! I cannot tell you how delighted I am to have your company. Since my husband died I have often been lonely. Ivo has been very good, but he has many other commitments, and cannot always be visiting me. You will be the daughter I never had. Do you agree?'

'You are…are almost too kind,' said Jossie in a low voice. 'I have not so far been a success as a daughter. I…I hope I don't disappoint you.'

'Oh, you won't, you won't!' said Lady Frances bracingly. 'I shan't allow you to!'

Major Morley was only too glad to be rid of the daughter who had all her life given him nothing but her trust, love and admiration. To him she had merely become a burden, a source of disappointment and shame. It was not only her disgraceful behaviour at the ball which had upset him. Some of the disapproval felt among the neighbours for the Radstocks had, in his opinion, quite unjustly spilled over on to him, especially at his decision to marry Mrs Cherton. The sooner Jossie was in someone else's hands and out of Lyne St Michael the better as far as he was concerned. Little as he liked Lady Frances, she was undeniably highly respected, and Jossie's godmother, too. No one could criticise him in the least for leaving Jossie in her care, and he gave her *carte blanche* to do as she pleased with the girl.

In a very short time, therefore, Jossie and Lady Frances were on their way to Sudiham. Ivo would not be there. He had some business in London, but had promised his father he would be back as soon as he could. As they travelled Lady Frances gave Jossie some family background.

'My brother was at odds with Ivo for over a year, and he now regrets the lost time. Ivo tries to be at Sudiham as often as he can, but he is, after all, young and active, with a large number of friends whom he likes to visit, some near Bath, and many others in London. Rupert often feels lonely, especially as Peregrine, Ivo's younger brother, shows no sign of wishing to leave Derbyshire. I think we are doing him a service coming to stay. At least, that is what I shall tell him!'

Ivo had already given his father the outlines of Jossie's story. The old man had condemned Peter Radstock with characteristic robustness, and though he was careful in what he said about Major Morley, it was clear that he disapproved of him, too. Even before she came he was prepared to support Jossie in any way he could, but she had not been at Sudiham very long before she and Lord Veryan were on excellent terms.

Lady Frances was relieved. Though Jossie had come a long way since July she was still a shadow of her former self, and Lady Frances had been afraid that her brother's somewhat abrasive style might upset Jossie's hard-won equilibrium. But Jossie liked his directness and took his comments in her stride. He was inclined to be more peppery and more prejudiced than his son, but she otherwise saw quite a lot in him which reminded her of Ivo.

For a while after their arrival the weather was good, and Lord Veryan soon persuaded Jossie to come out riding with him. Here there was no risk that she would meet any former acquaintance, or see any familiar landmarks. The park was extensive, with some beautiful views to the west and no reminders of her former home, and after a few days she was happy enough to join him. The greatest difference from her previous outings was that she now always rode side saddle, using Lady Frances's old equipment. She suffered her companion's blistering criticisms of her riding style with patience and a determination to improve. Soon her seat was once again excellent. No one would have guessed that she had ever done anything other than ride as a lady should.

Lord Veryan taught Jossie backgammon and cribbage, too, and they played endlessly when the weather was poor, competing, as she had with Ivo, for imaginary stakes. At first Lord Veryan won every time for the games were new to Jossie. But she watched and learned, and after a while Lord Veryan, much to his surprise, had to work hard to win. This did not put him out in the slightest. He had always enjoyed a good fight, and was delighted to find such a worthy opponent.

'That's the way!' he would shout. 'Beat me if you can, girl! No sense in playing if you don't intend to win. Games or life, it's all the same. No sitting back. Let 'em know what you're made of! Show 'em!'

Lady Frances sat and watched her brother and Jossie becoming fast, if competitive, friends. Her plan was working better than she could have hoped.

When Ivo came back some weeks later he found Jossie apparently almost back to normal. Almost, but not quite. Some of the fearless directness which had so enchanted him, the innocent vulnerability which had in his eyes made her special, had disappeared. The new Jossie, he thought, regarded the world with reserve. She would trust no one very far. He wondered what he could do about it. He and his aunt had rescued her from the ashes of her old life, but her future would be bleak if she continued living, as she had since that disastrous day in July, with no apparent aim or goal. It was time for Jossie to wake up again.

Then news reached Sudiham that Peter Radstock had married Rosalind Cherton with great ceremony in Lyne St Michael parish church. Bride and groom had apparently looked radiant with happiness. They were at present on a simple tour of the Lakes, but were planning to spend some time in London the following year. Jossie said nothing, but spent the rest of the day in her room. When she emerged in the evening she looked paler but more resolute, as if she had come to a decision.

Ivo wondered what form it would take. He didn't have long to wait, for Jossie herself brought the subject up at dinner. They had all so far carefully avoided any reference to the events in Lyne St Michael, but she said, with something of her old directness 'I notice that none of you has mentioned Peter Radstock's marriage. I'm not sure why—it is not as if it was unexpected. And I am not upset by it.'

'That makes me very happy. When you shut yourself up in your room, I thought you *were* upset,' said Lady Frances.

'No. I think I must have been waiting for it. It has woken me up. In fact, I spent the day thinking about my own future.'

'You are welcome to stay here as long as you wish, my dear,' said Lord Veryan.

She gave him a grateful smile. 'The notion is very appealing, sir. But I can't stay here forever. And if I am to do anything with my life I must soon make other plans.'

'And those are…?' asked Ivo.

Jossie hesitated, then turned to Lady Frances. 'You once said that you would like to introduce me to society, ma'am. Are you still of the same mind?'

After a moment's surprise Lady Frances replied, 'Of course! There is nothing I would rather do!'

'Are you sure about this, Jossie?' asked Ivo.

'Oh, yes! Quite certain. Lady Frances has promised to prepare me. I shall need to learn how to behave in company—how to dress, to dance, what people talk about and so on…among other things.'

'My dear girl, of course I will! And Ivo will, too, won't you?'

'Of course.'

Lady Frances got up and threw her arms round Jossie. 'Dearest girl, this is the best news I've heard in a long time. You shall be the most perfectly prepared débutante in London! We shall have such fun, I promise you!'

'I fully intend to, Lady Frances!' Ivo looked up

sharply. His aunt seemed not to have noticed a slight undercurrent in Jossie's voice, but he was sure he had heard one. What was she up to?

They talked at length after that, but though there was nothing more that was significant in what Jossie said, or how she said it, Ivo's suspicion had been roused. Eventually Lady Frances looked at Jossie's pale face and heavy eyes and said, 'All this excitement! You look quite worn out, child. Off to bed with you! There'll be plenty of time tomorrow to talk some more. Goodnight, my dear! I think you will sleep very well tonight!'

After Jossie had left them Lord Veryan said, 'I shall be sorry to see her go, but she is absolutely right! And you'll have no difficulty in teaching her, Frances. I've seldom known such a quick mind.'

'Yes, she has. A very quick mind. And I would quite like to know what else she has in it,' said Ivo, slowly. 'Jossie Morley has never before shown the slightest interest in London, or its society.'

'I see nothing to wonder at in that!' said Lady Frances. 'She wants to make a complete break with the past. Don't be such a cynic, Ivo! You are going to help, aren't you?'

'I've said I will. Always remembering that I must tread carefully. Can you imagine the talk if I don't? You were the one to remind me how the county loves a scandal, and my reputation usually hangs me before I've done a thing!'

Lord Veryan grunted unsympathetically at the slightly bitter note in Ivo's voice. 'Don't sound so sorry for yourself, sir! You've had considerable amusement in the process of getting your damned reputation! You can't blame people for believing the worst. It's often been no more than the truth! What's more, I've never seen you worry about it before.'

'You're right, I haven't! But this is different. Aunt Frances was right! It's important that we are careful, not for my sake, but for Jossie's. We don't want any more gossip, she's had enough. Why do you think I kept away from Sudiham for so long after she arrived?'

The two older people exchanged a glance, and Lady Frances asked slowly, 'You're not by any chance falling in love with Jossie, are you, Ivo?'

He looked at her in astonishment. 'Good Lord, no! She's far too young. No, no! I regard her as a protégée…'

A sudden vision of the scene by the waterfall gave Ivo pause. The memory of how it had felt to have Jossie in his arms, Jossie responding with such innocent abandon to his kisses…the way he had felt… They were not the feelings one had towards a protégée! She had been so completely captivating, so spellbindingly seductive that he had lost all sight of how young she was… For those few moments of madness she had simply been a completely desirable woman! He stood up and walked round restlessly, oblivious to two pairs of eyes following him. Radstock was a fool! A crass idiot! Why the devil could he not appreciate what an extraordinary delight it would have been to teach Jossie the ways of love, to unlock all her sweetness, her passion…?

Ivo turned round to find his aunt and his father regarding him somewhat quizzically. He pulled himself together. 'A protégée,' he said firmly. 'That is all! But you see why I have to be careful.' He paused. 'However, I'd still like to know what she intends to do in London.'

'What an absurd question! She will meet the *ton*, of course. I fancy I still have some good friends in London who would welcome me back and receive a young friend of mine kindly. Jossie mustn't be allowed to dwindle into a disappointed spinster, and in London she might well meet someone who could persuade her to forget Peter Radstock. Between us we could introduce her to the very cream of Society. She could make an excellent match in her first season.'

Ivo did not find this notion altogether palatable. It seemed to him that his aunt was being over-hasty. Jossie would marry some time, no doubt, but he was not sure he wanted her to find a husband as quickly as all that.

'In due course, perhaps!' he said firmly. 'But not yet. I'd like her to have time to enjoy herself first. She mustn't rush into marriage with the first eligible man she meets!'

There was a little silence.

'Of course not!' said his aunt.

'Naturally not!' said his father.

Exasperated, Ivo said, 'Why the devil are you both looking at me in that absurd fashion? My interest in Jossie Morley is…is totally platonic, I assure you! I wish you would stop reading more than there is into my words!'

'All the same, it's time you thought of finding a wife, Ivo,' said his father mildly. 'Jossie would seem to me to be an excellent choice. I like the girl—and you appear to like her, too! You've known quite a few young women in your time, but I've never seen you take quite so much interest in their welfare before!'

Ivo took a deep breath and said patiently, 'You're quite right, I *do* take an interest in Jossie's welfare. She has been treated heartlessly by the very people who ought to have protected her most. I do take an interest in her welfare and will continue to do what I can to promote her happiness. Furthermore, I agree with you that she would be an excellent choice for any man lucky enough to win her. However, my own choice at present is to remain single!'

Fearing that the discussion was about to dissolve into a family altercation, Lady Frances decided to intervene. 'And I am quite sure, Rupert, that Jossie does not regard Ivo in the light of a possible husband, either. Indeed, she is in no state at the moment to think of marriage at all. Remember the extraordinary life she led before last July, dressed as a boy and behaving like one, too! Ivo is right. She must be given time to learn something of the world before she makes her choice. It is undeniable that she has the necessary looks and wealth to be highly acceptable to the *ton*.'

'Acceptable? She has the necessary spirit and originality to make herself a huge success! If that is what she wants,' said Ivo, whose mind was still half-occupied with questions about Jossie's real motives.

Chapter Nine

The weather had turned cold and frosty, and Lord Veryan declared that the ground was too hard for riding. So
the next day Ivo invited Jossie for a walk in the park
instead. A night's rest had not caused him to change his
mind, and his curiosity about Jossie's motives was as
active as ever. Why was she so full of enthusiasm for
his aunt's plan? Why was she as eager now to see London, as she had been hostile to the idea in the past? Was
it simply a desire for a change of scene as his aunt had
suggested? He doubted it. He doubted it very much. Jossie was not a girl to be thrilled by the thought of dresses
and balls and life in a big city. So why the change? A
walk on a cold, frosty day seemed to provide an excellent opportunity for finding out.

'I'm delighted that you are going to London, Jossie,'
he began. 'Though I never thought to see you there. I
thought you disliked the place.'

She gave him a look. 'As you said yourself, I have
never been there. How can I possibly judge? And since
Lady Frances was prepared to be so generous I decided
to go to see for myself. Who knows? I might even learn

to like the company of fashionable people! They can't all be as boring as the ones I have met so far.'

This touch of the old Jossie aroused Ivo's ever-ready sense of humour, but he kept his face straight as he said reproachfully, 'How unkind of you to say so! I am generally considered to be quite entertaining. But if you are bored…'

'Oh, no! I didn't mean you!' said Jossie, immediately contrite. 'I don't think of you as a fashionable person at all!'

'Worse and worse!' said Ivo. 'A dullard, either way.'

Jossie looked at him suspiciously. 'You're laughing at me!' she said.

'My dear child,' said Ivo, giving way to his amusement, 'I think you know very little about fashionable people! You might even like some of them! But I don't believe that your sudden wish to go to London has its roots in a simple desire to see the *ton*. Why don't you tell me what is in that head of yours?'

'What do you mean?' said Jossie, looking at him wide-eyed, her eyes green as the sea. She was certainly up to something!

'Come, my girl! You know you won't succeed in pulling the wool over my eyes for very long. We've played chess too often for that. You are up to something, Jossie Morley, and I would like to know what it is!'

Jossie frowned, obviously debating what she should tell him. Then her face cleared and she smiled at him and said, almost conversationally, 'Peter said he wanted to go to London during the Season. And I expect he'll be even more determined now. He'll want to show off that new wife of his, the elegantly lovely Rosalind. He won't find it difficult to persuade her. She'll want to shine in London as she shone in Lyne St Michael. Oh, and Bath, too, of course. She shone to such good effect there. They will probably be in London next year.'

'Shine! Rosalind Cherton?'

'Rosalind Radstock.'

Ivo ignored this. 'Jossie, it's quite clear that you really do know nothing about the world! Take my word for it, whatever the girl's name is she would arouse very little interest in London. She's pretty enough, but there are a hundred prettier young women there. Her manners are elegant, but there is no lack of elegant females, either. And that is all there is to her! To be a success in London, to shine, as you call it, a woman needs something more than insipid elegance. She needs…oh, I don't know… something more special. Character. Originality.'

'Really?' asked Jossie, looking pleased. 'You don't think she would be a wild success, then?'

'I am sure she wouldn't!' Ivo was beginning to see where Jossie's thoughts were leading. He added deliberately, 'But *you* could.'

He was intrigued by the mixture of feelings in her expression. A strong touch of doubt, mixed with eagerness, certainly. But there was more. Plans were forming in that busy mind.

'That's what I want,' she said. 'And I would give anything to achieve it. But I'd have to be sure… Do you really think I could do it?'

Ivo regarded her with a small smile. 'You have no idea, have you? Jossie, you could be a sensation in London! Believe me, I know what I am saying. I've seen a good few charming women in my time, but when I first met you I was bowled over.'

Jossie forgot her schemes for a moment. 'Bowled over indeed!' she said scornfully. 'When you first met me, Ivo, you thought I was a boy!'

'Well, the second time, then. I had forgotten the pistol affair for the moment.' He shook his head. 'That first time I thought you were an impudent scamp. It was a rude shock to find you were a girl.'

'You handled me very roughly.'

'I'm surprised I didn't do worse! You had just frightened me to death! But, may I apologise now?' Ivo stopped and took her hand with a touch of gallantry. 'If I had known what an entrancing creature was disguised in those boy's garments…'

He paused. Jossie was looking at him with something of her old derision. 'Be careful, Ivo! I'm not one of your flirts!'

He laughed delightedly and hugged her. 'No, you're not. And you never will be, I promise. But I *will* be your friend. What's more, if they are what I think they are, I'll help you with these plans you are busily hatching at the moment.'

She was silent. After a pause she said in quite a different tone, 'I believe you…I trust you. Why do I have such confidence in you, when I don't seem to be able to trust anyone else?'

'What about your godmother? My father? Surely you trust them?'

'I'm fond of Lady Frances, and I like your father. I cannot say how grateful I am for what they have done. But I couldn't talk to them like this. With you it's different.' She turned away from him, and spoke in a muffled voice. 'After that ball and the…the rest, I tried to shut the world out. You know I did. But I couldn't shut *you* out. I don't know why it is, but I feel a sort of bond with you.' She stopped and said abruptly, 'I'm not sure I like it. I would prefer to be free of such ties.'

'After what has happened that's understandable,' replied Ivo. 'But no one can survive entirely alone. I'm glad you trust me.'

They walked on in silence for a little. Jossie appeared to be deep in thought. Finally she spoke.

'That kiss…' she began. 'The one by the waterfall. Was it only imagination that made it so special? Because I believed it was Peter?'

'I don't think so,' said Ivo carefully. 'But this is dangerous ground, Jossie…'

'If you kissed me again like that…would it still work? That last time the effect was magical. Even though it was only a lesson, even though you were only trying to show me how to respond to Peter, I felt for a moment that I could do anything in the world, be anything you wanted me to be! It was a glorious feeling. If you kissed me again, would it be the same?'

'I don't think…'

'I so want to feel like that again! To feel as if I could attract anyone I chose. It's not very likely, is it, when neither Peter nor my father thought me much of a woman.'

Ivo exploded. 'They were wrong! Quite wrong!'

'Were they? Peter found something in that Cherton girl that I hadn't even thought about.'

'I would say he didn't exactly *find* it so much as have it put under his nose, my dear. She and her mother between them made him aware, probably for the first time in his life, of feminine attractions!'

Jossie nodded. 'Feminine attractions,' she said thoughtfully. 'That's what we're talking about. I didn't even know they existed.' She stopped again. 'I suppose it was stupid of me not to realise… I thought friendship was enough, you see. Till then I had never…never thought about…about setting out deliberately to attract anyone. I wouldn't have known how. I suppose that's the sort of thing that woman meant.' She looked at Ivo and said with a curl of her lip, 'I mean Mrs Cherton. My father was going to ask her to teach me! I would rather have died!'

'She could have nothing to teach you, Jossie, believe me!'

She gave him a twisted smile. 'I certainly couldn't have learned anything from her. It's odd that in the end it was you who showed me something of it all. It shows how much I trusted you, even then....' The smile vanished and she added bitterly, 'But it was all too late, wasn't it? Peter had already been attracted to someone else, someone who was more of a woman than I would ever be, he said. And my father thought the same. I was not only not the boy he wanted, I couldn't even make a decent girl. That's what he said.'

Her bitterness was so unlike the Jossie he knew that Ivo said urgently, 'Don't let it affect you, Jossie! They were fools, taken in by a pretty face with nothing behind it but an ambitious and determined mother. Rosalind Cherton hasn't half your quality. Girls like her are two a penny in London. But she's been taught from the cradle to make the most of her attractions, and she used them on Peter.'

'You're saying he was trapped? Without any sort of struggle?' She thought for a moment. 'I think you're right. Now I look back I can see that he was always rather easily led.'

'To the devil with Peter! The best thing you can do is to forget him!'

'Oh no! I shan't do that. Not yet. I shan't forget either of them.' Once again her voice had the undertone which had aroused his suspicions the night before.

He put his arm around her, then lifted her chin with his finger, forcing her to look at him. 'What exactly are you up to, Jossie? Tell me!'

Her eyes were shadowed. 'I can't. I'm not yet sure I can do it. It's early days and I still have a lot to learn. How to behave, how to dress, how to dance… You know the sort of thing. But more than that I want to learn how to appeal. I want to learn the arts of attraction.' She stopped, then added, 'Except that I would prefer to call them the arts of war!'

'Take care that you don't get hurt again.'

'Hurt? You couldn't be more mistaken, my friend,' she said softly. 'I doubt anyone will ever again be near enough to *touch* me!' She stopped again, then said slowly, 'Except, perhaps, you.'

She turned and looked into his eyes. Then she moved closer to him, holding her face up to his. Ivo found it impossible to resist the unspoken invitation. He bent his head and kissed her. She responded instantly, with a mixture of passion and a desperate desire for comfort. After a while the kiss intensified, grew deeper. It was even more intoxicating than the first time…

Ivo lifted his head and gently put her away from him. 'I think that's enough,' he said softly, proud of the steadiness of his voice. 'What you need at the moment is someone to trust, Jossie. A friend, not a lover. You mustn't confuse the two. I shall try to give you all the comfort, all the reassurance, I can. But if that kiss had gone on much longer it would have been a lover's kiss.'

She turned away. 'I don't understand!' she said. 'It happened again! I felt such…such…a sense of contentment, such comfort, as if I could find the answer there in your arms. You made me feel like…like a queen among women!' She turned to him. 'I don't understand,' she said again. 'Why couldn't I feel like that with Peter?'

For a moment Ivo had a lunatic temptation to give in, to show her just how much had been missing in her relationship with Peter Radstock, to make her even more aware of her womanhood, to demonstrate how supremely appealing he found her... But he put temptation aside. He had no wish to go down such a dangerous road, for his own sake just as much as for Jossie's. It would be all too easy to find them both trapped...

She was still looking at him with bewilderment in her eyes. Ivo pulled himself together, and, putting these thoughts firmly behind him, grinned at her, saying lightly, 'Aren't you forgetting something? I'm very good at kissing—remember my reputation!'

To his relief Jossie laughed and responded in kind. 'Of course! The worst flirt in the county.'

'I don't wish to boast,' said Ivo gravely, 'but there are some who would say I'm the worst flirt in Europe!'

'Really?' said Jossie, looking impressed. She went on, 'That explains it, of course. I imagine all successful flirts must have a particular talent for kissing. I wonder where they learn it? It would hardly be at their mother's knee!'

Ivo was amused. Not one woman in a hundred would have replied as Jossie had. Some would have pretended to be shocked, others would have been sickeningly coy. But it took a Jossie Morley to enter into the spirit of his claim and manage to sound objectively interested, as if she really wished to know. As perhaps she did.

But after a moment's thought she went on, 'But perhaps you were right. I lack experience, of course, but I think you're *very* good, Ivo. I don't think we'd better try again.' She nodded. 'I'd rather have a friend.'

They walked on in silence. Ivo was a little piqued,

but at the same time relieved by Jossie's unselfconscious manner towards him. How did she manage to switch so easily, one minute behaving like a courtesan, the next like a child? She enjoyed his kisses, so much was obvious, but she seemed to be completely unconscious of any romantic resonances between them. She still regarded him as a trusted friend, nothing more.

But below his usual air of self-possession he was puzzled by his own mixture of feelings. He had been sincere when he had denied being in love with her, and equally sincere when he had sworn that he wanted only to be her friend. He liked Jossie, she amused him, he enjoyed her company. But he was not in love with her! So why did he suffer from such an inexplicably strong reaction whenever he had Jossie in his arms? When some of the most beautiful and experienced women in London could kiss him and leave him absolutely sober, why did Jossie's kisses have such an intoxicating effect?

As they made their way back along the drive he stole an occasional glance at his companion. She was such an unlikely source of temptation, about as far removed from the usual object of his desire as she possibly could be. She might wear girl's dresses now, but she still had a long way to go before her boy's coltish stride turned into the graceful steps of a young lady. She might have learned to ride side saddle, but she still had no idea how to behave the rest of the time. She was very young—in the ways of the world she was even younger, perhaps, than her years would suggest—and there was not the slightest suspicion of coquetry, not even a hint of any awareness of him as a personable male. Ivo smiled to himself. There was something surprisingly seductive in the total lack of any attempt to attract him.

He pulled himself together again. Seductive...? The

very thought was absurd! He regarded himself as a sophisticated man of the world, nearly thirty years old and
an unrepentant cynic. How could he possibly imagine
himself to be in any danger from an eighteen-year-old
innocent? Ridiculous! The child had a talent for kissing
which was unrivalled in his experience, her kisses went
to a man's head like champagne, but she knew less about
the arts of attraction than a nun in a convent! What the
devil had been *wrong* with Peter Radstock? He was supposed to have been in love with her. How could he have
known her all those years and failed to recognise the
potential passion which lay below Jossie's matter-of-fact
surface?

Or was the answer really very simple? Had the two
never truly been in love? If that were so then, in spite
of her present misery, it was possible that Jossie had had
a lucky escape. She would have been infinitely more
miserable tied for life to a country clod with little feeling
and less wit. She deserved someone more discerning,
someone who could appreciate the pure gold of her...
someone like himself.

Ivo cursed below his breath and told himself not to
be ridiculous. He had no intention of falling in love with
Jossie Morley! He wanted to help her, not seduce her!
She was too young, she didn't know the rules by which
he lived. He must remove himself from temptation before this temporary aberration got out of hand. His feelings about Jossie would soon disappear once he was
away from her—he had managed it once before, and he
would again. Indeed, in the months before he came back
to Somerset for that damned birthday celebration he had
enjoyed one or two very pleasant interludes in London
with women of experience, women who understood the
rules of flirtation. No danger there—and no thought of

Jossie either! He must remove himself to London and seek out some distractions. Then, by the time his aunt brought Jossie to London for the season, he would hope to be himself once more, able to support Jossie in the way she needed. As a friend. He would look forward to being her friend in London.

The gods were kind. The very next day they provided the excuse Ivo needed. Kate Calthorpe had given birth to a healthy baby boy a few weeks earlier than expected, and Adam had written to remind Ivo that he had volunteered to act as a sponsor to the child. No one could criticise a prospective godfather for wishing to make the acquaintance of his godson as soon as possible! He would be away from Sudiham within the week.

At dinner that night the discussion once again centred round Jossie's début. But when Ivo was consulted he said slowly, 'I'll do what I can, though I'm afraid it won't be much at the moment. I haven't had the opportunity to tell you yet, but I'm off to visit the Calthorpes before the end of the week. I learned just today that I have a new godson.'

He suffered a slight pang of conscience at Jossie's look of dismay, but she soon rallied and she and Lady Frances set about begging him for more details of the new arrival. Adam's letter had said little other than that Kate and the baby were perfectly healthy, and the baby was to be called Thomas Adam Ivo. But Ivo promised to send an answer to all of their questions as soon as he could.

When the excitement died down he said, 'About London. There is little enough I can do down here for Jossie at the moment. But I shall have a word with the Calthorpes. Kate was introduced to society just a couple of years back and had quite a time of it, encountering a number of the pitfalls on the way. I'm sure she would give any advice you wanted. Perhaps you could even stay with the Calthorpes on your way to London.'

'So when shall we see you again, Ivo?'

'I'm not sure,' he said easily. 'There are one or two people in London I want to see, so I thought I would go straight there from Calthorpe. I could easily do some business for you while I'm in town. The house in Charles Street has been shut up for years—it will need an army to put it into order before you come. And unless you take your household with you, you will need to hire servants and so on. Shall I see to some of that?'

'Thank you, Ivo. I should like you to.' Lady Frances went on, 'I intend to do this in style, with London servants, and my own carriage. Perhaps you would check the stabling.' She turned to Jossie with a smile. 'The Trenchard London house, thank goodness, is large enough for us to entertain any number and it has one of the best addresses in London. Charles Street leads directly into Berkeley Square. Thank heavens there is not the slightest necessity for economy. Everything shall be of the best!' She turned to Ivo. 'But I warn you, we shall expect more help than this after we arrive! Surely you can act as escort to your aunt and her goddaughter without arousing gossip? I know you feel a need to be circumspect, but—'

'It would be the first time in his life if he was!' said Lord Veryan tartly. 'But your aunt is right—you look after her and Jossie, my boy. Never mind the tabbies!'

Ivo nodded. 'Is there anything I can do before I go?' he asked. 'Aunt Frances? Jossie?'

'Yes, there is,' said Jossie coolly. 'These arts of attraction. I thought you were going to help me to acquire them. How can you do that if you aren't here? I hope you'll promise to show me in London! And if I wanted to be a flirt, how would I set about it?'

Lady Frances was scandalised. 'Jossie!' she protested, 'You mustn't ask things like that! And especially not so…so bluntly!'

'I haven't time to be polite, Lady Frances. Not in private. But you can teach me how to be diplomatic in public. If there is one thing I've learned recently, it is that you are judged by your shell, not by what is inside. Well, if I am to go to London, I intend to adopt a new shell! What I am inside…' She paused and for a moment her face was hard. 'What I am inside is my own business.'

Ivo left for Calthorpe soon after. At first Jossie was somewhat cast down, but she soon recovered and worked hard to learn what her godmother was teaching her. If Lady Frances had an uneasy suspicion that Jossie had more in her mind than a simple desire to be a success in London, she was too delighted at the change in her protégée's spirits to give it voice. The lassitude, the depression, were now things of the past, and Jossie was soon as active and as eager as ever, devoting her considerable energy and talents towards achieving her objective.

But as time went on Lady Frances began to wonder whether something of the old Jossie, the qualities which had made her so special—her delightful transparency, a spontaneous warmth of heart—had been lost forever on that disastrous evening in July. The new Jossie might have the appearance of openness, but was in fact considerably more reserved than before. If she hesitated now before speaking, it was not because she felt lost. She was taking time to consider the effect of what she was saying.

It had been thought that Peregrine might come home for a short time, but he sent to say that he was unable to leave Derbyshire, so Christmas and the early weeks of January passed quietly without the company of either of Lord Veryan's sons. Jossie and Lady Frances were invited to be present at the wedding of Major Morley and Mrs Cherton shortly after New Year, but not only did Lady Frances develop a bad cold, but the weather turned so severe that it would have been foolhardy for the ladies to attempt the fifteen miles along country roads to Lyne St Michael. No one was disappointed when they were forced to send their apologies.

But for Jossie the days were busy enough. She was a willing and intelligent pupil, and Lady Frances was soon delighted with the girl's progress. Her memory was excellent and she seldom needed to be told anything twice. Names, dance steps, conventions, all were quickly mastered. And, far from being a handicap, the active life she had led at Lyne now stood her in good stead, too. As her confidence in social skills increased, it was seen that she moved with natural and unconscious grace. Though her carriage was upright, it was not at all stiff or awkward. She held herself beautifully.

For a while she found it difficult to remember to limit her boyish stride to the smaller steps conventionally required of a lady of fashion, but soon that too was mastered. Lady Frances constantly gave her advice and instruction in the ways of London society.

'You mustn't think of London as a huge city,' she said one day. 'The part of it you will know is actually very limited and you will quickly learn your way about in it. Not that you will ever go out unaccompanied, Jossie. You must always, always be accompanied by a footman, or, at the very least, a maidservant. Which reminds me—we must find a suitable maid for you.'

'I promise to remember, Lady Frances, but when will you tell me the more interesting things? Rules of behaviour and the like are all very well, but they are very bor— I mean, do we really have to spend so much time on them? I want…I want…'

'What do you want, my dear?' asked Lady Frances gently.

'I want to be a great success! To fascinate them all! To show them! You all said I could, but I still don't know how!' Jossie got up and walked restlessly round the room. 'I wish Ivo were here,' she said suddenly. 'He must have known so many fascinating women. He could tell me how they do it.' She turned to Lady Frances. 'Could you?'

Lady Frances shook her head at Jossie. 'I wouldn't recommend some of the ways Ivo's ladies fascinate, Jossie!' she said a trifle austerely. 'But if we are talking of the more respectable kind… I'd say the most important thing is *not* to change, not to try to be someone different. Have the confidence to be yourself.'

Jossie instantly rejected this idea. 'Oh, no! That would never do. You know it wouldn't. Jossie Morley was an ungraceful, unappealing creature, incapable of capturing or holding any man. She liked winning arguments, not using honey words and sweet smiles. She preferred to waste her time riding over the hills, not using it to advantage in front of a mirror in her bedroom. Oh, no! Jossie Morley must be replaced! But with what? That's what I don't yet know. To learn *that* is more important to me than learning what to say or do if the Duchess of Sutherland should happen to speak to me.'

Lady Frances was firm. 'I mean what I say. You must be yourself.' She held up a hand when Jossie tried to protest. 'No, don't argue! Whatever you think, Jossie Morley was and is quite special. You must believe that.' She held Jossie's eye until Jossie shrugged and nodded. Lady Frances went on, 'Let me try to explain what I've been trying to bring about. Do you remember what you felt like last summer when you were made to attend all those balls and parties? I don't think you enjoyed them.'

'I hated them!' said Jossie with feeling. 'I had no idea what to do.'

'Exactly! So you spent your time staying in the background and wishing you were somewhere else. *Not* a way to success! But you will never have to worry again. The rules which govern behaviour in the polite world have now become second nature to you. You can walk, talk, dine, dance and perform all the other activities demanded of you as gracefully, as easily as the rest of the world. Indeed, I would say better than most. In the future, you will never wonder whether you are doing them properly. You will know that you are. They will all come instinctively.'

'I see…' said Jossie after a moment.

'Furthermore,' Lady Frances went on, 'a moderate amount of time spent in front of a mirror in the privacy of your own bedroom is *never* wasted, if it means that you can move about in company afterwards without thinking twice about how you look. Together with your maid you have done your best and you can now forget about it. There is nothing so un-fascinating as women—or men—who are forever worrying about their appearance.'

'You're talking about confidence, aren't you?'

'Yes. A woman who is quietly confident, at ease with herself, is halfway to being fascinating to others, Jossie. And when she has youth, beauty, wit and an interest in the rest of the world, she is very nearly there!'

'I'm not at all sure that I am as far along the road as you suggest, but I see what you mean. Where do we go from here?'

'Clothes!' said Lady Frances promptly. 'And I don't mean the draper's shop down the road, either!'

'Are we going to Bath?'

'Perhaps. For the less important ones. But most of your dresses will be bought in London. I wonder if Madame Rosa is still in Bruton Street? I'll write to Ivo—he'll know. Meanwhile I have some fashion journals upstairs which we shall examine tonight.'

Chapter Ten

Ivo returned briefly in March to spend Easter at Sudiham, and afterwards he escorted his aunt and Jossie to Calthorpe Court, where they were to spend some time before continuing to London. Jossie bade Lord Veryan farewell with regret, but cheered up noticeably when he promised to come to London in June to see how she was faring. Sudiham had been a safe haven for her ever since the previous summer, and though she was no longer the pitiful ghost who had come to stay then, it was still a wrench to leave it and face the world outside.

She was not altogether looking forward to staying with the Calthorpes, either. Lady Calthorpe had written everything that was kind, but Jossie was still nervous of meeting them. Thanks to Lady Frances she had come a long way in confidence, and was ready to deal with every conceivable social occasion, but she couldn't help wondering what the Calthorpes would make of her, all the same. There was even a touch of jealousy in her feelings towards them, for they were Ivo's closest friends, and she suspected that he admired Lady Calthorpe more than any other woman he had met.

But she need not have worried. Kate Calthorpe was a

warmly affectionate person, whose own great happiness spilled over everyone around her. Her lord adored her, and though she had a teasing, laughing relationship with Ivo, it was quite clear that she was very much in love with her husband. Their infant son was the centre of their existence, but he was not by any means allowed to dominate the scene. On the contrary. Lady Calthorpe took a lively interest in plans for the come out of 'Miss Calverton Morley', and spent a considerable time with her, talking of London, showing her some of her dresses, and regaling her with tales of Adam's and Ivo's exploits.

Lady Calthorpe even persuaded Kendrick, her somewhat daunting personal maid, to arrange Miss Calverton Morley's hair and give her advice on styles and colours of dress which would flatter her. Kendrick was critical of the gowns made in Bath, but unbent a little when she was assured that Jossie was to have a completely new wardrobe made in London.

It wasn't long before Jossie was invited to call Lady Calthorpe by her first name.

'Ivo is such an old friend, it seems absurd for you to be addressing me as Lady Calthorpe when we are all otherwise so informal. Do call me Kate! But what am I to call you? Helena or Jossie? Ivo has always referred to you as Jossie, but he introduced you to us as Helena. Which would you prefer?'

Jossie hesitated. Ivo had introduced her to the Calthorpes as Helena Calverton Morley at her request. In her distress after the débâcle of the ball at Lyne, she had passionately rejected the name of Jossie, along with a life she wished to forget. And she was as determined as ever to be known in London as Helena Calverton Morley. But Ivo and Lady Frances had continued to call her Jossie, and over the months she had grown used to it again, regarding it now as a nickname, a sign of affectionate intimacy. Did she wish to admit the Calthorpes to this inner circle? She looked at Kate and the warmth of Kate's smile made up her mind for her. 'I should like you to call me Jossie,' she said awkwardly.

From that moment the friendship prospered. Once she could see that Jossie was at ease with the Calthorpes, Lady Frances left her and went on ahead to London to stay with friends and vet the arrangements Ivo had made for them. Jossie was more than content to stay behind. Kate was not much older than she was, and it was a new and very pleasant experience for her to have a friend of her own age and sex to talk to. She watched and learned a good deal from Kate. Together they drove about the countryside, dined with the neighbours, danced, listened to music, played cards and had long conversations, and Jossie put into practice what she had been learning at Sudiham during the past year. Lady Frances had taught her well. Jossie knew the rules by heart and seldom put a foot wrong. But it was Kate Calthorpe who showed her how to infuse them with warmth and charm.

Ivo accompanied his aunt to London, but frequently returned to spend a few days with his friends in order, he said, to make the acquaintance of his godson. But he spent a lot more time with Jossie than with young Thomas.

It seemed to him that Jossie was improving with every visit. No doubt the attentions of Kendrick had something to do with it, but there was more than this. Jossie had always been a fast learner, and now she was learning a great deal more from his friends. He noted with amusement how closely she watched Kate, and how often touches of Kate could be seen in her manner, and in her voice.

'I approve of the new Jossie,' he said one day when they were out together for a walk in the late spring sunshine. 'But don't lose the old one completely. I should miss her.'

'Would you?' she asked, doubtfully. 'I don't think anyone else would. Besides, it's not the old Jossie who wants to go to London.' She pirouetted round and gave him a dazzling smile. 'It's Helena Calverton Morley, beautiful Helena, irresistible Helena, the feminine counterpart of the worst flirt in all Europe, Helena the breaker of hearts! Do you think she will manage it?'

Ivo looked appreciatively at the figure before him. Lady Frances had decided to wait till they were in London before dressing Jossie in style, and she was still clothed modestly enough in a grey pelisse and a simple bonnet. But the radiance of her smile and the grace of her movements were very appealing.

'I am sure she will,' he said with a smile. But he went on more seriously, 'Is that what you really want, Jossie? It can be a dangerous game for a woman.'

'I want it more than anything. And I doubt there will be any danger in it for me. But if there were I would welcome it.'

Ivo considered her carefully. That curious tone was in her voice again. He said slowly, 'There's something about it that I don't altogether like…'

'You don't think I can do it? You're afraid I shall fail?'

'I'm afraid you'll succeed! Oh, don't think I want to spoil your fun! You'll be a success, all right. I can see it getting more likely every time I come down here. You'll dazzle them. And the world owes you something after what happened last year. To be acknowledged as a beauty, to enjoy the admiration of the *ton*—yes, I can sympathise with that ambition. But a *heartbreaker*? I'm not sure I like that idea.'

'It isn't the admiration I want, Ivo,' said Jossie, suddenly fierce. 'It's the power. The power to make my father take back what he said, the power to show Peter Radstock—and Peter Radstock's mother—that he made a mistake—' She stopped abruptly.

'You surely aren't still in love with him?'

'I despise him!'

'Then don't waste your time on him!' Ivo gave her a sharp look. 'You're not planning anything so stupid as revenge on Peter Radstock, are you?' He waited and when she said nothing he gave her a slight shake. 'Are you, Jossie? If you are, then don't count on me to help you!'

'You said you would!'

'I said I would help you to enjoy London! And as long as you don't do too much damage, I'll watch with pleasure while you capture a few susceptible hearts. Capture, Jossie. Not break. But leave Peter Radstock alone!'

'Why?'

'He's married, and, what is more, he really isn't a worthy victim. I could name you two or three very presentable young men who would be a much greater challenge.'

Jossie eyed him speculatively. 'Too great a challenge?'

'Well…they've been on the town for a year or two now, and so far they've eluded all attempts to capture them. And they've left more than a few broken hearts and disappointed hopes behind them.'

'Are you one of those men?'

'Jossie! Hasn't Kate told you? I never flirt with hopeful young ladies.'

'Why not?'

'Because I have a dislike of hurting the vulnerable.'

'How very noble!' said Jossie mockingly. 'And, besides that, there's always the danger that you might get trapped into marriage, isn't there?'

'Very true! How well you know me after all!'

'So who are these young men?'

'I'll point them out when we get to London. But don't place your hopes too high.'

'You don't think I can do it!'

'It would be amusing to see you try. It's time they had a lesson. I suppose it wouldn't do you any harm to test your charms on one of them...'

'Not all three?'

'Oh, no! One mustn't look for the impossible.'

'Impossible, Ivo?' said Jossie. She gave him a slow, provocative look from sea-green eyes. 'You think it impossible?'

Ivo laughed delightedly. 'Excellent! Perfect! You've been practising!'

Jossie relaxed and grinned. 'I'm glad you like it. I thought it was rather good myself. I call it my siren look. You have no idea how long it took to get it right!' She put her arm through his and gave him another conspiratorial grin.

'Have you others?'

'Of course! There's the fresh as a daisy look, the flighty maiden look, the deeply serious look—oh, I have any number of others. But that one was the most difficult. I kept having to stop myself laughing.'

Once again Ivo found himself marvelling at the sudden changes in this girl—one minute a siren, the next a mischievous child. But he then corrected himself. Not a child any more. Jossie was unmistakably a woman, and a damned attractive one, too. He wondered how this adventure in London would turn out. It was becoming clear to him that she would need more than his help and guidance. The game she had decided to play had its dangers, dangers which she was still too innocent to see. She would need his protection. And he must see to it that she didn't rouse too much adverse gossip. That wouldn't do her any good at all... Ivo smiled inwardly. The creeping boredom which he had experienced in Brussels had recently begun to make itself evident in London. But now it looked as if that was all about to change. Boredom would be the least of his concerns!

'Well, Helena, my lovely enchantress, we'll see what you can do,' he said, adding warningly, 'But there are two men at least, whom you must leave out of your web. Peter Radstock is one.'

'Who is the other?'

'Me!'

'*You*, Ivo?' Her astonishment would have been comic, thought Ivo, if he hadn't felt just slightly piqued by it. She went on, 'I wouldn't even try to use any wiles on you. You'd see through them straight away. Besides, one doesn't use wiles on a friend. Though...'

'What?'

'You'd let me *practise* on you, wouldn't you?'

And, though he had some reservations about the wisdom of this, Ivo nodded, unable to resist the coaxing note in his protégée's voice.

In the privacy of their bedchamber Kate Calthorpe could not help speculating to her husband about Jossie and her relationship with Ivo.

'I simply don't understand it, Adam,' she said with a frown. 'From what the Leversons were telling us last week, Ivo is as much of a flirt as ever. Last month he set the *ton* by the ears with his pursuit of Lady Hartley, and before that it was Sybil Montague. They are already discussing who is to be Ivo's next.'

'What is there in that to puzzle you, my love?' asked Adam. 'I would find it strange if Ivo stopped flirting! He hasn't changed in all the years I've known him.'

'You think not?' said his wife with a glint in her eye. 'I suppose, in all those years you have known him, he has looked after any number of girls just like Jossie— just eighteen and about to make their début?'

'Well, not exactly…' said Adam.

'I suppose you will tell me that he has been scrupulously careful to avoid causing gossip about *hundreds* of young ladies, who have, like our young friend, been seen in his company?'

'He has certainly never worried about gossip,' said Adam with a reminiscent smile. 'Ivo used to keep the tabbies busy wherever he went. But I can't remember seeing him in the company of many *young* ladies at all!'

'Exactly!' said Kate, triumphant. 'So why does he spend so much time and trouble on the girl? Why is he so protective of her? Can it be possible that he has fallen in love at last?'

'In love? Ivo? With Jossie Morley? My dear Kate, you must have windmills in your head! I can't imagine Ivo in love with anyone, and certainly not with such an innocent! Ivo's inamoratas are always thoroughly experienced women. He avoids débutantes like the plague.'

'I'm not talking of that kind of love, Adam. I mean real love, commitment, marriage, even.'

Adam burst into a roar of laughter. 'Ivo Trenchard! What an absurd idea!'

In the face of his wife's silent disapproval he calmed down and said patiently, 'Have you seen anything at all romantic in his behaviour to suggest such a thing?'

'Of course I haven't! There isn't anything. That is precisely why I am so suspicious.'

'Er...' Adam was uncertain. His Kate was still capable of puzzling him on occasion. 'I am not quite sure I understand you.'

'Ivo is never "romantic" with Jossie. They are remarkably matter of fact with each other. But he watches over her like a mother hen with her chicks! He disguises it pretty well, I'll grant you that, but it is there all the same. I don't think the girl herself suspects it.'

'Is she in love with him? I hope not. Ivo is not the most constant of lovers.'

'You can really be exasperatingly stupid, Adam,' said the wife of his bosom. 'That is precisely what I have been saying. Ivo is not behaving like a lover at all! He isn't *flirting* with Jossie, he's looking after her. As for Jossie... She is not so easy to read. But I am sure the thought of falling in love with Ivo has not entered her head. Not yet.'

'Less easy to read? I find her charmingly frank and open.'

'Her manner is delightfully so, I agree. But there's something below the surface... It's quite clear to me that she has suffered a body blow of some kind. Ivo hinted as much when he came to Baby Tom's christening.'

'Do you know what it was?'

'Not exactly. Jossie herself never talks of it, and Ivo is always very discreet. But do you remember? When he visited us last July he told us a little about Jossie and said he was going to meet her again at a coming-of-age party in Lyne St Michael. He gave us the impression that she was involved with the young man whose party it was. Now neither the party nor the young man are ever mentioned. Nor the girl's family. Whatever happened to hurt Jossie, Adam, happened about that time, I am quite sure, and it was serious.'

'Why do you say that?'

'It has left her very wary of involvement. I certainly don't think she's ready for any of the more tender emotions. But she trusts Ivo. It could be a beginning.'

'You mean you'd be pleased if they made a match of it?'

'She is just what he needs! He is already used to looking after her. And she may be innocent, but she is by no means naïve. Look how quick she is at cards. It's a revelation to see how she can keep us all on our toes! It's my belief she is well up to all of Ivo's tricks—and he loves it. She keeps him amused. Moreover…' She gave her husband a mischievous look. 'She is so beautiful, and so lively, that Ivo won't have any time to flirt with anyone else—he'll be too busy fighting off the competition! Yes, I'd like them to make a match of it.'

Adam had had enough of his friend's affairs. He drew his wife to him. 'Well, dearest Kate, I'm just a simple soldier. I don't understand all these subtleties. I wish Ivo well, but just now I want to know how much *my* wife loves *me*. A little?'

'More than that, Adam,' murmured Kate and set about proving it.

Kate was still interested in Ivo's attitude towards Jossie. One night at dinner she brought up the question of how they had met.

'Ivo told us that you pursued him with a gun? Is that true, Jossie?'

Jossie shot an impish glance at Ivo. 'Perfectly true. He was trying to steal my horse.' Ivo uttered a protest, and she added, 'At least I thought he was.' She grinned. 'I've never seen a man so frightened.'

'Really?' murmured Adam. 'I always thought the Hussars were more show than go, but…*frightened*? Ivo!'

'Don't look at me like that, Adam! You'd have felt exactly the same. I saw the horse in the middle of nowhere and had merely stepped forward to take a closer look. How do you suppose I felt when I turned round to face a scabby little urchin pointing a loaded pistol straight at my head! I expected it to go off at any moment.'

'I thought he was a gipsy horse thief,' said Jossie by way of explanation.

'A gipsy horse thief! *Ivo?* Now that I find that very hard to imagine,' said Kate, eyeing the immaculately elegant figure opposite her.

'I…er…I had had rather a rough night before that. I dare say I didn't look quite my best,' said Ivo defensively.

'But how could you have thought Jossie a scabby little urchin?' asked Kate. They all looked at Jossie. The light from the candles caught the laughter in sparkling blue-green eyes, it glowed warmly on artfully arranged dark curls, and followed the beautiful curves of cheekbone and chin. The rose of Jossie's lips was echoed faintly in the delicate bloom of her cheeks. Finely moulded throat and shoulders rose from a virginally simple white silk dress. It would be difficult to conceive of a creature less like a scabby little urchin.

Kate turned for her answer, but Ivo's eyes were still resting on Jossie with an expression in them which she found difficult to interpret. Pleasure, certainly. But then Jossie was a pleasure to look at. A touch of reserve. Why? And, intriguingly, a slightly possessive pride. With every moment Kate grew more curious about the situation between her two guests. She wondered what would happen in London...

Ivo answered finally. 'She wasn't dressed like that when I first saw her.' He hesitated, and Jossie stepped in.

'I was wearing breeches,' said Jossie. 'He thought I was a boy.'

'Oh, you cannot imagine how often I have wanted to do that!' cried Kate. 'They seem so much more convenient. Did you ride astride, as well?'

When Jossie nodded she went on, 'Quite right, too! It's high time women were allowed to ride sensibly instead of the ridiculous way we have to perch at the moment!'

Adam exclaimed in horror, 'Good God! I'm married to a revolutionary!'

Ivo started to laugh. 'Don't tell me you've only just discovered it! Do you know how Adam once described his ideal woman to me, Kate? A quiet little blue-eyed blonde, affectionate, obedient—'

'Stop! Stop! What are you trying to do, ruin my marriage? Kate, don't listen to him—'

'Oh, I don't mind!' said Kate comfortably. 'I know you had a weakness for blue-eyed blondes. Julia Redshaw was your ideal, though whether she would have been either obedient or affectionate is another matter altogether!'

'Most unlikely, I'd say,' Ivo interposed. 'Do you know that the lovely Julia has persuaded Balmenny to bring her to London for the coming season? I suppose it's a reward for doing her duty and presenting the Viscount with not one but two heirs last year.'

'Julia has had twins?' asked Kate in amazement.

Ivo nodded. 'Both boys and both healthy. And since the Balmennys spent most of the months beforehand closeted in their castle in Ireland, Balmenny can be reasonably certain they are his. He's over the moon.'

Kate turned to Jossie, who was looking somewhat bewildered. 'Julia Redshaw lived next door to Adam when they were young. I rather think they were childhood sweethearts, but Julia married Viscount Balmenny almost as soon as she was out.' Kate paused, then said, 'She is very lovely, but I have to confess I never liked her. Perhaps motherhood has improved her.'

'It may, but I doubt it,' said Ivo. 'She is apparently quite happy to leave her sons behind her for three months while she enjoys the season in London.' He turned to Jossie. 'What Kate was too scrupulous to tell you, Jossie, is that Julia's husband is considerably older than she is, but very rich. Before he bore her off to Ireland she was a flirt of the first order.'

'Ivo!' said Kate scandalised. 'That may well be true, but you shouldn't say so! You ought not to prejudice Jossie against Lady Balmenny before she has even met her.'

'Oh, Jossie will not think less of Julia for being a flirt,' he said. 'Indeed, she would probably welcome her as an object for study—Viscountess Balmenny is, or was, a living embodiment of every art of attraction, Jossie!'

'But not, in the end, attractive,' said Adam. His deep voice was serious. He looked at Kate and smiled. 'I'm glad I came to my senses in time,' he said.

Kate said softly, 'So am I!' Then she turned to Ivo and said briskly, 'But tell me, Ivo, what would your ideal wife be like?'

'You mean, if I were in the market for a wife? As much like you as possible, Kate!' Ivo replied with a winning smile.

'Flummery! Save your charm for the ladies in London, my friend. I would never do for you. But seriously, I'd really like to know. What would you look for in a wife?'

Ivo thought for a moment. 'Seriously, Kate, I have no idea. I cannot imagine marrying anyone. I like my life too well as it is at present—I have no plans to change it. But I certainly wouldn't want the sort of wife who would regard my philanderings with complaisance! That could only come from indifference or timidity, and I wouldn't be content with either of those. As you know, I like women of spirit.'

'Ah!' said Adam reminiscently. 'Shades of Heloise de Leiken... What a pity she was already married!'

'Heloise de Leiken was a delightful companion but I wouldn't have wanted her for a wife!'

'Why not?' asked Kate. 'She sounds just right. What was wrong with her?'

'Oh, she was very nearly perfect. Accomplished, exquisitely beautiful, witty, elegant...you were never bored in her company. She had all the requisites for a perfect partner, except the one essential one.'

'She didn't love you?'

'I think she did, a little. In her fashion. But love is a chancy business, Kate. There are so many kinds of love.

How can anyone define it?' Ivo's eyes rested for a moment on Jossie, then he went on, 'No, what Heloise de Leiken lacked was any kind of loyalty. You may find it surprising, but I think keeping faith with one's partner is a first consideration…'

Then he laughed and shook his head. 'What a bore I am! Kate, you're asking me the wrong question. I don't know what my ideal would be. I've told you, my choice at the moment is not to marry at all!'

Adam cast a look at his wife and smiled. 'You'll change your mind when the right woman comes along, Ivo. Then it's not a question of choice. You'll find you have to marry, and marry only her. Nothing else will do. You'll see when the time comes.'

'There you are, then, Kate. Ask me again in a year.'

Kate persevered. 'What about you, Jossie? Have you dreams of an ideal husband?'

Jossie had been following the conversation with amused interest, but now the laughter faded. 'I'm like Ivo,' she said. 'I really have no interest in acquiring a partner for life.'

'You sound very sure. Isn't that the object of taking part in the season?'

'Not for me,' said Jossie with a charmingly apologetic smile.

'You must excuse my wife, Jossie,' said Adam, who had begun to think that Kate's curiosity was going too far. 'She means well. The point is, she has been so lucky in her choice of husband herself that she wants everyone to be as fortunate. I keep telling her that men like me don't grow on trees, but she still persists. And now I should like to hear that duet you two ladies have been practising. Shall we go into the saloon?'

The conversation broke up amid protests and laughter,

and Adam made sure the subject was not brought up again. However badly Kate wished to see a match between Ivo and Jossie, it seemed to him that it was most unlikely, at least for the foreseeable future. The question was best left alone.

When the time came to leave Calthorpe Jossie was filled with regret. At Sudiham she had felt safe, and had left with apprehension. Here at Calthorpe she had been reassured, able to relax for a short while, in the warmth of the Calthorpes' undemanding friendship. She had seen a truly happy marriage at work, had observed the interests, the humour, the respect, and the deep love the Calthorpes shared. And though she did not lose sight of her own aims, the memory of her time with Ivo's friends was stored away, and ultimately had a healing effect on her own damaged feelings.

Kate had one further gift for Jossie. A day or two before her departure she invited Jossie into her bedroom.

'I have been thinking of this for some time, Jossie, but you have only to say no and it shall be forgotten. I gather that you have not yet engaged a proper personal maid?'

'Lady Frances preferred to wait till we were in London before engaging any staff. But the girl I brought with me has done well, don't you think?'

'She is excellent! For the country. But in London you will need someone more experienced. Someone like Kendrick, for example. What would you say if I offered to release Kendrick? I engaged her for my own début two years ago, and she has been with me ever since. She's a first-class lady's maid, and I am very happy with her, but she's wasted down here. I know she would jump at the chance of working in London for someone like you, who was about to make her début. You would find her invaluable.'

'Do you mean it? I would love to have Kendrick, in spite of the fact that she frightens me half to death. But how would you manage?'

'I would find someone else. I don't need the high standards Kendrick imposes now, and I would really like her to have something more satisfying to do. Would you like me to speak to her?'

'Please do!'

As a result of this conversation Jossie set out for London with a maid who would have been snapped up by any one of a dozen London society ladies the minute it was known she was free. Kendrick herself was very happy. She left Lady Calthorpe with regret, but domestic bliss in the country was not what she looked for. To have such a promising candidate as Miss Calverton Morley for top honours among the débutantes in the coming season was exactly what she would have wanted. And if Kendrick knew anything of it, her new mistress would not be permitted to do anything but conquer.

They left Calthorpe early one morning, stayed the night in Hungerford with some cousins of Lord Veryan's, and by the evening of the next day they were in Charles Street in the heart of fashionable Mayfair. Jossie had never travelled so far in her life before, but Ivo's carriage was well sprung, and the journey had been enjoyable. The presence of Kendrick in the carriage precluded any very personal conversation, but Jossie had been given so much to think about that she hardly noticed. It was strange that her thoughts turned more than once to the mysterious Countess Leiken. Was she fair or dark? Had she really been so beautiful? And had she been as amusing as Ivo had said? Jossie would have given much to have the answers. It sounded as if the Countess would have been someone to use as a model. There was Julia, Viscountess Balmenny, too…but it was Heloise Leiken that Ivo had really liked…

Jossie settled herself back against the squabs and let her imagination take over. She was dancing in a large ballroom, surrounded by an admiring crowd, her father and Peter standing in amazement at one end. Two lovely ladies, both wearing coronets, one Irish, one Belgian, were standing close by, looking deeply envious as she floated past them. Her partner was holding her close, guiding her faultlessly through the steps of the waltz, his dark blue eyes smiling down into hers. She had seldom felt so secure, so happy…

But the next day, when Ivo took his two ladies for a drive through London to the park, she suddenly felt apprehensive. She looked at the stylishly gowned and coiffured ladies and immaculately dressed gentlemen passing by, listened to their drawling voices as they stopped to exchange greetings with Ivo and her godmother, endured their well-bred stares as Lady Frances introduced her. As they went along she looked at the grand houses and wide streets, was deafened by the bustle and noise, and her panic grew. What was Jossie Morley, a tomboy, a hoyden, rejected by her father as well as her childhood friend, doing in this sophisticated world? How had she thought she could possibly rival the elegance, the assurance, the style of these fashionable people? The *ton* would laugh her to scorn… She looked at Ivo in despair. How could he understand? He was more elegant, more assured, more stylish than any of them! How could she ask him to waste his time helping to launch a country nobody?

Ivo leaned forward and gave her hand an encouraging squeeze. 'Be brave,' he said softly. 'Give yourself time. I've told you. You'll dazzle them all.'

Chapter Eleven

Lady Frances wasted no time in introducing Jossie to one of London's foremost modistes. Madame Rosa of Bruton Street was as famous for the dictatorial style she adopted toward her clients as for the beautiful gowns she created for them. But no one could deny that she had a touch of genius, and most people accepted her advice without demur. Lady Frances had already been to see her for her own requirements, and had been treated with the deference due to a former valued customer. Her new wardrobe was already well on its way. Today it was Jossie's turn.

'So thees is Mademoiselle Calverton?' said Madame, circling Jossie with the predatory eye of a hawk about to swoop. Sallow, thin as a rake, with snapping black eyes and hair in a tight bun, she looked disparagingly at her new client. 'Mademoiselle is tall, hein? And thin. The figure—it is there, but it needs more emphasis. That dress is *impossible*. It 'as neither cut nor style. She needs something quite different... Walk about, *mademoiselle*!'

Jossie walked.

'Ah! She 'as grace, this one! And a good carriage. Look at me, child!'

Jossie, somewhat indignant at these peremptory commands, gave Madame Rosa a straight look.

Far from being displeased by this, Madame clapped her hands and exclaimed to her assistant, *'Mais, regardez, donc! Quels beaux yeux! Quelle couleur ravissante! Quel esprit!'* She soon recovered herself, however, and turned to Lady Frances to say condescendingly, 'I might be able to do something for your goddaughter, milady. We shall take 'er measurements, and then you may leave it with us. One week today for the fittings?'

A somewhat bewildered Jossie was led out. 'But, Godmama! Have we no say in the matter? Does Madame Rosa know what I want? All she has said so far is that I am thin!'

'She knows what you *need*, Jossie. And don't forget that she likes the colour of your eyes. And your spirit.' She gave Jossie an amused look. 'It is enough. You may trust her. And she and I have already discussed the number of dresses and all the rest you will require for your début.' When Jossie still looked rebellious she said, 'Forgive me if I'm wrong, my dear. I thought you weren't interested in clothes?'

'I'm not! But—'

'Then you may leave it to Madame Rosa and me to see that you are suitably dressed. Don't worry. She knows what she is doing.'

Though Jossie was not altogether satisfied she decided not to argue. Other questions were occupying her mind.

During that first week, while Ivo was showing his aunt and her goddaughter round London, he adopted in public an attitude of avuncular indifference towards Jossie. The last thing he wanted was to arouse any kind of speculation about his relationship with her—for his own sake as much as for hers. How the world would laugh if it were known that Lord Trenchard, the devil-may-care threat to husbands all over Europe, was personally concerned about an eighteen-year-old unknown from Somerset! No one would believe that his interest was purely platonic, even though he, his aunt and Jossie herself all knew it to be so. But it was not difficult to forestall gossip. Ivo Trenchard's views on débutantes were so well known that no one who knew him would really believe that he was taking any serious interest in the pretty young thing staying with his aunt in the family mansion. The polite world was soon persuaded that Lord Trenchard was merely showing a laudable sense of responsibility in spending so much time on Lady Frances and her young protégée, and the gossips turned their attention to the more interesting question of who would be his next amour among the ladies of Society.

Jossie herself was content to stay quietly in the background. All her study of warfare had demonstrated the importance of knowing the ground before planning an attack, and London to her was not very different from a battlefield. It was still early in the season, but she found enough to study and absorb. She soon set about winning the approval of a few important personages who held the key to acceptance in society. Her godmother was a valuable ally in this. Lady Frances had numerous influential friends who were delighted to see her again. All doors were open to her, and wherever she went Jossie accompanied her. There were even one or two older people who remembered Jossie's grandparents, Sir Robert and Lady Calverton, and who were more than pleased to make the acquaintance of their granddaughter. Soon 'Miss Helena Calverton' (Jossie quickly dropped the 'Morley') was generally held among the older members of the *ton* to be a delightful girl with a charmingly modest manner. Especially as she was widely known to be the heiress to the Calverton fortune.

Ivo soon saw through Jossie's tactics, approved of them, and derived great enjoyment from observing her at work. Previously he had always avoided afternoons and evenings spent with the more worthy members of his aunt's circle of acquaintance, dismissing them as excruciatingly boring. But now he accompanied her without hesitation. It was worth it, just to see Jossie sitting demurely next to old General Cartwright, listening to his rambling dissertation on Waterloo with all the wide-eyed admiration of an ingenue. As he knew to his cost, Jossie had the details of the battle at her fingertips, and her patience with factual errors was non-existent. But far from being subjected, as he had been, to scornful corrections, or impatient interruptions, the General was heard in admiring silence. Ivo didn't doubt that, if the old man had told her that Wellington had fought for the French, she wouldn't have blinked an eyelid!

'Charmin' girl, charmin'!' was the General's verdict. 'Not a flibbertigibbet like the rest of 'em. Sensible head on her shoulders! Knows how to listen.' And his daughter, Lady Phelps, who just happened to be one of the more influential ladies in Society, smiled favourably on Miss Calverton, and invited her to her ball the following week.

'I can see I'd have done better to be in my dotage,' said Ivo when they arrived home that night.

'Why do you say that?' asked Lady Frances, amused.

'Jossie would have treated me much more kindly two years ago. She allowed General Cartwright to talk a fine load of nonsense tonight without so much as a squeak

No such forbearance in the past when I made any mistakes.'

'You know very well why I allowed the General to talk such nonsense, Ivo,' said Jossie calmly.

'I do, my little schemer. To win the general's daughter's approval! What are you doing? Seeing to your support group?'

'What on earth are you two talking about? What support group?' asked Lady Frances.

'We're talking tactics, Aunt Frances. Jossie here is about to launch an attack on Society, and she's making sure of her ground.'

'If you are saying that Jossie is making sure that she is accepted by the people who matter before she attempts to make her mark on the rest, then I approve. Er...are you planning anything outrageous, Jossie?'

'Oh, no! But if my new dresses are as flattering as you say they will be, I shall become...a little less... inconspicuous, shall we say? Acceptance by the people who matter is only the beginning.'

Lady Frances laughed. 'Good luck to you, my child. Enjoy yourself. Ivo and I will see that you don't come to grief.'

The new dresses were more than Jossie could have hoped for. Madame Rosa had created a wardrobe for every mood and every occasion. Floating voiles, stiff taffetas, delicate muslins, heavy silks, trimmed with lace, or edged with satin... Even Jossie, who was not a girl to rave over clothes, was enchanted with the collection. There was a preponderance of white, of course, as befitted a débutante, but no insipid pinks, washed-out blues or wan-looking yellows. Instead, Madame had taken inspiration from Jossie's indignant eyes, and the dresses were full of touches of brilliant sea-green, or dark sky-blue, and one or two glittered with hints of gold and crystal... The whole collection was full of individuality, unmistakably made for Jossie, without once overstepping what was suitable for a débutante.

'My dear Jossie! My dear! Madame has excelled herself,' cried Lady Frances. 'You must have made such an impression on her. I've never seen anything so lovely as this dress! Or this one! And just look at this one! I cannot wait to see you in it. You must wear it for your first appearance at Lady Phelps's ball. The world will be there, and this would be perfect for it.'

Even Kendrick, who was not given to enthusing over anything, was impressed. She went so far as to say that one or two of the dresses would not have disgraced Miss Payne. 'And she, miss, was the toast of London! Before she became Lady Calthorpe, that is.'

By the evening of Lady Phelps's ball Jossie had already achieved her first two goals. She had the approval of what Ivo called 'the tabbies', and she had a wardrobe of style and distinction, which was fit to impress the most demanding of critics. The Season was now getting under way, and this ball was the first of many in the social calendar. If Jossie wished to make her mark in the wider world of London society it was time to begin, and Lady Phelps's ball would be her début.

On the evening of the ball she dressed with the greatest care. Not a detail was overlooked. A coiffeur had been the day before to cut and shape her hair, and now feathers of dark curls framed her face and drew attention to the delicately lovely lines of her bone structure. Kendrick brushed and dressed the rest of her hair into a gleaming crown, then carefully finished it off with a very pretty pearl hair ornament.

'Where did that come from?' asked Jossie.

'Her ladyship sent it in, miss. A present for your début, she said.'

Jossie stared, then shook her head and swallowed hard. She wasn't used to being given presents. She waited quietly while the maid finished her work, and then, when her godmother came in, she went to her and kissed her. Jossie was not usually demonstrative, and Lady Frances looked surprised.

'Thank you for your present,' Jossie said simply. 'I can't say how touched I am. I've never had such a pretty thing before. Indeed, I can't remember ever being given such a present at all!'

'Oh, tush, child, it was nothing! I thought it would look well with these.' Lady Frances was carrying a jewel case, and she now opened it to reveal a rope of perfectly matched pearls lying on a bed of velvet. Jossie stared at them, then at her godmother. They were so beautiful, but where could they possibly have come from? Was Lady Frances proposing to lend them to her?

'They were your mother's,' Lady Frances said, as she took them out and fastened them round Jossie's neck. 'And now they are yours.' She added with a touch of satisfaction, 'I remembered to collect them from your father before we left for Calthorpe, along with the rest of Lucinda's jewels. He wasn't very pleased, but he couldn't argue. He knew they belonged to you. Your mother had a wonderful collection of jewellery, but these are the most suitable for tonight. Now let me see you!'

She held her goddaughter away from her and took a long look. Jossie was wearing a simple slip of white peau de soie. Over it was an overdress of silk gauze scattered with tiny embroidered forget-me-nots. Sleeves and bodice were held in with dark blue-green velvet rib-

bons. White gloves, and white satin slippers completed
the ensemble. The soft sheen of the pearls matched the
sheen of the silk, the deep colour of the velvet was re-
flected in Jossie's eyes. Lady Frances took in a deep
breath of satisfaction, then she nodded to Kendrick 'My
congratulations, Kendrick! You've done well!' Her eyes
softened as she turned back to Jossie and kissed her.
'You look beautiful, child! How proud your mother
would have been of you tonight!'

They went downstairs. Ivo was waiting in the saloon.
As they entered he held up his quizzing glass and examined Jossie. For a moment his face was quite still.

'Will I do, Ivo?' she asked nervously, impatient for
his verdict.

'Oh, you'll do, Jossie. You'll do very well,' he said
with a curiously wry smile. 'It's just a little breathtaking
to see something I foretold actually coming to life.' Then
he seemed to pull himself together and with a flourish
produced a small parcel wrapped in silver paper. 'With
my congratulations and best wishes for your début.'

Jossie looked at him in surprise. 'Another present?
What have I done to deserve all this?' She unwrapped
the packet. It was a small, exquisitely painted ivory fan.
'Ivo! It's lovely! Oh, thank you!' She smiled brilliantly
at him, then spread the fan and held it up, looking at
him provocatively.

Ivo nodded, still with that slightly wry look in his
eyes. 'A prop, Jossie. I'm sure you'll use it to devastat-
ing effect.'

In spite of this evidence of support from her friends,
Jossie was very nervous when she followed Ivo and her
godmother into the ballroom, and she maintained her air
of calm with some difficulty. Ivo looked over his shoul-

der at her. 'Go for it, my girl!' he said softly. Then he bowed gracefully and disappeared. After a moment or two he was back with a pleasant-faced young man, a few years younger than himself, in tow.

'Aunt Frances, Helena, may I present Captain Fanshaw? The Captain was a subaltern in my company in Spain, and he's relatively civilised. I think I can vouch for him. Harry, this is my aunt, Lady Frances Danby, and her goddaughter, Miss Calverton. You're a lucky fellow, Harry! Miss Calverton is newly in London and looking to be amused.'

Captain Fanshaw bowed gracefully. 'Lady Frances, Miss Calverton...' The admiration in his eyes as he turned to Jossie made it plain that he, too, thought himself lucky. 'Are you by any chance free to dance with me, Miss Calverton?'

From then on Jossie's fears were forgotten. Captain Fanshaw had several friends only too anxious to be introduced to Miss Calverton, and she was soon surrounded by a laughing group of very presentable young men, most of them former officers known to Ivo, and each vying for her favour.

Ivo, standing some distance away, looked on with satisfaction. Jossie's eyes were sparkling, she was smiling—she was enjoying her first ball in London. He watched her for a while, then set off in search of amusement for himself. He soon found it, of course, and was as charming as ever. But his partners failed to hold his wholehearted attention. His gaze strayed more often than he realised to where Jossie was laughing, talking, dancing with such grace, such bewitching charm. She had wanted to shine, and that was exactly what she was doing. He remembered their first meeting and marvelled at the change in her. The potential had always been there, he had known it almost from the first, but it was still a revelation to see how she fitted in to the most demanding, the most exacting Society in the world. She looked as if she had been born to it. In his eyes at least, even accredited queens of society, women who had long been acknowledged as diamonds of the first water, lost some of their brilliance when put beside her. He was pleased for her, proud of her, and, though it was ridiculous, he was more than a little envious of the young men who surrounded her.

In the days that followed Jossie found herself much in demand. She rode with Captain Fanshaw, went driving in Richmond Park with Lieutenant Camden, visited Somerset House with Sir Richard Endicott... Her list of escorts was seemingly endless. And she was careful to keep it so, seeing to it that no one was more favoured than anyone else. Like Ivo, she wanted no broken hearts. Not among his friends.

If she was sometimes a little depressed that Ivo himself did not seem to have time to spend on her, she took pains to keep it to herself. After all, Ivo was well known as a flirt, and could find any number of ladies, of vastly greater experience and sophistication than Jossie Morley, eager to oblige him in this agreeable pastime. She frequently watched them doing so.

In fact, she sometimes wondered what would happen if she marched up to him and *demanded* that he should flirt with *her*! She was sure she could please him. She had watched those ladies, and was quite certain she could look as enticingly, smile as seductively, make him laugh as often as any of them. And she already knew how pleasant...how very pleasant...how *easy* it was to respond to Ivo's kisses! But in the end she knew she would never risk it. It would be useless. Ivo regarded her as his protégée, as a friend, someone he looked after somewhat in the style of a kindly uncle. He was remarkably indulgent, but he would never think of her as a candidate for any lover-like attentions. He might even laugh at her. Look at the way he had distanced himself in the past after kissing her, when she would have been perfectly prepared to continue! No, Ivo would never take her seriously, it was better not to try.

Soon, Miss Calverton was generally acknowledged to be a reigning Beauty. It became the mode to be in love with her, and many a susceptible young sprig of fashion, who had possibly not exchanged more than two sentences with the lady, claimed to have been slain by one glance from those mysterious sea-green eyes. Indeed, the exact colour of her eyes became a matter for eager debate among her admirers, some raving of sapphires and turquoises, others waxing lyrical about jade and emeralds and the like. The rooms of the house in Charles Street were filled with posies of every description, and nearly every morning brought at least one written effusion, sometimes poetic, sometimes not, and subject to Ivo's derision. Jossie was annoyed and said so.

'They mean well, Ivo. You shouldn't make fun of them.'

'I have never accepted meaning well as an excuse for poor performance. They haven't even any originality. Your name is Helena, so of course more than half of them compare you with Helen of Troy. You can't possibly enjoy such obvious bits of rubbish, or find them flattering!'

Jossie said fiercely, 'On one occasion, an occasion which I assure you I shall never forget, Mrs Cherton stood beside her exquisitely dressed daughter, and laughed at the very idea that my name was Helena. ''How unsuitable!'' she said. ''I can quite understand why you prefer Jossie!'' She didn't mean it kindly, of course. She just wanted to imply that the boy's name suited me better. You probably think so too.'

'Jossie, I—'

He was ignored. Jossie went on, 'The notes may be as badly written as you say, but I find the notion that Jossie Morley can be compared with Helen of Troy extremely agreeable! I don't believe I could possibly have too many messages like that.'

Ivo looked troubled. 'Does it still hurt so much, Jossie?' When she said nothing he went on, 'Listen to me! I do think Jossie a better name for you. For me Jossie is someone special, someone unique! There are several women in London who are just as beautiful as Helena Calverton, and could more aptly be compared with Helen of Troy—who was, when all is said and done, just a faithless wife with nothing to recommend her but her beauty!'

'Ah, but that's what you prefer, isn't it, Ivo? People like Mrs Dart, Lady Handwood, Alicia Farden. And the rest.'

Ivo started to look offended, but then he shrugged his shoulders with a laugh. 'Don't be impertinent! My *affaires* are none of your business.'

Jossie turned her head away. He waited for a moment, then he said, 'Don't waste your time making a catalogue of my *affaires*, Jossie. They are not important.'

'Then what is important to you? I'd really like to know!'

He looked at her in silence. Then he said, 'I don't

know. I'd like to see you happy, that's one thing. But for myself? I don't know.'

Lady Frances was particularly pleased with Jossie's reaction to her success.

'Jossie has always been so matter of fact,' she said to Ivo one day. 'But I am impressed how sensibly she is taking all this adulation. Any girl might easily lose her head, but from what I can see Jossie remains just the same. It is almost as if she is waiting for something.'

'She is. She's waiting for the arrival of her father and the Radstocks.'

'Of course! The poor girl wants to show them... I cannot blame her for that, Ivo.'

'Nor can I.'

'Then why are you looking so severe?'

'I hope that is all she wants to do.'

'She isn't any longer in love with Peter, if that is what you're afraid of.'

'No.' Ivo smiled. 'I dare say I'm worrying quite unnecessarily. About that, at least.'

He continued to keep a careful eye on Jossie, observed her bewitching an elderly General, or a severely critical dowager with the 'fresh as a daisy' or the 'deeply serious' look. He saw how she enchanted half a dozen young men with a sparkling smile and a look which said that she found them all as captivating as herself. But, to his relief, he had not yet seen her use what she had called the 'siren' approach. With the wrong sort of person there could be danger in it, a danger which she in her innocence would not see. He should have said so when she first used it on him at Calthorpe, of course, but he had been so entertained by it, and, yes, intrigued, that it hadn't occurred to him to warn her against using it in earnest. He must ask his aunt to say something to her. The idea of Ivo Trenchard acting as nursemaid was so absurd that he could only hope no one ever learned of it!

But more than once, indeed quite often, his decision to keep his distance from her in public seemed very difficult to maintain. Memories of how much he had enjoyed dancing with Jossie at Calthorpe kept intruding. There they had danced just with one or two other couples, to a piano played not very well by one of the doctor's daughters, but the rhythm, the grace, the rapport he had felt in Jossie had far outweighed these disadvantages. Here in London it seemed to him that most of her partners, not having had the benefit of working on the Duke of Wellington's staff, had no idea how to hold a girl in the waltz! They either grabbed her like a parcel, or held her at such a distance that the poor girl was not sure which way her partner wished to turn! His impatience grew and one evening, without quite knowing how it happened, he found himself in front of Jossie, asking her to dance the next waltz with him. She regarded him in astonishment, the colour rising in her cheeks.

'You want to dance with *me*, Ivo? Why?'

'I see that you have the tabbies' approval for the waltz. I thought it time you danced one with me,' he said, smiling charmingly down at her.

'Is it because you're trying to make someone jealous? Lady Alicia, perhaps?'

'Using you?' he asked, raising an eyebrow. 'Of course not.'

'Oh,' she said, sounding flat.

'Shall I say that I wanted to dance with the most beautiful woman in the room?' he went on, giving her a little bow.

She shot him a suspicious glance. 'You're teasing, Ivo. You've never tried before. Why now?'

'I was being circumspect, little Jossie,' he said ruefully. 'But I couldn't resist one waltz.'

When she saw that he was absolutely serious, a lovely colour rose in her cheeks. 'I'm not sure…' she stammered, looking flustered. 'I must look at my card…'

He took the card from her and put it back in her reticule. 'Don't try those tricks on me, my girl. They don't work. Will you dance or not?'

'Aren't you being a little high-handed? Here comes Lieutenant Cotter to claim me for the waltz at this very moment!'

Ivo regarded the young man benevolently. 'I'm afraid, Lieutenant, I am about to pull rank. It's one of the few compensations of age. Miss Calverton presents her apologies, but she is about to dance this waltz with me. I do beg you to excuse me. Jos…er…Helena?'

With an apologetic glance at Lieutenant Cotter, Jossie allowed Ivo to lead her on to the floor. 'Very high-handed!' she muttered as they took their places.

At first they danced in silence. Then Ivo asked, 'So how do you find the fashionable world, Jossie?'

'At the moment I like it. It wouldn't suit me forever, though.' She sighed. 'I'm not sure what would…'

'Have you had any offers yet?'

'My *affaires* are no more your business, than yours are mine, Ivo!' she said with a provocative look at him.

'Rubbish! You're too young to have *affaires*! I am considerably older and wiser than you. And I have made you my business, you know that! How many offers have you had?'

Jossie looked mutinous for a moment, then she shrugged and said, 'You know the answer, anyway… It doesn't matter how many I've had, I wouldn't accept any of them. I've told you before. I'm not looking for a husband.'

'What, never?'

She said sombrely, 'I cannot imagine ever again wanting to marry anyone.'

'Don't say that! You're too young to let that spineless fool ruin your life! You'll meet someone better than Peter Radstock, I'm sure. Why, I'd marry you myself rather than allow you to live a spinster for the rest of your life!'

'You would? And how would you persuade me to agree?'

There was a glint in his eyes as he replied. 'As long as you weren't in love with anyone else, I could persuade you—we both know that. But it wouldn't do.'

'Of course it wouldn't!' Jossie said quickly. 'But why do *you* think so?'

'I'm too old for you! Too old in every kind of way…'

'I don't want to marry, anyway! You could flirt with me, if you wished…' she said, smiling seductively at him. She had observed Lady Alicia employing just such a look earlier in the evening, and Ivo had seemed impressed with it. She was sure hers was every bit as good…

He was impressed now, but not in the way she had hoped. 'I thought Aunt Frances had told you to forget that look,' he said sternly. 'Didn't she explain?'

'Oh, she said something,' said Jossie airily. 'And I must say I was disappointed. Lady Frances is not usually so stuffy.'

Ivo regarded her coldly. He said, 'Come and sit down!'

Jossie was surprised, but allowed him to lead her to a bench in a corner of the room. 'Why are you cross with me? Is it because I suggested you might flirt with me? It would only be in fun, Ivo! It wouldn't...wouldn't mean anything.'

'I've told you. I shall never flirt with you. But that's not what I want to say. Listen to me! Aunt Frances was not being stuffy. You mustn't look at others as you've just looked at me, Jossie.'

'I don't quite understand you. How did I look?'

'You looked at me in an excessively provocative manner. You once told me you called it your siren look. I suppose between friends it's amusing. But you mustn't, you *must not*, direct it at anyone else!'

'But Lady Alicia used it on you! I don't see why I shouldn't try it.'

'Lady Alicia can look after herself. But, believe me, it could lead you into trouble.'

'What do you mean?'

Ivo took a breath. 'Jossie, I flirt. It amuses me. And Lady Alicia is experienced and well aware of what she is doing. But, surprisingly enough, I have scruples. There are plenty of men in London who have none. If you should happen to use that look on one of them, he might well regard it as an invitation to...to...the sort of...of...intimacy which you would find repugnant. Your innocence and youth would not stop him.'

'Oh, but I can take care of myself—'

'No! With such a man you couldn't! He would be quite ruthless about taking what he thought you were offering. Don't do it, Jossie!'

'Don't be absurd! I'm not a weakling, you know! I

may have learned how to be a lady, but I still remember a trick or two from my days as a boy.'

Ivo looked at her in exasperation. Then, after a pause, his expression grew enigmatic and he said gently, 'Would you care to have a walk outside, Jossie? It's warm in here and the Manchesters have a very pleasant garden.'

Jossie was suspicious, but decided to agree. They went out through the long windows which led into the garden. Lanterns had been hung on trees which bordered a path leading down into a sort of wilderness. Shrubs and early flowers scented the night air.

'Mind the step,' Ivo said, and he tucked her hand through his arm. 'It isn't too cold for you, is it? Shall we go a little further?' This was Ivo at his most charming, and even though Jossie was still wondering what he was about, she found herself walking along with him.

They reached the end of the path. Lights and the sounds of music came from the house, but here it was almost completely dark, except for a stray beam of moonlight.

'Now…' Ivo slid his arms round Jossie's waist. He drew her to him. Jossie's doubts grew. She tried to keep her distance, but Ivo's arms were too strong. She was pulled inexorably closer until they were touching breast to breast, thigh to thigh. She could feel their two bodies moulded to one another. His face was close, so close… But he looked different in the moonlight. His usual expression of lazy good humour had vanished, he looked…harder, less kind. His eyes were filled with mockery, his teeth gleaming white in a devilish smile…

Jossie panicked. 'Ivo—'

'Hush, Jossie,' he whispered. 'Let me kiss you!' He bent his head but it was her throat he kissed, then his lips moved further down... One hand came to push aside the lace of her bodice, to caress her breast. For one sudden, shameful moment Jossie was swamped by a sensation of fiercely burning desire, but then shock and outrage took over. She fought to pull back from him.

'No! How can you...? Stop this, Ivo! Let me go!'

Ivo's hand was withdrawn, but he still held her in an iron grip. She could not move. He gazed down at her grimly. 'You've had enough? Frightened, perhaps? You needn't be afraid of me. I'm not going to do another thing. I am quite sober, quite in control, and I mean you well. It was only make-believe, Jossie.'

Jossie gasped angrily. 'I don't find that sort of make-believe amusing!'

Still holding her fast, he said sternly, 'I didn't mean it to be. It was a demonstration of the very least you might expect from a man who is possibly half-drunk and certainly ruthless. If such a man accepted your invitation he wouldn't stop where I stopped.'

'But, Ivo, I can—'

'I know. You can take care of yourself. Try! Try to get away from me. I think you'll find you can't.'

Jossie tried all the tricks she knew, but Ivo's superior strength foiled her easily every time. In the end she had to admit defeat.

'Let me go. You've made your point,' she said sulkily. He set her instantly free. She added, 'But you didn't behave very gentlemanly.'

'Dammit, these are not gentlemen!'

'I could have screamed—'

'You wouldn't have been heard from here—not with all the music and chatter in the house.'

She was about to argue, but the expression on his face stopped her. For once she could see that beyond the façade of the good-humoured man of fashion, the light-hearted flirt, there lay a determined fighter, the cool but absolute authority of an officer in command. She gave in. 'Oh, very well, Ivo, you've made your point. I agree. I'll be careful in future.'

'Good! Now let me help you tidy yourself up.'

'No, thank you! I can manage,' Jossie said hastily. The thought of Ivo's fingers even tying a ribbon was too unnerving at the moment. She knew that he would take no further liberties, that was not the reason. But she could still remember that feel of his hand on her flesh, the mad, wicked moment when she would have granted him whatever he wanted… Shock, she told herself. She had been in shock. It was purely shock.

But that night in bed she lay awake, wondering what would have happened if Ivo had been serious. What would he have done next? And how did his real mistresses behave when his fingers touched them, as he had touched her that evening…?

Chapter Twelve

When Jossie came down the next morning she was relieved to hear that Ivo was out.

'In fact, I'm not altogether sure where he is,' said Lady Frances. 'It was past one o'clock when he brought us home this morning, but he went out again almost immediately afterwards. You had already disappeared upstairs, and I followed you soon after. I didn't hear him come in again.' She added carefully, 'Of course, Ivo is his own master...'

'Of course,' said Jossie. She had a sudden vision of Lady Alicia looking deliciously abandoned in a floating robe, her white and gold loveliness half-covered, half-revealed...Ivo's dark head was bent over her... Jossie jumped up.

'I'm sorry he isn't here,' she said brightly. 'I rather hoped to go for a ride in the park this morning.'

'Well, if you take your groom you should be safe enough. You're looking rather pale, a breath of air—such as it is in London—might do you good. Off you go! I propose to rest in my room and answer a few letters.'

Jossie sent a message to the stables to have her mare brought round and went upstairs to change.

In half an hour she was trotting sedately through the park gates. It was still early. Apart from servants and tradesmen few people were about. Jossie was glad. The events of the night before seemed to have removed the last veil from her understanding. The process which had begun on the night of Peter Radstock's coming of age was almost complete. She needed to think...

During her sojourn in London she had observed, she had listened, and she had learned a great deal. She was no longer the ignorant simpleton, the green girl of the year before, who hadn't thought twice about asking Ivo to show her how to kiss. She realised now how incredibly naïve she had been, isolated as she was from normal human society, brought up as a boy with a despotic father, and single-mindedly absorbed in her plans to marry Peter. The only women who had played any sort of part in her life had been Lady Radstock and her godmother, and their influence had been strictly limited. Peter's mother had confined herself to reprimanding Jossie for her careless behaviour, for being late, for looking untidy, for keeping Peter out till all hours roaming the countryside... And Lady Frances's opportunities for serious conversation had been severely restricted by what Jossie now knew to be her father's antagonism.

As a result she had been a very odd creature indeed when she had met Ivo—almost wholly ignorant of the world and its relationships, and ridiculously unaware of Ivo as a powerfully attractive male animal. The very idea of physical attraction had never occurred to her. Her childhood friendship with Peter had changed, she had thought, into love, but when Peter asked for a demonstration of that love she had been mystified and distressed. So she had turned to Ivo, who was so much older and so much more experienced, and who by that time had become a trusted friend.

What must he have thought of her? Not many men would have treated her request so seriously, so honourably as Ivo had. Now that she knew more of the world, she was astonished at his forbearance, his respect for her innocence.

And she had been so stupidly, so dangerously, innocent! Even when Ivo kissed her and she had felt for the first time the delight, the wonder, the exhilaration of desire, even then she had not recognised it for what it truly was. She had assumed that Peter's kisses would give her the same pleasure once she had got used to the idea, had thought that it was only a matter of time and patience.

Now she knew differently. She had suspected it for some time, but the events of the night before left no room for doubt. She would *never* have felt the same with Peter. Peter had held her close, but in a perfectly gentlemanly manner, he had kissed her, but gently, taking care not to frighten her. There had been no threat. But she had felt stifled in his embrace, repelled, had wanted only to escape.

Which brought her back to Ivo's treatment of her in the garden the night before. He had set out quite deliberately to frighten her, had overmastered her efforts to escape from him, had kissed her against her will, treated her with little respect, determined to prove how powerless she was in the hands of an unscrupulous and determined man. He hadn't meant it seriously, of course, he had merely intended to teach her a lesson. If his first lesson in Somerset had shown her the delights of a kiss, his second in London had been meant as a warning. None of it had affected him personally.

It was only stupid Jossie Morley who had been haunted ever since by the sudden rush of desire she had felt when he touched her. And she now recognised it as the darker side of a passion she had experienced before in Ivo's arms. Shamefully, she both feared it and longed for it again.

Worst of all, she had a suspicion that it was not Ivo, the expert in dalliance, the famed lover whose *affaires* had long been the talk of Europe, who had evoked these feelings, but Ivo the man himself. If she wasn't very, very careful, she would find herself in love with Ivo Trenchard. And if that happened, her case would be desperate. She had heard his views on love-sick débutantes often enough. If he ever believed that she thought of him as anything more than a friend and protector, he would remove himself from her life. She would lose even his friendship.

For a moment or two she felt miserable, but her natural optimism soon reasserted itself. She was no worse off than she had been before. As long as she suppressed these inconvenient feelings, as long as she kept the fears they brought with them strictly to herself, she and Ivo could continue as before. He was her friend and protector. That was all! That must be all!

Nor should she forget her main purpose in coming to London. Not to find a husband, but to show them! To show her father, Peter, Lady Radstock and the rest how wrong they had been. That had been her design from the beginning, and it was not yet fulfilled. She would concentrate on that, and forget these stupid thoughts about Ivo.

As she turned for home, she saw him in the distance.

She urged her mare to a faster trot and caught up with him just by the gate. 'Ivo! Wait!'

The gentleman turned. To her confusion she saw that she had been mistaken. This was not Ivo, but a stranger. There were resemblances, but this man was several years younger, and his features were somehow less well defined.

'I...I'm sorry,' she faltered. 'Forgive me, I thought—'

'That I was my brother?' The stranger smiled. 'I believe we are quite alike at a distance. I'm Peregrine Trenchard.'

'Oh! We thought you were in Derbyshire, sir!'

'I was till three days ago. I heard last week that my father was coming to London, so I decided to visit some old friends here and see my family at the same time.'

'You are not going to stay in Charles Street?'

'Er...no. But, please! Tell me who you are! Are you related to Lady Frances? I heard she is in London.'

'I'm her goddaughter, sir. My name is J...Helena Calverton.'

Peregrine Trenchard looked at her with a curious smile, but said merely, 'I am delighted to make your acquaintance, Miss Calverton! May I accompany you back to Charles Street?'

'Of course! But your father hasn't yet arrived, sir.'

'In that case I shall be more than pleased to escort you.'

His remark puzzled Jossie. It was said in a most amiable fashion, but, if she had understood his meaning correctly, he was not being particularly pleasant towards his parent.

'Is my brother Ivo likely to be at home?'

Jossie stayed calm, though her heart jumped. 'I'm not sure. He comes and goes a great deal,' she said with tolerable indifference. 'He wasn't in this morning when I came out.'

'Better and better,' murmured Peregrine. He saw her surprise and added, 'It means I can devote more of my time and attention to you, Miss Calverton.'

As they rode back through the London streets Jossie wondered what sort of man this was. He didn't seem to like either his father or his brother. Why had he bothered to come to London to see them?

Lady Frances was delighted to see her younger nephew, only protesting at his decision to stay in Half Moon Street with friends.

'Come, Aunt Frances! You know very well that if my father and I stayed under the same roof he would be bellowing at me before a day had gone by. It's much more comfortable for everyone if I stay elsewhere and visit you often but briefly. When is he due?'

'Any day now. But he's changed, Perry. I think Jossie has tamed him.'

'Jossie?'

Jossie blushed and said awkwardly, 'Your aunt calls me by my old name, Mr Trenchard. I used to be known as Jossie Morley.'

'Helena suits you better,' said Mr Trenchard. 'May I call you Helena? Neither Miss Morley nor Miss Calverton sounds very friendly, and if you've tamed my father you must be the best friend I have!'

Jossie smiled and gave him permission, but inwardly she was still doubtful about Peregrine Trenchard. She liked Lord Veryan, and she found his younger son altogether too frankly critical. She studied him as he chatted to Lady Frances. The resemblance to Ivo was not so marked now she was close. Peregrine's hair was as dark as Ivo's, but his eyes were a lighter blue, and, though he was equally tall, his build was slighter, less powerful. His manner was different, too. He seemed more anxious to please, less confident than his brother. Knowing Lord Veryan as she did, she could well imagine that his younger son's diffidence would irritate him.

She did not see Ivo until that evening. He had stayed out all day, and in the end it was Peregrine who escorted them to their evening engagement, a soirée with music and dancing at Crewe House. Peregrine proved to be an excellent dancer and an amusing companion, and Jossie found she liked him a great deal better than she had thought. He had a fund of amusing anecdotes, which kept Lady Frances and her friends entertained throughout the evening. The ladies were not averse to gossip, however, and the talk eventually turned to the subject of other recent arrivals in the capital.

'Of course, Mr Trenchard, you must not think you are the only newcomer. There has recently been a positive influx of visitors. I hear the Balmennys arrived yesterday, as well,' said one lady. The chill of disapproval which descended on the group at this news was almost palpable.

'I hear she is as lovely as ever,' said one. 'And as flighty. Motherhood hasn't improved her.'

'A pity,' said another dowager, and added with a significant nod, 'However, since they spent almost the whole of last year on his estate in Ireland, Balmenny can at least be sure the children are his!'

Lady Frances was shocked. 'Maria!' she said.

'Facts are facts, Frances. And it cannot be denied that Julia Redshaw was never in love with her husband. Poor Balmenny has had a devil of a time with her.'

Jossie's interest had been caught by the mention of Julia Redshaw, and she listened to this exchange with amusement. Heaven help those who offended these gently bred members of Society! They were quite ruthless in their destruction of a character—though what they were saying about the lovely Viscountess Balmenny only confirmed what she had heard from the Calthorpes. But then the ladies went on to discuss other arrivals with equal charity, and her attention wandered. She looked around the room…

On the other side, almost opposite her, was Ivo. He had clearly just arrived, and seemed to be searching for someone. When he saw Jossie and her companions he nodded and came towards them. She felt her face grow warm and turned away. To her relief he first greeted Lady Frances, then nodded to Peregrine.

'I heard you were in town,' he said. 'I'm glad to see you, Perry. How are you?'

The brothers talked for a while, thus giving Jossie time to recover. She was even able to be amused at the manner in which her godmother's friends were eyeing Ivo. They obviously felt they ought to disapprove of him, but were unable to resist his charm. He was, after all, so very handsome! Jossie was reminded that one or two of these dowagers had been famous beauties in their day, and they were smiling now as if they, too, were remembering… She cast a quick glance at Peregrine, inviting him to share her amusement, but was surprised to see that he was looking at Ivo with an expression which Jossie found hard to define. But it wasn't friendly.

Ivo's conversation with the ladies finally came to an end and he turned to Jossie. 'Will you dance?' he asked.

Jossie started to refuse, but Ivo insisted. 'Please!' She

hesitated, then gave him a nod and led the way without speaking to the ballroom.

By the time they started she had herself under control, even managing not to stiffen when he took her hand in the dance. 'I don't expect you thought you would see your brother here tonight,' she began lightly.

'On the contrary, I heard he was in town, which is why I came.'

'Oh.'

'Or rather, it's one of the reasons I came.'

Jossie took a breath and said calmly, 'There's another?'

'Two. They both concern you.'

She felt herself colouring again. 'If you mean to say anything about last night, I would rather you didn't.'

'I must. I deeply regret what I did, and I beg you to forgive me.'

Jossie managed a little laugh. 'Goodness, Ivo! Don't sound so grave! You did me a service. I am grateful to you for the warning, and intend to take it seriously. I ought to apologise to you for being such a nuisance. Looking after such an idiot can't be very amusing.'

'You're not—' He stopped abruptly. After a moment he said, 'I hope we're still friends?'

'Of course!' Ivo looked so unlike himself, so concerned, that she found it easy to reassure him. She gave him a perfectly genuine smile. 'What would I do without you to save me from further stupidities? Though I think I *am* learning more about the world. There may even come a time when I shan't need you.' He couldn't reply immediately as they were separated for a moment by the dance.

When they came together again he was frowning. It looked as if he was still annoyed with himself.

In an effort to distract him she said, 'I wish you had been here earlier. The ladies were talking about Julia Redshaw, and they were even less kind than the Calthorpes about her. They say she is in London. After all the things I've heard I can hardly wait to see her. Is she really as beautiful as they say? Was Adam really in love with her?'

'Yes, I think so. Before he joined the Army. But once he met Kate…'

'You liked Kate, too, didn't you, Ivo?'

Ivo said with some reserve, 'Yes, I liked her. I still do, very much. But I didn't allow myself to fall in love with her, if that's what you're asking. Adam's friendship was more important to me. And now they are both very good friends of mine.'

Jossie nodded. 'You're fortunate. They're very nice people. I should love to meet them again. Do you think they will come to London?'

'I'm afraid not. Not this year.' He paused, then said slowly, 'I haven't yet given you my other reason for seeking you out tonight.'

'What is it?'

'Your father is here in London.'

Jossie nearly missed a step, but rallied. 'My father?' She gave a little laugh. 'With his new wife, no doubt.'

Ivo nodded. 'Together with the Radstocks.'

'What a delightful family party!' Jossie said lightly after the briefest of pauses. She had lost colour, but her voice was under control. To a casual listener she would have sounded perfectly normal.

'Quite!'

'So Rosalind has had her way… Lady Radstock will be pleased, but I wonder what Sir Thomas makes of it? He hates towns.'

They were parted again for a moment.

Ivo, watching Jossie carefully, thought she was taking it almost too calmly. He noticed that she had not mentioned Peter. When they came together at the end of the set, she said, 'It should prove interesting. For everyone. Do you mind if we go back to Lady Frances?'

Lord Veryan arrived the next day, and the house was in something of a bustle until Lady Frances had seen to it that he was suitably installed in his own bedchamber, with his extra pillows and his special chair, and his valet in the dressing room next door.

'Don't get old, Jossie,' he said irritably. 'People always make such a fuss about your comfort. As if I can sleep anyway in this rackety place! Never liked London and never shall!'

'Then I'm all the more grateful to you for coming,' said Jossie. 'And I shall cancel my engagement for tonight.'

'What nonsense is this? I'll come with you, girl! I want to see how you're doing. Where is this engagement?'

'Oh, I won't be noticed tonight! It's at Marchant House, and the Carterets are hosting a reception for the Duke of Wellington.'

'Dammit, you mustn't miss that! Isn't he your hero?'

'The trouble is, the world and his wife all wish to be there,' said Lady Frances doubtfully. 'An invitation might be difficult to come by.'

'Carteret's an old drinking partner of mine. He'll let me in easily enough,' said Lord Veryan. 'Who else is going?'

'Ivo is one of his Grace's party. And Perry—'

'Peregrine? Is he in London?'

'Didn't you know?'

'I wouldn't be asking if I did, would I? What's the young fool doing in London?'

'He's here to meet you, sir,' said Jossie with a laugh. 'I hope you won't frighten him off!'

'Hmm. He'll be there tonight, you say?'

'Yes. He's acting as our escort,' said Lady Frances.

'You don't need him when you have me!'

'But will you be fit enough, Rupert?' his sister asked patiently. 'And, if you do come, will you promise to keep your temper with Peregrine?'

'There's no need to tell me how to behave, Fanny!' said his lordship testily. Since he knew perfectly well that Lady Frances hated to be called 'Fanny', Jossie could only assume he was being deliberately provocative. The journey had clearly upset him more than he would admit.

'Have you brought your backgammon set with you, sir?' she asked.

'Never travel without it. D'y want a game?' Jossie nodded. 'Now?'

Jossie nodded again and said, 'There's a corner in the library that is perfect. But of course you know that. Shall we go there?'

Lady Frances heaved a sigh of relief, and gave Jossie a warm smile of approval.

Others were looking forward to the reception at Merchant House. The Morleys and the Radstocks had been lucky enough to get invitations, too. It was to be the climax of the Morleys' visit to London. The Radstocks were to stay several weeks, but to his wife's chagrin, the Major could not afford to spend more than a few days in a London hotel.

'I have to say, Gerard,' said Mrs Morley in a complaining voice, 'that I think you have arranged things very badly. Surely you could have persuaded the Radstocks to invite us to stay on with them? You know I never complain, but it is very hard not to spend longer in London, now that we have finally got here. I think the Radstocks are being monstrously selfish. But you refused even to ask them!'

'Because, as I have told you more than once, my dear, Sir Thomas is not a particular friend of mine and would have been very surprised if I had. Think of the embarrassment if he had refused! Where would we have been then? We have at least been invited to dine with them while we are in London.'

'I still think you could have taken a little more trouble, Gerard! My previous husband...'

Major Morley uttered an oath, went to his own room and stared resentfully into the long mirror there. Why was he always cursed with such bad luck? Mrs Cherton had been a charming lady before she married him. Just what a man not yet past his prime had needed, especially after the fiasco of that coming-of-age ball. She had soothed his lacerated nerves and been ready to sympathise when some of the neighbours had been most unpleasant. He had been sure that in time when the world saw him with such a beautiful, elegant wife at his side, he would once again be admired and envied, instead of being pitied, or even criticised, for having such a failure of a daughter.

But the new Mrs Morley was far from being what he had expected. There had been some very awkward scenes when she learned that the Calverton fortune was not his but Jossie's, and from then on she had been much less amenable, much less inclined to minister to his feelings. And now, with increasing frequency, she had taken to comparing him unfavourably with her first husband! It was too bad! Jossie might have had her faults, but she had never criticised him! Gerard Morley looked at himself in the mirror. He looked very well in his dress uniform. What a damned shame it was that he had had to give up his career! He might well have been the guest of honour tonight, not Arthur Wellesley. But Wellesley had always had all the luck. Luck was all it needed. Just a bit of luck, and he would have given the Duke of Wellington a run for his money!

'I hope you are not going to commandeer that mirror for very much longer, Gerard,' a voice behind him said acidly. 'The one in my room is impossible!'

Marchant House was particularly suited to grand occasions. It had a huge ballroom at the back of the house, and the reception rooms in the main building were also very handsome. But even the resources of Marchant House were stretched to their limit on the night of the Carterets' reception. By the time the Duke's party arrived, the way through to the ballroom was lined with most of the polite world, all craning their necks to get a glimpse of Waterloo's hero.

The Radstocks and the Morleys had managed to find quite a good vantage point with a clear view of the procession as it made its way along.

'By Jove, look, Morley!' said Sir Thomas. 'Isn't that the Trenchard fellow? Lady Frances's nephew?'

Sir Thomas's voice was penetrating, and Ivo could hardly fail to hear it. He looked over, and bowed slightly without leaving his place behind the Duke.

'Friends of yours, Ivo?' asked the Duke in a side whisper.

'Not exactly, sir. Neighbours.'

'Don't like 'em, eh? Never mind, you needn't talk to them. I'll keep you busy.'

And the Duke was as good as his word. Ivo and his fellow officers, all former members of the Duke's Staff, were sent here and there to escort one or other of the more important personages who wished to have a word with the great man, keeping at bay the ones the Duke didn't wish to meet. But after an hour and a half even great men get bored.

'I've had enough of this,' he said. 'I've done my duty for long enough. Ivo, you usually have a line on good-looking women. I'd like to have a chat with a beautiful face for a change, and I haven't had time to find my own old friends. What about it?'

'Sir, some of the loveliest women in London would be honoured to meet you.'

'Well, get on with it, then! Is there to be any dancing? Ellington, you go and arrange it with Carteret. Duty's done, it's time for enjoyment, gentlemen!'

Ivo was nothing if not tactful. He took care to bring first ladies who were certainly good-looking, but also had some other claim to the Duke's attention, such as, for example, the Princess Lieven, Lady Cowper, and others. After that he brought one or two of his own choice. The Duke chatted with all of them, and danced with one or two.

'You're doing well, Ivo!' he said genially. 'But how about one of the younger ones now?'

Ivo smiled, looked thoughtfully round the room, and made his way through the crowds to where Lord Veryan was sitting with Jossie at his side.

'Father. I'm sorry I haven't had a chance to talk to you. My former commander has kept me busy all day.

We must have a good session tomorrow. But meanwhile, may I borrow your lady friend for a moment? His Grace wishes to meet Jossie.'

Jossie almost dropped her reticule. 'Me! Ivo, I can't!'

'Of course you can! He's as susceptible to beauty as any of us—more so, if anything. Don't keep him waiting.'

Jossie walked with Ivo up the room to where the Duke was standing and gave him a deep curtsy.

'Miss Helena Calverton, Duke,' Ivo said. 'I've warned her not to talk to you about Waterloo.'

The Duke was eyeing Jossie with approval, but at this he turned to Ivo and said, 'Why not? Does it offend her feelings to talk of battles?'

'On the contrary. It's your feelings I worry about, Duke. Miss Calverton is quite likely to correct you if your memory plays false.'

'What's this, what's this?'

'Please, your Grace, don't listen to Lord Trenchard. He talks a great deal of nonsense.'

'He does, doesn't he? Ivo, you are dismissed. Come back for Miss Calverton later.' He took Jossie's arm and led her to the floor. 'So, miss, I suppose you think I talk a great deal of nonsense as well, eh?'

Jossie shook her head and gave him an impish glance out of blue-green eyes. 'I am quite sure no one would dare tell you so, if you did, your Grace. I've heard stories of your setdowns.'

The Duke laughed delightedly and swung her on to the floor. 'Wit as well as beauty! I can see that I must tell Ivo to be on his guard.'

They passed two other dancers. Peter Radstock almost fell over. He clutched his wife's arm and said dazedly,

'That…that's Jossie! No, it can't be—I must be dreaming.'

'Where?'

'Dancing with the Duke.'

'Peter! Don't talk such nonsense. Jossie Morley? Are you mad?'

'I think I must be. But I could have sworn…'

He took Rosalind's hand and walked determinedly off the floor. When he reached his parents he interrupted their conversation to say, 'Father, that girl dancing with the Duke. Did you see her?'

'No. Why?'

'Look at her now! Does she remind you of anyone?'

They all looked. The girl did a graceful turn, then laughed up at the Duke as he said something. He was quite clearly very taken with his partner.

'It looks like… Who do you think it is?' asked Sir Thomas.

'It's Jossie!'

Mrs Morley laughed. 'Don't be absurd, Peter! That's quite out of the question. Look at the girl's style, her clothes! They are in the first stare of fashion.' Her eye rested a trifle discontentedly on her daughter. Since her marriage Rosalind had taken to wearing some very unstylish dresses. Mrs Morley blamed Peter for it.

'I don't think it can possibly be Jossie, dear,' said Lady Radstock. 'Remember how she hated to dance? That girl is unmistakably enjoying it.'

Peter turned to someone standing next to them. 'Excuse me,' he said. 'Can you tell me the name of the girl dancing with the Duke?'

'That's Helena Calverton, the latest sensation. Lovely, isn't she? The Beau always had an eye for a beautiful woman.'

'You see?' Mrs Morley was triumphant. 'I knew it couldn't be Jossie.'

'Yes, but...' Lady Radstock hesitated. 'Jossie's real name is Helena. And her mother was a Calverton.'

Ivo returned as ordered to collect Jossie at the end of the dance. The Duke was most complimentary on his choice of companion, and it took some skill to extricate her.

'Ivo, thank you!' said Jossie with a glowing look. 'What an experience! I shall never forget it!'

'I haven't finished with you yet,' said Ivo.

'What about your duties?'

'I think I've done enough for the time being. I've asked Colonel Ancroft to cover for me. Besides, the Duke is due to go into supper with the bigwigs any moment. Look! They're collecting him now. I must take you to meet someone else.'

He looked so serious, that Jossie guessed what he was going to say before he spoke. 'My father?'

'And Peter Radstock, yes. All of them, in fact. They're all here.'

Jossie stiffened. She said coolly, 'How on earth did they manage that? I thought invitations were at a premium? They were very fortunate to get any at all, let alone six!'

'I made sure they did,' said Ivo calmly.

'You? But why?'

'I wanted them to see you tonight. Having a triumph. Not very worthy of me, was it?'

Jossie regarded him with surprise and admiration. 'You clever thing!' She started to laugh. 'So you organised it all! The invitations, the dance with the Duke, all of it. And you called *me* a schemer!'

Ivo took her hand to his lips. 'You deserved any help I could give. I know what it means to you. You've worked hard and come so far in the past year, Jossie.'

Jossie's colour rose. 'Ivo,' she said nervously. 'You're not being very circumspect. People will say that you're flirting with me, if you're not careful.'

'As I've told you many times before, I will never flirt with you.'

They had reached the end of the room where the Radstocks were waiting. Jossie's father was standing to one side of them, looking furiously disbelieving.

Chapter Thirteen

The hand resting on Ivo's arm stiffened and Jossie's fingers gripped him painfully. This was the first sight she had had of her father since that dreadful confrontation in the Radstocks' garden the year before, and Ivo was not surprised that she was as tense as a coiled spring. But when he glanced down at her he could see no sign of this in her face. He was filled with admiration and pride. Jossie was showing nothing but serenely polite pleasure.

'Father,' she said, curtsying. 'How are you?' She turned to her father's wife, and curtsied again. 'Ma'am.'

Mrs Morley gave a slight nod, but her eyes were fastened on Jossie's dress. It was one of Madame Rosa's most beautiful, a masterpiece in silver and white. Tiny silver beads and drops of crystal decorated the bodice and hem of diaphanous white silk worn over an underdress of satin. A delicately wrought crescent of the same silver and crystal nestled in her dark hair, and a scarf of silver gauze was draped over her arms. The only touches of colour were found in the faint rose of her cheeks and lips, and the intensely vivid turquoise of her eyes. The effect was stunning. She looked not quite of this world—

a moon goddess. Mrs Morley's face settled further into lines of dissatisfaction.

Major Morley made no move towards his daughter. 'What's this Calverton nonsense?' he asked. 'You're called Morley. Jossie Morley. Or isn't my name good enough for you?'

Jossie gave him a wry smile. 'The last time we spoke, Father, you made it painfully clear that you didn't consider me good enough for your name! So I prefer to use ''Helena Calverton''—it carries no such unfortunate memories. But don't let's spoil the occasion by disagreeing about something which happened quite a long time ago. You remember Lord Trenchard, of course?'

Her father could hardly say more in such a public place, so he gave Ivo a stiff nod. Ivo bowed but didn't speak, and moved on instead to exchange courtesies with Mrs Morley.

Jossie went on to speak to the Radstocks. 'Lady Radstock, Sir Thomas. What a surprise to see you here! Are you staying in London long?'

Lady Radstock, looking somewhat dazed, responded politely, but Sir Thomas took Jossie's hands and held them in a firm grip. 'Eh, it's wonderful to see you looking so well, Jossie girl! You look bonnier than ever and that's a fact! But what's all this? I thought you didn't like towns and suchlike any more than I do! What are you doing here?' He shot a glance at Ivo. 'Are you...'

'No, no! Lord Trenchard is merely taking me back to my godmother.'

Sir Thomas's face cleared. 'Oh, you're with Lady Frances, are you? For a moment...'

'Lord Veryan and Lady Frances are in the next room, Sir Thomas. I now live with my godmother, as I dare say you know, and she has been sponsoring my come-out in Society. I cannot tell you how kind she and Lord Veryan have been. And Lord Trenchard has been nothing more than a true friend. The best I have. Nowadays.'

Sir Thomas looked very uncomfortable. 'Yes, well... I'm sorry, lass. It was cruel of us...'

For a moment there was a flash of the old Jossie in the warmth of the smile she gave him. 'Don't say another word! *You* were never cruel.' She moved on.

Peter and his wife were next. Ivo made sure he was standing close beside her as Jossie said, 'And here are your son and daughter-in-law! You're looking very well, Peter.'

Peter flushed to the roots of his hair. He stammered, 'Jossie... You look so different. I hardly recognise you...I didn't...didn't realise—'

'That I would change? People do, you know. Sometimes overnight. But I don't believe I ever congratulated you on your marriage.' Her gaze included both the young Radstocks as she said charmingly, 'Let me wish you all the happiness you deserve.'

Ivo coughed, there was a little silence, then Jossie said, with a laugh, 'Oh dear! That isn't very tactful of me, is it? I wish you both happy—that's much better, I think.' She paused, then added, 'Kinder.'

Ivo gave her a straight look and said firmly, 'I think it's time we found the rest of our party, Jossie. They must be wondering what has happened to us.'

Lady Radstock hesitated and said, 'If your aunt has time I should very much like to see her again, Lord Trenchard. She has been much missed in Lyne St Michael.'

'I'm sure she would be delighted if you called on her,' replied Ivo. 'She's at home most afternoons. You know our direction?'

'Charles Street. Yes.'

'Excellent! She will look forward to it. Can she expect you all?'

'Unfortunately not,' said Lady Radstock, adding, with very little sign of regret, 'Major and Mrs Morley are leaving London tomorrow.'

'How sad,' said Ivo with equal sincerity. 'But my aunt would be pleased to see you and your family, at least.' He turned to Jossie. 'Come along, Jossie. Princess Lieven wishes to have a word with you, but first we must rejoin the others.' He led her away.

The Morleys and the Radstocks were left behind to wonder and conjecture.

'I would never have believed it,' said Lady Radstock, her eyes following Jossie's progress through the room. The progress was slow enough. She stopped every few paces, to curtsy to Lady Jersey, blush at a compliment from one of the Royal Dukes, or laugh with one or other of Ivo's friends. Her position as a reigning beauty was undeniable. Lady Radstock blinked. 'Tell me I'm not dreaming!'

'I've a good mind to make her come back and live with me,' frowned the Major. 'That godmother of hers had no right to take her away. We could do with some-one like her at the Manor, the place hasn't been the same without her.'

Mrs Morley had no wish to see herself and her own daughter eclipsed by the return to Lyne St Michael of a wildly successful prodigal stepdaughter. 'I shouldn't if I were you, my love,' she said, sweetly. 'I doubt Helena, as she now calls herself, would come. And the village wouldn't take it too kindly if you forced her. It would only start the talk again, and you know how you hated it.'

'Well, I say, good luck to her!' said Sir Thomas. 'And good luck to the lucky man who gets her! What a girl, eh? A real beauty! Charmin', lively and with a fortune, too...' He cast a disparaging glance at his daughter-in-law.

Peter had been silent, staring at Jossie as if he still couldn't believe his eyes. But at these words he turned to his wife and said, 'Come and dance, Rosalind. I always enjoy dancing with you.' And with a defiant glance at his father he took Rosalind on to the floor.

For the rest of the evening Jossie herself put on a brave front, chatting gaily, dancing every dance, and refusing to admit how much the encounter with her father and the Radstocks had taken out of her. But after a while Lord Veryan announced that she could dance the night through if she wished, but he was going home to bed, and he advised her to do the same. So, with the exception of Ivo who, as the Duke's aide, had to stay to the end, the Charles Street party went home comparatively early.

But though Jossie excused herself and went to bed almost as soon as they got in, she found that she could not sleep. She was still taut, unable to relax. So much had happened that evening. To have danced with England's hero, the man who had saved Europe, beaten so many French generals in Spain, and ended by defeating Napoleon himself at Waterloo...! The thrill of that alone was excuse for a sleepless night.

Then there was the rest, the less glorious, but no less agitating, experience of meeting once again all the actors in the drama that had been played out on the night of Peter's coming of age. The triumph had been everything she had wanted. Because of Ivo's machinations she could not have appeared to them in a more impressive light, and she hoped and believed her performance had repaid his efforts.

But the drama seemed so long ago and so much had happened in the year since. She had both feared and looked forward to meeting her father and the others again, she had been so determined to show them. This was what had driven her for nearly a year, had made all the effort seem worthwhile. Now it was done, she was surprised to feel a sense of anticlimax, a curious sense of loss. The Jossie of those early days would have danced in the streets tonight at the discomfiture of her enemies. But somewhere along the way that girl had vanished, along with the girl who had worshipped her father and imagined herself in love with Peter. The desperate girl, who thought that her life had come to an end when they had both rejected her, simply no longer existed...

But what sort of person had taken her place?

She went to the window, quietly drew back the heavy curtains, and opened it. Her room looked on to the street, which at this hour of the morning was deserted. It was a clear night and she could see a narrow strip of sky above, brilliant with stars. The moon was still full enough to cast a faint light on the road below. She sat for a while gazing at the stars. Where was Ivo now? Was he with Lady Alicia? Or was another of his amours delighting him tonight? She realised with a pang that her success with the *ton*, her triumph over Peter and her father, would have counted for less than nothing if Ivo had not been there to share it with her. She would give up all the admiration she had seen in other men's eyes, every bit of the amazement she had seen on the Radstocks' faces tonight, if Ivo would only look at her as he looked at Lady Alicia and the others. He never would. He would never see her like that. She was his friend, his protégée. She sighed and turned to go to bed.

As she did so her eye was caught by a lone figure striding along Charles Street, in the direction of the house. It was Ivo. His head was slightly bent—he seemed to be deep in thought. Jossie drew back a little, but still watched him. He looked tired.

Then to her horror she saw another man creeping up on Ivo from behind, holding what looked like a heavy stick in his hand. Her heart gave a thump, then seemed to stop...

'Ivo!' she shouted desperately.

Ivo looked up, then, suddenly alert, turned as the thief attacked, and partially dodged the murderous blow aimed at him. If it had landed squarely it would surely have killed him. Ivo recovered his balance and promptly tackled his assailant, and a short, sharp fight ensued, which ended when the stranger broke loose and fled back down the street. Ivo stood for a moment, then made for the house again. But he staggered as he turned and had to hold on to the railings for support. He was injured! Jossie threw on a wrapper and ran down two flights of stairs at breakneck speed. She arrived at the front door just as one of the servants was opening it. Ivo almost fell into the hall.

'Don't just stand there! Help me!' she said to the servant. Between them they supported Ivo to the nearest room on the ground floor, the library. Here they helped him into a chair, where he sank back with a groan. Another servant came hurrying in, carrying the lamp from the hall.

'We shall need water and cloths,' Jossie said, carefully examining the ugly wound on the back of Ivo's head.

'And see if Lord Trenchard's man is awake. If not, rouse him. Quickly!'

'Don't wake anyone else, Foster,' said Ivo with an effort. 'I don't want my father or her ladyship alarmed. They sleep at the back, they won't have heard anything yet. And tell any other servants to go back to their beds.'

'But oughtn't we to send someone after the man who attacked you?'

'Useless! He's long gone. And fortunately he didn't get anything. You ought to go back to your bed, too, Jossie.'

'As if I could!' She turned to the man carrying a basin of water and cloths. 'Good! Put it down here, if you please. Now.'

The next few minutes were difficult. Jossie was as gentle as she could be, but Ivo's hair was matted with blood, and it took some time to clean the wound. Fortunately his manservant arrived halfway through and, after watching her in silence for a moment, he offered to take over.

'Let him, Jossie. He knows what he's doing. Kealy was with me in Spain.' Ivo tried to grin. 'He's seen worse than this! Send for some brandy and then get off to bed. I'll soon be perfectly fit.' He looked at the other servants. 'Make sure the door is locked and then you be off too. Quietly! Thank you for your help. Goodnight.'

Jossie went over to the decanter and glasses on the library table and poured out a small brandy. She brought it back and held it to Ivo's lips. His face was white, and when he reached to take the glass his hand was ice-cold.

'Ivo!' She kept hold of the brandy, made sure he drank it, then put the glass down. She put a cashmere shawl, which had been on the back of one of the chairs, over his knees, then knelt on the floor beside him and took his hands in hers.

While his man busied himself with basilicum powder and bandages, Jossie knelt close to Ivo, cradling his hands to her, giving him the warmth from her own body. She couldn't quite stop herself from thinking how like and yet how very unlike it was to what had happened just a few nights before, and when she looked up Ivo's eyes held a gleam which showed that, injured though he was, he was thinking of it, too. She smiled at him. This was different. On this occasion there was no threat, no compulsion, nothing forced or cheap about it. She was freely giving him what comfort she could through the warmth of human contact. The feeling was very precious. Ivo's eyes closed... For a few minutes there was silence in the room, except for the small noises made by the servant, as he tended Ivo.

'I think that will do, my lord,' he said finally. 'I'm pleased to say the wound is superficial. It will hardly show tomorrow.'

Ivo opened his eyes and stared at Jossie. He removed his hands from her grasp and slowly traced a line down her cheek with the tips of his fingers, ending by cupping her chin in his hand. He held it so for a moment, looking deep into her eyes, then he released her and sat up. 'Thank you, Kealy,' he said. 'Now, will you please see Miss Calverton safely to her bedchamber, then come back here and clear up the mess. With your help I think I can make it to my room.'

'But, Ivo—!'

'Do as I say, Jossie. Let Kealy take you. You mustn't be found here.' His voice was tired but determined. Jossie, feeling bereft, got to her feet and nodded. Ivo didn't want to be accused of compromising her, and he was right.

'Good night,' she said stiffly. Now that the crisis was over reaction was setting in. She could hardly speak for the ache in her throat. 'I'm glad you're not badly hurt.'

'Thanks to you. I was half-asleep as I came along that street. I couldn't have defended myself if you hadn't woken me up.'

She nodded. Kealy was holding the door, and she walked slowly out of the library and up the stairs. When she reached the door of her bedchamber she turned to Kealy. 'Don't let your master do too much,' she said.

'I wouldn't, miss. The thing is, I don't know how to stop him! But I think he'll do. This knock is nothing to what he's had in the past.'

She smiled. 'Thank you, Kealy. Good night.'

Inside her room she slowly took off her wrapper and examined it. The sleeves were stained with traces of blood. Ivo's blood. How close she had come that night to losing him altogether! She stared at the wrapper and gave a twisted smile. So much for her resolve not to fall in love with him! It was too late. She was already there. She trusted him, she was grateful to him, she respected him—all of these. But this strange mixture of loving tenderness and hungry desire, this longing to stay with him, look after him, be with him…this was different.

Deep down it had been there almost from the beginning, of course. It explained why she had responded so ardently to Ivo's kisses, and so reluctantly to Peter's, though she had been too blind, too naïve, to see it at the time. Now it was clear enough, even for her. This love of hers for Ivo Trenchard was not that of an untutored girl. She now longed for everything that love would entail, perfect harmony of body as well as of mind. And she wanted this man for her lover, her husband, her companion for the rest of her life. This man and no other. How foolish she was! How madly, stupidly foolish!

Jossie got into bed. She lay there for a while, thinking of the scene in the library, wondering what Ivo's look had meant. He had gazed at her seriously, a little sadly—almost as if he was saying goodbye... She dismissed the thought as absurd. His head had been hurting, that was all. Then she folded her hands to her, and relived the moments when she had cradled Ivo's hands to her breast, giving him life and warmth... Finally she fell asleep.

Meanwhile Ivo had made his way to his own room and removed his stained coat and shirt. Then, in spite of Kealy's protests, he sent the man to bed and sat in a chair at the window in his dressing gown. His head was aching, his body felt as if he had been in the saddle for a fortnight, but his mind was as awake as it had ever been.

He had now finished what he had set out to do for Jossie. She had been as successful in London as he had foreseen, and was now securely established in the eyes of the *ton* as someone worthy of a place in the highest echelons of society.

Furthermore, he had helped her to prove herself to those who had injured her so badly at that accursed coming-of-age ball. Her wounded spirit must have been healed by tonight's demonstration... He hoped so, at least. He had occasionally had a suspicion that Jossie wanted more than satisfaction, that she wanted revenge, but to his relief there had been no sign of that tonight. Ivo smiled involuntarily. The little minx, wishing Radstock and his wife the happiness they deserved! And the look on their faces!

His smile faded and he sighed. So what was left for him to do? Fade tactfully from the scene? Jossie would now surely forget her determination to remain single. She could marry any one of a dozen extremely eligible young men, and that was undoubtedly what she ought to do...

He sat up. No, dammit! It was not. Jossie belonged to him! He'd be hanged if he let her marry some young stripling who would never value her as he ought. Jossie might be far too young for Ivo Trenchard, but who else could possibly appreciate how very special she was? Who else would watch her as she needed to be watched, protect her from dangers she was too trusting to see?

He sank back into the chair again. He mustn't go too quickly. If Jossie was persuaded to marry him, it would mean giving up his old ways forever—the flirtations, the *affaires*, the pursuit of a new quarry.... They would all have to go. He wouldn't, he couldn't, offer her anything but complete loyalty. She had been hurt once before, she mustn't be hurt again. Not ever. The choice was simple enough—his old, very enjoyable, bachelor existence, or marriage to Jossie. There was no halfway, no compromise. Was he ready to decide between them?

He smiled ruefully. Adam had been right, after all! It wasn't a question of choice. Marriage no longer seemed a necessary duty, a trap, a limitation of his freedom. Life with Jossie offered everything he wanted, and nothing else would do.

Of course he was ready! He ought to have realised it the other night. While he was teaching Jossie her lesson in the garden at Manchester House, he had congratulated himself on managing to remain quite objective, perfectly cool. But how he had paid for it afterwards! He had been haunted by Jossie's reproachful eyes, the hurt shock in her voice, and, worse than that, he had been quite unable to forget the feel of her lissome young body under his hands... It had seemed a good idea to banish these thoughts with a visit to Lady Alicia. And what had happened? For all her charms, all her experience, the lady had never before seemed so unattractive, nor he so unable to respond. The whole visit had been a disaster. Indeed, she might never forgive him for the manner in which he had left her. And then he had walked the streets of London till dawn...

No, there wasn't much danger that he would be tempted to stray if Jossie married him. The difficulty would lie in persuading her that he was the one for her. Yes, there was one lesson he still had to teach Jossie— the most important lesson of the lot. Ivo Trenchard was the one for her, the only *possible* one to be her lover, her husband, the father of her children...

Dawn was breaking. Ivo got up, stretched and stared down at the street. He knew at last what it was he wanted from life. Now he had to work out how to achieve it. He would have to go warily. Jossie might well be willing to marry him out of gratitude, or for friendship's sake, or even to avoid loneliness. And, from the evidence of their past encounters, he could probably seduce her into marrying him, too. But it wouldn't be enough. He wanted her to come to him because she loved him in every way there was, body, heart, and soul. No other reason would do. She must love him as completely, as irreversibly, as he loved her. But with *his* reputation, how the devil was he to convince her of his sincerity?

By noon the next day, which was when everyone got up, Ivo was himself again. There was no sign, either on his person or in the library, of what had taken place the night before. Jossie raised her eyebrow as she greeted him, but he only smiled reassuringly and invited her for a drive that afternoon.

'Jossie tells me that the Radstocks wish to visit us,' said Lady Frances. 'I have no objection to receiving Sir Thomas and Lady Radstock, but I have to say I should prefer not to see Peter and his wife. But I suppose I must if they are brazen enough to call. Do you think they might come this afternoon, Ivo?'

'We didn't make any definite arrangement. However, I should imagine they would leave it a day or two.'

'Peregrine said he would visit us this afternoon. I've told Rupert he's to be kinder to the boy. He was quite short with him last night. I do wish he wouldn't always compare him with you—I could see Perry didn't like it. I hear he has done very well in Derbyshire. Why doesn't your father talk of that?' She paused. 'Mind you, Derbyshire isn't London, and last night was quite an occasion, was it not? I was very proud of you myself. It's clear that the Duke thinks highly of you.'

'You wouldn't think so if you heard what he says to me! But one of us certainly had his total approbation last night.'

'It is not to be wondered at! Jossie, you looked superb, and danced divinely! I was so proud of you! I remarked to Perry, as Ivo brought you back to us, what an impressive pair you made!'

'That will have delighted my brother,' said Ivo drily. 'You must have pleased him almost as much as my father did!'

Later, in the afternoon as she sat beside Ivo in the phaeton, Jossie asked him, 'What is it with you and Peregrine? Why are you so cool with each other?'

The lazy good humour which was Ivo's normal expression disappeared for a moment as he said abruptly, 'It's an old story, Jossie. Perry and I were good friends in the old days, but he served me a very ill turn three years ago.'

'What did he do?'

'He kept my father and me apart for over a year, including the months before Waterloo... That's something I find hard to forgive. But I'd really prefer not to talk about it.' His tone was final. 'Tell me, what did you think of the meeting with your father and the others? Were you satisfied? Do you think you "showed" them, as much as you wanted to?'

'More than I could have imagined! Thank you again, Ivo. I cannot say how grateful I am to you! But—'

'I don't want your gratitude, Jossie.'

'That's absurd! I owe you practically everything! But...'

'What is it?'

'Well, Sir Thomas was his usual bluff self, but the rest don't seem to be very happy, do they?'

'Good God! Do you think they ought to be?'

'I suppose not....' She paused for a moment, then said, 'It's just that in the old days I was the one Peter always looked for when he was miserable...'

'And now he has a wife,' said Ivo firmly. 'You've done what you wanted to. Now you must leave them alone!'

'Yes, of course! I know I must.' She looked away. 'In any case, he deserves to be a little unhappy, don't you think?'

This preoccupation with Peter Radstock was not at all to Ivo's liking. It seemed he had been wrong in assuming that Jossie would now be able to put her old life behind her. He said, 'What Peter Radstock feels really doesn't concern me. Nor should it concern you. It's time to move on.'

His tone disconcerted Jossie. It was so cold. 'Of course!' she said brightly. 'Do you plan to go to the Duchess of Sutherland's soirée?'

'Jossie, I—'

'Or are you accompanying us to Vauxhall? Perry has hired a boat.'

'Neither,' said Ivo with something of a snap. 'I've arranged to see Colonel Ancroft tonight. Shall we go back?'

He had decided to postpone any attempt to talk seriously to Jossie. It didn't seem to be the right moment.

When they got back to Charles Street they were surprised to find Lady Frances entertaining the Radstocks and Perry and Rosalind to tea in the saloon.

Jossie sat down next to Sir Thomas, and before long they were deep in conversation about the changes he was making on his land.

'Sir Thomas! I'm sure agriculture is the last thing Jossie—or should I call you Helena, my dear?—wants to talk about in London!' said his wife.

'She'll always be Jossie to me, Lady Radstock! And she still knows a thing or two about the land. I feel I've got something to talk about with Jossie.' His eye rested briefly on Rosalind, who was sitting, looking rather pale and subdued, next to Lady Frances. He turned back to Jossie with a sigh. 'Eh, the times we had with the two of you! I was never sure which of you would be in a scrape next, you or Peter! What a pair you were!'

Not altogether surprisingly, this led to a moment's awkward silence. It was broken by Lady Radstock, who gave her husband a severe look and said, 'Tell me the name of your modiste, Helena. That dress you were wearing last night was exquisite.'

Lady Frances eagerly picked up the topic, and the ladies talked for a while of dresses. Jossie moved over to join them, but was soon bored with the discussion. She looked around. Ivo and his father were clearly enjoying a lively conversation with Sir Thomas. Perry was sitting to one side, leaning back in his chair and quietly observing the three of them. Peter was standing by the window with his back to the room. His shoulders were drooping.

Before she could stop herself she went over to him. He turned. 'I haven't seen my father so happy since...' He paused, then went on, 'Since I came of age. He's never forgiven me, you know.'

'I'm sorry.'

Peter gave a bitter little laugh. '*You're* sorry! What a thing to say, Joss! I don't suppose you'll ever forgive me, either.'

'I already have.'

'How can you expect me to believe that? What I did was cruel! I can't even forgive myself!'

'The manner of it was cruel, I won't deny that,' said Jossie with a twisted smile. 'But I've come to see that you really did us both a service. We should never have suited.' She put her hand on his arm. 'You must forgive yourself, Peter! Be happy!'

'I...I can't,' he replied in a stifled voice.

'Why not?'

'I can't tell you here. Joss, I need to talk to you. I must talk to someone!'

'Careful! Your mother has her eye on us!'

Peter grinned fleetingly. 'That's what you always used to say in the old days. remember?'

'I remember.'

He was serious again. 'Please, Jossie, can we meet somewhere? You always helped in the past. Help me now!'

'You're asking a lot.'

'Too much?' His eyes were fixed anxiously on hers, and she was swamped in memories. She couldn't bring herself to refuse him.

'Where?'

'In the park? Tomorrow morning?'

'Very well. I often go for an early ride. We can go together. At ten?'

'At ten. I don't deserve this, Jossie, I know. But I don't know where else to turn.'

Jossie nodded. It was time to end this tête-à-tête. Lady Radstock was looking concerned. And when she looked further she saw that Peregrine Trenchard's eyes were now on them, too. Ivo still appeared to be engrossed in his conversation with Sir Thomas.

'Ten, tomorrow,' she said.

Ivo was not as unaware as he had seemed, but the failure of his attempt to talk seriously to Jossie in the park had left him at something of a loss. The expedition to Vauxhall might have offered a better opportunity to straighten things out between them, but his engagement to dine with Colonel Ancroft that evening was perfectly genuine and one he was reluctant to break. Since Waterloo he and his commanding officer had seen a fair amount of one another, first in Paris and now here in London, where they both still worked as aides to the Duke when needed. The more time Ivo spent with the

Colonel the more he liked him. By now they were reasonably at ease in each other's company, so much so that over dinner that night Colonel Ancroft was prepared to tease him about Jossie.

'I do believe you're serious at last, Ivo. I never thought to see it. But she's an enchanting creature! You'll be a lucky man if she'll have you.'

'I think so, too, sir. The devil of it is, I'm not sure I can persuade her to take me seriously.'

Colonel Ancroft laughed. 'I can see that might be difficult—but you only have yourself to blame! However, I'm sure you'll succeed. And I hope I'll still be here in London to see it.'

'You're going away?'

'Soon. I…I have things to do in the north.' Colonel Ancroft sighed and stared moodily at his wine glass. 'I can't delay much longer, much as I would wish to.'

Ivo waited, then said carefully, 'Has your journey north anything to do with the recent death of Lord Coverdale?'

'Who told you that? Or was it a lucky guess?'

'The Duke mentioned something. Are you…are you the heir, sir?'

Colonel Ancroft got up and walked restlessly round the room. 'Yes, dammit! And I wish to heaven I wasn't! But I suppose I always knew I'd have to go back one day unless Boney got me first.'

His tone was so bitter that Ivo looked for something to divert him. 'How will you travel? Not in a mule cart, I dare swear.'

'No, by heaven! That's one thing I can thank the peace for—no more Spanish mules! No, I'm taking my own carriage. And my own team of horses.'

'Surely that makes for a slower journey? More stops for resting the horses?'

'I…er…I shall have a companion. I've agreed to escort someone up north. A lady.'

'A…a friend of the family, perhaps?' said Ivo carefully.

'No, I don't know her from Adam—or should I say Eve?' his companion replied. 'I haven't yet met her. She's a widow.'

'I see,' said Ivo. 'A widow.'

Colonel Ancroft laughed. 'I thought that would intrigue you. But I'm afraid I have to disappoint you, Ivo. No intrigue there! The lady is elderly, infirm, and of a nervous disposition. I understand that she is taking her husband's ashes back to his birthplace in the north, and is convinced she will be attacked on the road.'

Ivo was astounded. 'And you've agreed to look after her?'

'To accompany her party. She has her own attendants.' When Ivo continued to look surprised he went on, 'I'm doing it to oblige a friend—someone to whom I owe a lot. He knew I was going up to Yorkshire, y'see. To take up my new responsibilities.' The Colonel looked grim. 'Yes, it means the journey will take longer, but I'm not sorry about that. My memories of the place are not happy and I'm not exactly eager to see it. Escorting this lady will give me something else to think about.'

'When do you plan to leave?'

'I'm not sure. She hasn't arrived in London yet. But I shall certainly hope to see you before I go. Meanwhile, good luck with Miss Calverton!'

Chapter Fourteen

Peter was waiting for Jossie when she arrived the next morning at the Chesterfield gate. He had clearly been there for some time—both he and his horse were restless.

'Shall we go to the far end of the park?' she asked.

'A good idea—this creature needs some activity, and so do I! But...I'd like some privacy,' he said, his eye on Jossie's groom. Jossie hesitated, then told her man to wait for them at the gate. Then she turned to Peter.

'Let's break all the rules and have a good gallop, Peter! Come on!'

She set off with all her old impulsiveness down the bridle way. They raced to the end of the path, and came to a halt on the other, unfrequented, side of the park.

Jossie sighed. 'That was glorious! But for heaven's sake don't tell a soul! I should be ruined if the tabbies got to hear of it. A sedate trot is the most that is permitted to the ladies of the *ton*.'

Peter regarded her with admiration. She was flushed, her eyes were sparkling, and she was smiling at him in the old way...

'Jossie!' he said. Her face changed.

'What is it you wish to say?' she asked, with a touch

of reserve. 'I won't listen to anything indiscreet, Peter. Nothing disloyal.'

'I don't intend to be disloyal!' he said hotly. 'I love Rosalind. Still. In spite of—' He stopped. After a short silence he went on desperately, 'I need your help, Joss! I need help to sort things out. But I do love Rosalind.'

'Good! I couldn't listen if you didn't.' Then she added, 'But why do you need *me*? Why can't you talk to *her*?'

'She's part of the problem.' He stopped again.

Jossie said impatiently, 'For goodness' sake, Peter, get on with it! We haven't all day.'

He looked hurt at her brisk tone, but pulled himself together and began. It was a sorry tale, but not uncommon. His father had never approved of his marriage, and, though not actually unkind to Rosalind, he seldom made himself agreeable to her. Lady Radstock did her best to make the girl feel part of the family, but she was hampered by the fact that Rosalind's mother spent far too much time with her daughter.

'I thought Lady Radstock liked Mrs Cherton?'

'She liked Mrs *Cherton* well enough. But Mrs Cherton is now Mrs Morley of Calverton Manor, and very ready to queen it in the neighbourhood. My mother resents it, and quite right, too!' Peter said indignantly. 'Mama has been the first lady among the neighbours ever since old Lady Calverton died. And it's not even as if your father is the real owner of the Manor!'

'No,' Jossie agreed. 'It must have been a nasty shock to Mrs Cherton to discover that. But, Peter, this all sounds rather petty. I don't believe your mother could be so upset by this that she would take it out on your wife.'

'No, but that's not all. Mrs Morley criticises me, too.

She's always hinting that I don't spend enough time with Rosalind, that I don't give her a big enough dress allowance, that…oh, everything!'

Rosalind's mother was a fool, thought Jossie drily. The one sure way to antagonise Lady Radstock, irretrievably, was to criticise her son.

'And now I'm badgered on all sides. My father can't understand why I don't spend more time on the estate. Rosalind doesn't understand why I can't spend every minute with her. My mother can't understand why I let Rosalind spend so much time with her mother. What am I to do?'

'But why are you telling *me* this? What on earth do you think I could do?'

'Oh, I don't know… Give a hint to your father, or your stepmother? Have a chat with my mother? Or even…' Peter's face brightened. 'Have a word with Rosalind. Explain to her how important it is for me to ride round the estate.'

'I know why you ride round the estate, my friend! You enjoy it! Why don't you take Rosalind with you?'

'She's not like you, Joss! She doesn't like riding rough.'

Jossie suffered a pang as she had a sudden memory of riding with Peter over the hills and fields round Lyne St Michael. She had been so happy, so unaware…the land had seemed so precious then. She had almost forgotten it in London.

She pulled herself together and said firmly, 'You must know I can't do any of that! The idea is absurd. My advice, for what it is worth, is to restore the Dower House and go to live there. You and your wife need time alone together, away from both mothers. You're not short of money—increase Rosalind's dress allowance, and take her to Bath to find some new dresses... Or, better still, buy her a few dresses while you are here. I'll introduce her to Madame Rosa, if you wish. No, I'm serious, Peter! Clothes are very important to Rosalind. It's surely worth a little time and money to keep her happy, isn't it? As for the rest... Why don't you consult Lady Frances? She is in a much better position than I am to do something.'

'I couldn't! You know what she thinks of me, especially after...'

Jossie nodded and faced the inevitable. Peter had always tried to get other people to do difficult tasks. 'Would you like me to speak to her?'

'Oh, Jossie! If you would!'

'I'll see what she has to say. Meanwhile, try talking to Rosalind while her mother is out of the way. It might be a chance to get her to listen to you.' She waited until he gave a reluctant nod. Then she said, 'I must get back to Charles Street. They'll be wondering where I am.'

His face fell. 'But we've had no chance to talk! I thought we might have a chat like old times.'

Jossie regarded him with a mixture of regret and exasperation. Why had she never before realised how childishly selfish Peter was? How blind. 'But it isn't old times, Peter,' she said impatiently. 'This isn't Lyne St Michael, and we aren't children any more. And you are married.'

He looked so disconsolate that she added more kindly, 'I'll do what I can. For old times' sake. I'll try to have a word with Lady Frances today. Perhaps I can see Madame Rosa today, too. Shall we meet tomorrow at the same time?'

'At the gate. I'll be there. And, Jossie!' She had already started off, but she stopped and looked back.

'I know I ought not to ask for your help,' Peter said, looking slightly ashamed. 'After what I did to you. But there's no one else I can turn to. I'm grateful, I really am.'

'So you've already said, but I really don't want your gratitude. In the end you did me a good turn. We should never have been happy together.' Peter looked somewhat put out at this direct reply, and Jossie wondered fleetingly whether he had, deep down, thought he could revive her old affection for him. Well, enough of it was left for her to want to help him now. But not much more.

They rode back at a more suitable pace. It was as well. Several other people were out for an early ride, among them Peregrine Trenchard. He eyed them curiously, and Jossie felt herself colouring, but she saw no reason to explain herself. She greeted him calmly, and bade Peter farewell without referring again to their next meeting. Mr Trenchard was too interested, as it was.

Indeed, Mr Trenchard *was* interested. He was so interested that he mentioned it to Ivo.

'I don't wish to interfere, Ivo, old chap,' he said later that day. 'But if I were you I'd get Aunt Frances to give a hint to young Helena. She really ought not to go riding with young men in the park, especially not without her groom. People are bound to talk.'

Ivo looked coolly at his brother. After a moment he drawled, 'I don't know why you can't mention it to Aunt Frances yourself, Perry. Or even to warn Jossie yourself. She won't bite you. If, as I suspect, what you really want is to tell me that Jossie has had a secret assignation, then why don't you come right out with it? However you try to disguise it, you're still a tale-bearer.'

Peregrine reddened but said, 'This is rich, coming from you!'

'What do you mean?'

'It can only have been you who told Father about Charlotte Gurney and the way I kept your quarrel with him going. You know he sent me to Derbyshire because of it?'

'No, I didn't. I thought you went because you had at last seen sense and got away from Sudiham. He hasn't said a word about forcing you to go. But why are you so sour? What's wrong? I thought you liked Derbyshire?'

'I do. But I didn't like being sent away like a naughty schoolboy, because of what you told him.'

'Perry, Father isn't a fool. He can work things out for himself. As a matter of fact, I didn't tell him anything at all. Not about Charlotte, nor even about your lies to keep Father and me apart. What is more, he wouldn't have liked it if I had. He doesn't like tale-bearers any more than I do. Which brings us back to the present issue. Supposing Jossie *is* meeting someone in secret— which I doubt. What do you think *I* could do about it?'

'I thought you liked her?'

Ivo regarded his brother in silence. Then he said quite pleasantly, 'I do. Very much. And I assure you, that if you tell any of your stories about her, or do her any harm, I won't waste time telling my father or anyone else. I'll break every bone in your body.'

Perry laughed nervously. 'There's no need to be unpleasant. I didn't mean any harm. But I wasn't lying. I saw them together. In the park. Helena and Peter Radstock.' He retreated hastily as his brother's face changed and he took a step forward. But whatever Ivo had intended he changed his mind. He stopped short, then, with an expression of disgust, he turned on his heel and walked out of the room. Perry breathed a sigh of relief. And smiled.

Lady Frances was not as sympathetic to Peter's difficulties as Jossie would have hoped.

'He's quite hopeless!' she said. 'A handsome face with nothing behind it. No strength of character, no determination, and not very much wit. Anyone could have foreseen that Mrs Cherton would be a difficult mother-in-law, and taken steps to protect himself against her!'

'My dearest Godmama!' said Jossie, half-laughing. 'What could poor Peter possibly do?'

'Poor Peter! You can still call him that?'

'Yes, I can,' said Jossie seriously. She went over to her godmother and took her hand. 'Thanks to you and Ivo, I'm a sane, healthy, rational being again. I bear no grudges—well, perhaps a slight remnant of one towards my father. Apart from him, I have completely forgiven all of them. I would like them all to live happily together, especially Peter and Rosalind.'

'You're not thinking of dying young, are you, Jossie?' asked Lady Frances suspiciously. 'This is far too saintly for my taste.'

'Certainly not! Why can't you believe that I am grateful to have had such a narrow escape? If nothing had happened to stop it I would have married Peter Radstock and been unhappy for the rest of my life. I might not even have realised why. I admit, that, at the time, I would have gone under if you and Ivo had not been there to rescue me. But you *were* there, and you *did* rescue me, and I shall never cease to be grateful to you both.'

'Is that all you feel for Ivo? Gratitude?'

Jossie hesitated. 'No. Not only. But without wishing

in the slightest to be rude, I don't propose to discuss what I feel for Ivo with anyone else.' She gave a wry smile. 'It's of no significance to anyone but me. Can we do anything for Peter, do you think?'

'I think you've already done something by giving him a sympathetic ear. And I agree with you—the young couple should have a home of their own. If we were in Lyne St Michael I might be able to talk to Lady Radstock, but the opportunities in London for such a talk are non-existent. Peter will have to do more for himself. He has always been very spoiled, of course. From what I've heard, he spends too much time at the races with friends, or hunting anything that moves. That can't make him much of a help to his father, nor much of a companion to his wife. He could satisfy both of them, if he would only give up a few of his own pursuits.'

'And in London, meanwhile?'

'Meanwhile, it's a good idea to persuade him to make more fuss of Rosalind while her mother isn't here to poison his efforts. By all means introduce them to Madame Rosa, though whether she will wish to make anything for Rosalind remains to be seen. She won't do it for everyone. But, Jossie…' Lady Frances looked serious. 'Be careful! If Peter's wife is feeling sensitive at the moment, she wouldn't take it kindly if she learned that he is seeing you. Make tomorrow's meeting the last time you see him alone.'

Mindful of Lady Frances's warning, Jossie remained by the gate for her meeting with Peter the next morning, and kept it brief and businesslike. She reported what her godmother had said, then went on, 'I went to see Madame Rosa yesterday, too. She is prepared to see Rosalind, and take her on as a client.'

Peter was not particularly grateful, though it had taken some hard persuasion from a valued customer to get the modiste to agree. 'Dresses! How will that help?'

'Peter, try to show a little understanding. I know clothes were never important to either of us. But they are very important to your wife, and you must try to put yourself in her place!' said Jossie patiently. 'A dress from one of the foremost mantua-makers in London would give her a great deal of pleasure—and confidence. Even I have learned that. Have you managed to talk to her yet?'

'I tried,' he said gloomily. 'She wasn't very receptive.'

'Well, try again! And ask her if she would like to see Madame Rosa. Trust me on this! I know what I'm talking about!' In an attempt to impress on Peter the importance of what she was saying, Jossie leant forward and spoke very earnestly. From a distance it looked almost as if they were touching.

Ivo saw them. He was on his way back from Tattersall's, and was passing Chesterfield Gate just at this moment. It was unfortunate. He had set out that morning with no thought of Peregrine's insinuations in his mind. Indeed, if he had remembered them, he would have taken another route back to Charles Street, in order to avoid the slightest suspicion that he might be spying on Jossie. But he did see her. And she was talking confidentially with Peter Radstock—for the second morning running, if Peregrine had been telling the truth. He spurred his horse on and passed as quickly as he could. Jossie was too preoccupied to notice him.

When he reached the house Ivo found he was trembling with rage. He had been angry before, but he had never before been so angry, so beside himself, because of a woman. No woman had ever before meant enough to him. For a while, until reason prevailed, he paced his room like a caged tiger, furious both with himself and the whole female sex. Jossie was a fool! A witless, idiotic, deceitful fool! They had been practically *kissing* each other! How could she possibly—*possibly*—want to win back Peter Radstock? Could she still not see him for what he was—a weak, spineless, dithering, spoilt, *child*? Radstock would never grow up, whatever age he lived to... Was she really prepared to nursemaid him through life? And what about his wife? Had Jossie forgotten that he was married?

Ivo started to calm down. He didn't believe it. Jossie couldn't possibly want to entice Peter Radstock away from his wife. Even if she loved him, she would still not attempt it. She was brave enough and scornful enough of convention for herself, but Radstock was neither. She must know that he would never stand the total ostracism from his own small world which would surely ensue.

But, in that case, why was she meeting him secretly in the park?

He threw himself into a chair. Was he wrong in his assumption that Jossie still felt some kindness for Radstock? He had sometimes suspected her of planning revenge. Was *that* her game? To make Radstock fall in love with her again, and then throw it back in his face?

Surely not! The Jossie he knew would not stoop so low.

Ivo got up again and poured himself a glass of brandy. Deep in thought, he stood at the window, slowly sipping his drink. Was he right to trust his instinct? The girl he had known before the previous July had been an enchanting creature, direct, original, brave and loyal. And clever. But on that night in July that girl's world had exploded in her face. It was not surprising that she had changed. Had she changed so much that she would deliberately set out to exact some kind of revenge on Radstock? He hoped not. He sincerely hoped not.

Ivo put his glass down and went slowly downstairs. The sad thing was that he was as much of a besotted fool as any of the lovers he had so despised in the past! Whether she was a witless fool, or a devious seeker for revenge, he loved Jossie Morley all the same. He was still concerned for her, still ready to protect her from any unpleasant consequences, to be her champion still. Faithful unto death like an idiotic knight in a romance! He smiled bitterly. Who would have thought that he, Ivo Trenchard, cynic, experienced campaigner, as wise as any man in the ways of women, could be so deeply in love with Jossie Morley that he was prepared to defend her, *whatever* she did. How his friends, how all the polite world, would laugh if they knew!

Ivo dismissed the reactions of the polite world. What did they matter? He would have to speak Jossie, if only to warn her. Peregrine could not be trusted. If he could make trouble he would, and others might have seen what he had seen in the park. Possibly quite harmless in itself, but dangerous in the hands of a malicious manipulator. Perry had been clever enough to see that he could hurt Ivo by hurting Jossie, and he was unscrupulous enough not to care who else might be hurt in the process. Yes, he must speak to Jossie.

Ivo found her in the library playing backgammon with his father.

'Come in, come in, Ivo! Celebrate with me! I've just trounced Jossie, and that's a rare enough event. What can we do for you?'

'Congratulations, sir. I've come to ask Jossie if she would like a walk.'

'A very good idea. She certainly wasn't on form during that game.' He leaned forward and patted Jossie's hand. 'You look pale, child. Too many balls and the like. Too many Dukes wanting to dance with you. Take some air, it'll do you good.'

He sat back comfortably, but his eyes were sharp as he watched Ivo and Jossie leaving the room.

Ivo took Jossie to Hampstead, and, leaving the carriage in the care of the coachman, they made their way on to the Heath. They walked in silence for a short while. Jossie seemed subdued, and Ivo was trying to find a way of opening a conversation which he was very reluctant to embark on.

'I saw you earlier today,' he said at length.

'Where? I didn't see you.'

'At the Chesterfield Gate. I'm not surprised you didn't notice me. You seemed very preoccupied.'

Jossie was looking wary, but she answered calmly enough, 'With Peter.'

'You're surely not still in love with him, are you?'

'That's a very big leap, Ivo! If all the people who met in the park were assumed to be in love...'

'Not many meet at ten o'clock in the morning and ride off into the distance without taking a groom with them.'

Jossie's eyes narrowed. 'We didn't do that this morning—we stayed by the gate the whole time. Peregrine has been talking to you.' She started to get angry. 'Did you send him to spy on us? And this morning you came to see for yourself, is that it?'

'No! I saw you by accident. What did he want?'

His imperious tone offended Jossie even more. She said coldly, 'I'm not sure you have a right to ask that, Ivo.'

'Of course I have a right! I've done my best to see you safely launched into the very cream of society, and I'm not having you now make a fool of yourself over Radstock! What did he want, Jossie?'

She looked at him thoughtfully for a moment, then said, 'Madame Rosa's address.'

'Dammit, this isn't a joke!'

'I'm not joking, it's perfectly true. Among other things, of course. But that's all I shall tell you.'

Ivo kicked a stone from the path, and swore under his breath. This was not going the way he had planned. He glanced at Jossie. 'I've done this badly, haven't I?' he said.

'Yes. I'm not sure why you're so annoyed.'

'When I saw you with Radstock you were practically kissing him!'

She looked at him in amazement. 'Whatever is wrong with you? You must be making that up! We never ever touched. How could you think…? Look, Ivo, you don't deserve this, but I give you my word that since last July I have never even thought of Peter in that way.'

'Then why are you meeting him?' he demanded.

His tone affronted her at first. Then her expression changed and she gave him a mocking smile. 'You ought to be careful! You're beginning to sound like a jealous husband! What a reversal of role that would be for the worst flirt in Europe!'

'Stop prevaricating, Jossie! Why are you meeting him?'

She hesitated, then said firmly, 'I can't tell you. It's between Peter and me.' She stole a glance at him, and sighed when she saw that he was still frowning. 'I don't think this walk is doing either of us much good. Shall we go back?'

Ivo stood his ground. 'Not yet,' he said, pulling her round to face him. 'Listen to me, my girl! So far you've been lucky. You've managed to avoid the pitfalls there are for a beginner in society. But not everyone means you well, and any scandal could still do you real harm! If you don't wish to lose everything you've gained in the last few months, stay away from Peter Radstock!'

Jossie was so incensed by the force with which he said these last few words that she decided against telling him she had already made up her mind not to meet Peter in private again. Instead, she flashed out, 'I shan't let you dictate to me! I shall meet Peter when and where I like!'

Ivo gave her a shake. 'You exasperating little shrew! Why the devil can't you realise that I'm only trying to protect you?'

'I don't need your protection any more. I don't want your protection. Stop treating me as if I was a child!' Jossie cried angrily. 'I'm a grown woman, and I know what I'm doing. I don't need your interference any more! Leave me alone!'

Ivo was pale. Hurt and angry, he said stiffly, 'I'm sorry. I hadn't realised you regarded my natural concern as interference. Shall we go back?'

It was not a happy party which set out for Lady Porchester's ball that evening. They were only three, for Lord Veryan had decided to stay at home. Ivo was unusually silent, and Jossie's manner towards him verged on the icy. Only Lady Frances was her usual calmly cheerful self.

'I thought Perry was to accompany us tonight?' she said, as they went out to the carriage.

'He sent a message to say he was kept elsewhere. But he will see us at the Porchesters', I understand,' said Ivo briefly.

They sat in silence as they were driven at a snail's pace through the streets to Hanover Square. Lady Frances looked at each of her companions in turn. 'I haven't seen you wearing that dress before, Jossie,' she said at last. 'It suits you. Don't you agree, Ivo?'

'Very pretty,' her nephew replied in a bored voice. There was another silence.

Lady Frances tried again. 'Do you know if the Radstocks will be there tonight?' she asked.

'I believe so,' said Jossie. Ivo gave her a sharp look, which she returned defiantly, whereupon he looked away to stare out of the window. Silence fell again, and this time it lasted until they arrived. They joined a queue of carriages waiting to deposit their passengers at the door, and sat for some minutes as the line slowly moved on.

'Well,' said Lady Frances, 'The Porchesters' entertainments are notoriously dull—an evening with them is never wildly amusing. But it is going to be absolutely intolerable unless you two start talking to one another! I'm surprised at you both! Where are your company manners, Jossie? And as for you, Ivo, I cannot imagine what has got into you! Where is the polished rogue we all know and love?'

'I'm about to rediscover him, ma'am,' said Ivo, 'He was mislaid for a time while I misguidedly tried to help someone I thought needed it. But I now find the role of nursemaid beginning to pall. You may expect to see a change.'

'A welcome relief for us all,' snapped Jossie.

As they entered Lady Porchester's vast and gloomy entrance hall he said, 'I'm sorry to have disappointed you, Aunt Frances. But I see Peregrine coming this way, and the Radstocks are just beyond him. I have no doubt they will amuse you more. Both of you. Meanwhile I'll seek my own entertainment, and relieve you of the burden of my company.' With that he bowed and disappeared in the direction of the card rooms. Lady Frances gazed after him in astonishment.

'I have never, ever, seen Ivo in such a mood,' she said. 'Not even when his quarrel with Rupert was at its height. What have you done, Jossie?'

'What makes you think that he could possibly be affected by anything I could do?' asked Jossie. 'He regards me as nothing more than a troublesome child! If he is annoyed with me, it's because I won't do as I am told!'

Lady Frances looked sceptical, but was unable to comment. Peregrine was upon them, closely followed by the Radstocks.

It looked as if the younger Radstocks were feeling about as amiable towards each other as were Ivo and Jossie. Rosalind was pale and washed out, and noticeably avoided any contact with her husband. Soon after the groups had joined, Peter invited her to dance, but she turned away with a petulant toss of her head. An awkward moment followed. Peter was painfully embarrassed, grew very red, then turned defiantly to Jossie and invited her instead. After a moment's hesitation she accepted. He looked so desperately unhappy, that she simply couldn't bring herself to humiliate him further. She justified it by telling herself that it was an opportunity to find out how matters stood with Rosalind, though on the face of it the answer would not be encouraging.

As she and Peter went to the floor she saw Peregrine

stepping forward to Rosalind. Later she found it supremely ironic that she had been happy at the time, had thought that Peregrine might cheer Peter's wife up a little.

The dance with Peter was not a pleasant experience. He was full of resentment towards Rosalind.

'Your idea about Madame Rosa didn't do any good at all. Rosalind was furious when I mentioned her.'

'*Furious?* Whatever did you say?'

'That I thought she'd look a lot better if she had a dress made in London.'

'Peter! How could you be so tactless?'

'I thought I was being damned generous. She hadn't been particularly pleasant to me beforehand, you know. Most wives would have given me a kiss and thanked me. But not her!'

He clearly expected Jossie to comfort and reassure him. This was no part of her plan. Indeed, she was already ruing her decision to dance with him, when she caught sight of Ivo standing on the edge of the floor, frowning at her. She mustn't let him see how much she regretted not following his advice. She tossed her head and turned with a brilliant smile to her partner.

When the dance was over she gave an inward sigh of relief and returned gratefully to Lady Frances and the rest. Peregrine was leading Rosalind back, but they were deep in conversation, and stopped once or twice on their way. Rosalind was questioning Peregrine closely, shaking her head in disbelief, then apparently asking him to repeat what he had said. By the time they reached the corner of the room where the rest of the party was standing she was clearly in an extremely agitated state, paler than ever, eyes glittering, hands restlessly clutching her partner's sleeve. She confronted Peter, apparently oblivious to the rest of the room.

'Why didn't you tell me yourself?' she demanded.

'Tell you what?'

'Don't pretend you don't know! Never any time for me, oh, no! Never time to take *me* riding in the park, talk about dresses to *me*!' She gave a sob. 'How could you so deceive me?'

Shocked and concerned, Lady Radstock tried to intervene. 'Rosalind! My dear! Calm down! We can't have a scene here!'

Rosalind threw off her mother-in-law's restraining hand. 'I will not calm down! Wait till you hear what I have just been told, and then tell me to be calm! Your precious son has been meeting Jossie Morley secretly in the park. Early in the morning, so they will not be seen.'

'I don't believe it!' Lady Radstock turned shocked eyes on her son. 'Is this true?'

Sir Thomas said stoutly, 'Of course it isn't! Jossie would never behave in such an underhanded way, nor would Peter. The girl is raving.'

Sir Thomas's voice was loud and several of Lady Porchester's guests looked curiously in their direction.

Peter looked at his mother and said uncomfortably, 'It is true, but not the way she says it...'

'How can it be different?' cried Rosalind, now thoroughly distraught. She turned on Jossie. 'I know what it is! You think you're having some sort of revenge! You blame me for what Peter did to you, and now you're making me suffer the same fate! You've taken him back! How could you be so cruel?'

'Don't talk such rubbish, Rosalind!' said Lady Frances roundly. 'You're making a great deal out of nothing at all! Pull yourself together, girl! This is no way to behave.'

'How can I behave any other way? Don't you understand? She's not content with all these admirers of hers. She wants my husband as well!'

Jossie swallowed an angry retort, and spoke as calmly as she could. 'I assure you, you couldn't be more wrong,' she said firmly. 'Peter is yours. All yours.'

'Then why did you have to meet him in secret?'

'He wanted to—' Jossie stopped. How could she tell the girl the truth? 'Peter…Peter was worried about you,' she went on slowly. 'He wanted to give you a surprise. A new dress to cheer you up. And he asked me to recommend you to Madame Rosa. That's all. I was trying to help.' Even to her own ears this sounded rather lame, and, far from being mollified, Rosalind was even more upset.

'So it was you who told him I looked dowdy! I knew he couldn't have thought of it himself! It was you! Talking of your precious Madame Rosa… You must think I am stupid! Peter isn't interested in the way I look any more…he wouldn't think of buying any dresses. No, no! He just wanted to humiliate me. You've taken him away from me. Oh, I'm so unhappy,' she sobbed. 'I want my mama.' She cast herself on Lady Radstock's bosom.

By this time the people gathered near the Radstocks and Trenchards were looking in open curiosity. Several of them were whispering to each other in delight at the juicy scandal developing before their eyes. Miss Helena Calverton, darling of the *ton*, favourite of the tabbies, was being accused of stealing someone else's husband! Delicious!

Lady Frances gazed round frantically. A major catastrophe was rapidly unfolding, and, as far as she could tell, no one was doing anything to prevent it! Rosalind Radstock should have been removed from the scene as soon and as discreetly as possible, but her mother-in-law seemed to be paralysed, helplessly holding on to Rosalind without making the slightest effort to take her away. Sir Thomas was no better. Indifferent to the public at large, he was staring from Jossie to Peter in baffled rage. Neither of them seemed to realise how serious the situation was. Unless someone acted soon there would be a full-blown scandal which would destroy not only Jossie, but everyone else in the sorry tale. Lady Frances's eye met Ivo's in desperate appeal. He came over.

'For Heaven's sake, do something!' she whispered. 'Before we are all ruined!'

Ivo frowned, then nodded and moved to Rosalind Radstock's side. He took her from Lady Radstock and held both her hands. Then, exercising all his considerable charm, he said, 'Mrs Radstock, look at me.' Rosalind sniffed and raised her eyes. Holding her gaze, Ivo went on, 'Lady Frances was right, it is all nonsense. There is absolutely no reason for you to be so distressed. None whatsoever. The tale my brother has been telling you is quite false. It was my brother, wasn't it?'

'Yes,' said Rosalind, gazing up at him helplessly. 'I didn't know before—'

'Of course you didn't! There was really nothing to know.'

Ivo's charm was having its effect. Rosalind was calming down, though she was still unconvinced. 'Mr Trenchard said—'

'Mr Trenchard was mistaken. He saw your husband with Miss Calverton, that is perfectly true. But the rest was…a fantasy. He was wrong.'

'But how do you know?'

'I saw them myself. Miss Calverton is telling you the truth. She was trying to help an old friend, and that is all.'

'How can you be so sure?'

Ivo smiled and gently released her. He stretched out his arm and drew Jossie towards him. 'Because I know Miss Calverton better than anyone. We have no secrets. She tells me everything.' He smiled at Jossie. 'I know we hadn't intended to make it public before the end of the season, my love, but I think it would be better to let our friends know now, don't you agree?'

Jossie stammered, 'I…I…don't—'

'I think we must,' Ivo said firmly. 'You see, Mrs Radstock, Miss Calverton couldn't possibly have designs on your husband, or indeed any other man.' He cast a glance at the people surrounding them, and raised his voice a little. 'Miss Calverton and I are to be married. Quite soon.'

Chapter Fifteen

Shocked faces and critical whispers were all at once replaced with smiles of approval and cries of congratulation. In spite of his philandering ways Ivo was a popular figure, and nothing could have killed the incipient scandal more quickly than this announcement of his. No one questioned it. The world had seen how attentive Lord Trenchard had been to Miss Calverton almost throughout the season. They all nodded their heads in a knowing fashion—however he had tried to disguise his interest in his aunt's ward, they told one another, he had succeeded in deceiving no one. And now it was out! Rosalind Radstock was dismissed as an unimportant troublemaker, and she and the rest of the Radstocks were very quickly forgotten, elbowed out of the way by a crowd of eager well-wishers.

It was not every day that two of society's most prominent members announced their engagement in such a dramatic fashion, and the *ton* was amused, intrigued and, most of them, happy. Lady Balmenny was heard to remark that the girl was, of course, far too young for Lord Trenchard, but was silenced when a friend pointed out that Julia herself was at least twenty years younger than her own husband. Lady Alicia said she pitied poor Miss Calverton with all her heart, tied as she would be to a man whose affections were notoriously fickle. She did not look particularly comforted, however, when someone commented that Lord Trenchard had never before got as far as offering marriage to anyone else—not even to her... But apart from these and a few others, society looked on the match with favour, and was anxious to tell the happy couple so.

For the rest of the evening they were not allowed a single moment alone. It was quite impossible for Jossie to protest or to question Ivo's startling announcement in private, and to do so in public would have fanned the sparks of the threatened scandal into a full-blown fire. So she smiled and nodded, looked modest or flattered, walked about the crowded rooms accepting good wishes and congratulations, and was never once allowed to leave Ivo's side. There was little help to be had from Lady Frances. Whenever Jossie caught sight of her, she too was nodding and smiling, not at all modestly, but with the complacent air of a cat which is in possession of a particularly rich saucerful of cream. Her friends could have been pardoned for believing that she had known about the engagement for weeks.

It was well past midnight before they could all escape, and once in the carriage, Jossie sank back against the squabs and put her face in her hands.

'How could you! Oh, how could you!'

Ivo smiled grimly. 'There was no other way, my dear! Desperate situations need desperate remedies. You were heading for full-scale disaster.'

'He's right, Jossie,' said Lady Frances. 'That girl was bent on committing social suicide and taking you with her. To think I thought her a harmless, well-behaved mouse!'

'But what are we to do now? We're trapped!'

Ivo shook his head and said drily, 'You should moderate these ecstasies of delight at my proposal, Jossie. Who knows? I might get conceited.'

'Ivo! I didn't mean— Oh, you're teasing me! That wasn't really a proposal, you know it wasn't!'

'If it wasn't, it was a remarkably good substitute for one!' Lady Frances observed tartly. 'Half of London heard him. He might have difficulty in crying off, if you choose to hold him to it.'

'I wouldn't dream of doing such a thing! Ivo doesn't really want to marry me!'

Ivo's face was in darkness, and his voice held no expression as he asked, 'What makes you say that?'

'It's obvious! You were indulging in the very pastime I told you to abandon only today. Protecting me as if I was a child. You were right—it was stupid of me to meet Peter in the park. If I had known what would happen I would never have done so. But it was *my* mistake and I should have put it right in my own way! Now we are in a worse pickle than ever, and all because of this stupid conviction of yours that I need protection. Why don't you look after your brother instead? He was the one who stirred it all up, don't forget!'

'I haven't forgotten that. So you think I was merely protecting you? Conscience-stricken, perhaps, at my brother's ill-doing?'

'Yes, I do.'

After a slight pause Ivo said, 'Well, whatever might be my motives in the affair, I'm afraid the end result is the same. We are still committed to marry.'

'Don't be absurd! Of course we aren't!'

'I think we are.' When Jossie drew breath to argue, Ivo said with decision, 'No more, Jossie! I do not propose to argue with you here in this carriage, after a very trying evening. We are neither of us at our best.'

'Don't try to dictate to me!' said Jossie growing more agitated. 'I've told you before, I'm not one of your men! You can't announce to the world at large that I am to marry you without even consulting me first, and then expect me simply to fall in with whatever you decide! How dare you refuse to discuss it!'

Lady Frances said sharply, 'Jossie! Try for a little control. Ivo is right. This is neither the time nor the place for any argument.'

Jossie shut her mouth with a snap and stared out of the window, visibly struggling with her temper. When the carriage came to a halt she waited in silence, then got out and walked swiftly inside. Here she paused until Lady Frances and Ivo joined her. Ivo took one look at her stormy expression and said, 'The library?'

They entered in silence, and waited until the servants had withdrawn before speaking. Ivo stood by the fire, staring into its depths. Lady Frances sat in a chair nearby, frowning slightly as she watched Jossie walking restlessly about the room.

Ivo turned and said calmly, 'Now. You have made yourself painfully clear, Jossie. I'm sorry that the notion of marrying me displeases you so. Would you care to tell me why? Are you perhaps in love with someone else? Is that it?'

Jossie was tired and near to tears. She said angrily, 'Why must you think there has to be someone else? There isn't. But the sort of marriage you propose would be a disaster! You know it would! I won't marry you out of gratitude, Ivo. I have no desire to be eternally grateful, not even to you, and you would soon get bored with the role of benefactor, once you had to play it day in day out.' Lady Frances looked as if she was about to protest, but Ivo silenced her with a quick shake of the head.

Jossie went on, 'Besides, I'm not really a creature of society. I've enjoyed this season in London, and I'm grateful for what you and Lady Frances have done to make it such a success, but I'm still a country girl at heart. I don't quite know what I am to do in the future, but of one thing I am quite certain. How could we possibly be happy if you were saddled with a wife who dislikes all the things you most enjoy?'

Ivo's face was stern as he said, 'The outlook is bleak indeed. But it's a worse one for both of us if we now go back on our word. I refuse to be laughed at as a fool or condemned as a knave. Do *you* wish to be known as a jilt?' He held her by the shoulders and made her face him. 'Jossie, Society would never forgive you if you cried off now after tonight.'

Jossie's control broke. 'There must be a way out of this!' she cried in despair. 'There must! I can't marry you, Ivo! I won't!'

She tore herself free from him and ran out of the room. Lady Frances shook her head. 'Shall I try to talk to her?'

'No, Aunt Frances. Leave it,' said Ivo bitterly. 'She has made her position very clear. What the devil I am to do about it, I don't know. Is there any way of extricating ourselves gracefully from this tangle?'

Lady Frances raised her eyebrows at her nephew. 'Giving in without more of a fight, Ivo? That's not like you.'

Ivo regarded her morosely. 'It's a devil of a situation!'

he said. 'I can't really blame Jossie. She has never seen me as a possible husband. When we first met she was blinded by her infatuation with Peter Radstock, and since then I have been a sort of father figure, her rescuer and teacher. It's not surprising she can't imagine any other kind of relationship with me.'

'I refuse to believe that one of London's most notoriously attractive men couldn't persuade her to change her mind! She isn't made of stone.' Lady Frances waited a moment, then said briskly, 'This defeatism is not like you, Ivo! Pull yourself together! Falling in love for the first time in your life is no excuse for becoming a marshmallow!'

She laughed at Ivo's look of outrage, and said, 'That's more like it! You'll do!' She got up and went to the door. Here she paused and said, 'I'm very fond of you both, and, what is more, I think you are ideally suited. I'd like nothing more than to see you married. Don't let too many scruples get in the way. If necessary, remind her of what she owes you, and hold her to the engagement. You could always teach her afterwards to love you.' When Ivo shook his head she said, 'Gratitude isn't such a bad basis for marriage.'

'In this case it would be the very worst!' When she looked at him in surprise, he shrugged his shoulders and said, 'I suppose you think me absurd. But...do you remember Jossie as she was when I first met her? A free, confident, independent spirit? That's the girl I fell in love with, Aunt Frances. I don't believe in gratitude as a reason for marriage any more than Jossie does. I want Jossie to come to me of her own free will, and *only* because she loves me. After tonight I am afraid, really afraid, that that will never happen.'

* * *

The next morning Ivo decided to deal with Peregrine before seeing his father. He went over early to Perry's lodging, where he was told that his brother was not at home. With a grim smile he swept the manservant aside and strode in. Peregrine had been breakfasting, but when he saw Ivo he got up and stood behind his chair, as if seeking refuge.

'G-good morning, b-brother,' he said.

Ivo ignored this greeting. He stood frowning, pulling his riding crop through his fingers. 'Are you going to face me like a man, *brother*?' he said unpleasantly. 'Or shall I give you the thrashing you deserve?'

'No! N-Neither! I'm sorry, Ivo, I truly am! If I had known that Rosalind Radstock would make such a scene, I would never have told her a thing!'

'Don't lie to me, Perry. Face the truth for once. You're a cowardly liar.'

'I'm not! I'm not!'

'What else would you call a man who not only tried to destroy a marriage, but damned near ruined a girl who had never done him the slightest harm?'

'I didn't realise…I never intended to *ruin* anyone.' Peregrine tried to hold his brother's eye, but after a moment he said sulkily, 'I only wanted to stir up some trouble.'

Ivo regarded him in silence. 'Why?'

'I wanted to hurt *you*! You've always had everything! Everything! Charlotte Gurney laughed at me when I wanted to marry her. She wouldn't even consider it— I'm the younger son, I have nothing! You'll get the lot. And as if that wasn't enough, here in London you're the hero, Wellington's man, the favourite of all the ladies. And as for Father—' Peregrine broke off and went to the window. 'And to crown it all you were in love with

Helena Calverton, the jewel in Society's crown, the perfect bride. You had *everything*, Ivo. I wanted you to hurt, and the best way was through that girl. I tried telling you about her liaison with Radstock, but you wouldn't believe me. So I had to show you in front of the world, and Radstock's wife was the perfect weapon. I wanted you to hurt.'

Ivo cursed. He kicked the chair away and, taking hold of Peregrine's collar, pulled his brother roughly to him. His fingers round Peregrine's throat, he said softly, 'So just to hurt me you came close to ruining Jossie. And you may well have wrecked Rosalind Radstock's happiness as well. What sort of worm are you?'

'I know, I know,' Peregrine gasped, staring wildly into Ivo's menacing face. 'I...I swear that you can't say anything to me that I haven't already thought myself. When I saw how unhappy that girl was...Rosalind Radstock, I mean...I hated myself for what I had done...' He tried to pull Ivo's fingers from his throat. 'You're...you're choking me!' Ivo released him contemptuously and Perry staggered over to the window and stood there, drawing in gulps of air. After a moment he went on, 'It didn't even work. They all forgot the Radstocks when you told them you and the Calverton girl were engaged. I hadn't expected that.'

Ivo stood considering, his crop in his hands. The desire to make Perry even sorrier for his part in last night's excitement was still there. It was, after all, what he had come to do. But though it might satisfy his own feelings, it would hardly improve relations with his younger brother. He could feel his anger draining away, being replaced with the old feelings of pity and guilt.

'The Radstocks will manage. They're used to picking up Peter's pieces,' he said more calmly. 'But as for you—you'll leave London before the end of the week and you won't be back. Not while I'm here.'

'That's easy enough. I don't even like it in London. I'm happier in Derbyshire. The people there like me, they treat me as if I *am* someone.'

'Then stay there! Father says you're doing well at Arneston—he was talking of giving it to you.'

Perry's face lit up. 'Give Arneston to me? He would do that?'

'But he won't, if he hears of this latest affair.'

The change in Perry's expression was alarming. His face clouded over and he snarled, 'And that's what you'd like, isn't it? I suppose you're going to tell him!'

Ivo sighed. The charming, gentle little boy he had known years ago had vanished. Peregrine neither loved nor trusted the rest of his family. There could be no cure for his unreasonable fear of his father, nor for his childish resentment of his elder brother. And in spite of his quiet manner, he could be astonishingly ruthless when he considered he was being badly treated. The best thing for all of them would be for Peregrine to make his own life in the North, away from what he saw as a hostile world. He said wearily, 'No, I won't do that. You must leave here and make a proper life for yourself at Arneston, Perry. Go as soon as possible. I don't want to see you in London after next week.'

Peregrine looked at him suspiciously, then nodded and said with apparent humility, 'You will allow me to take my leave of Father before I go? I promise not to stay long. And I should like to make my apologies to Miss Calverton, too. Is that permitted?'

Ivo was not altogether happy at Perry's way of expressing himself, but the request was reasonable enough.

'Of course,' he said coolly. 'You can certainly have time for that.'

It was still early when Ivo got back to Charles Street, but his father was waiting for him in the library.

'What's this I hear?' he demanded as soon as Ivo came in.

'Sir?'

'This engagement business. Is it true? Why didn't I hear of it from you?'

'How *did* you hear?'

'Never you mind. What does it all mean?'

'I've asked Jossie to marry me.'

'Good! Splendid! This is the best news I've had since you came back from Waterloo. Fetch her, fetch her, my boy!'

'Er…there's a problem. A big one.'

'Nothing that can't be overcome, I'm quite sure. She's a good girl, we're all very fond of her. And it can't be about money—you've both got more than you would ever need. So what is it? Sit down and tell me about it.'

'What have you heard about this engagement?'

'Not much. Just that it's all over the town that Ivo Trenchard has got himself engaged at last. I was hoping you would tell me more—when you got round to it, that is. What's wrong?'

'Jossie is at present refusing to carry it through.'

'Carry it through…? What d'y mean? Either you're engaged or not, there's no halfway. Is the girl mad?'

'Let me tell you what happened.' Ivo then gave his father an account of the events of the night before, leaving out only the malice behind Perry's actions.

'So… Let me just make sure—you *are* engaged? Jossie didn't deny it in public, or anything like that?'

'No. I think she was too dazed.'

'Well, then! All you have to do is to make her stick to it.'

'I thought you knew Jossie?'

'I do. And I know you.'

'I don't know why the rest of the world is so sure I can manage Jossie Morley,' said Ivo irritably. 'I'm damned uncertain myself!'

'That's not such a bad thing,' said his father, sounding pleased. 'You're usually too cocksure for your own good.'

Ivo had decided that he had had enough of his family for the time being and was on the point of taking his leave when his aunt and Jossie came into the library. They looked as if they were about to go out.

'What's this, what's this?' demanded Lord Veryan. 'No time to spare for your future father-in-law? Come here, girl!'

'I...I...' Jossie threw an anguished glance at Ivo, then said, 'Hasn't anyone told you the truth?'

'Ivo said something about it not being perfectly decided, but I took no notice. You'll marry him, of course you will. You wouldn't disappoint an old man, would you?' When Jossie looked as if she might, he went on, 'Besides, you can't cry off. You can't want to make my son look a fool!'

Jossie looked desperately at Ivo. 'I hadn't realised what it meant...but—'

Ivo came over to her and took her hands in his. 'Don't listen to him, Jossie. You mustn't do anything you don't wish. If you could bear to leave things as they are for the moment, I am sure we can find a solution to this mess before very long. But don't look so unhappy. That's the last thing I want.' He kissed one of her hands before he let it go. Then he went on in a cheerful voice, 'Where were you ladies going? Can I escort you some of the way?'

'We've decided to call on Lady Radstock, to enquire after Rosalind. And to make sure that all misunderstandings are at an end,' said Lady Frances.

'That's an excellent idea!' Ivo said. 'And it would be an even better one if I came with you! Do you agree, Jossie?'

They all waited. If Jossie agreed to Ivo's company on a visit to the Radstocks, it meant she was willing to let the engagement stand, too. When she nodded Lord Veryan and Lady Frances breathed a sigh of relief. But Ivo sounded quite matter of fact as he said, 'Good! Shall we go?' He ushered the ladies out, then, struck by a sudden thought, he excused himself and returned to the library. 'I forgot to tell you, Father. Perry has decided to go back to Derbyshire. He wishes to visit this afternoon to take his leave of you. Is it convenient? I said it would be.'

'Yes, yes! I shan't know what to say, mind you. I never do!'

'Why don't you let him know how much you approve of his management of Arneston? You might even tell him what you said to me—that it could soon be his.'

His father shot him a sharp glance. 'Still promoting Perry's interests, Ivo? I should have thought you were tired of that.'

'I promise you, I don't intend to do much more of it. But I'd be easier in my mind if Perry was happily settled in Derbyshire. Dammit, he ought to have *something*, Father!'

'Very well, very well. Leave it now. Don't keep the ladies waiting.'

* * *

Lady Radstock received them with a certain air of constraint, but thawed slowly when she realised they had come merely to enquire after her daughter-in-law's health.

'She and Peter are out, I'm afraid, but Rosalind is much better, thank you. I am sure she regrets…she is sorry—'

'Please!' said Jossie. 'Please, Lady Radstock! Rosalind may have been mistaken about my motives, but I was very thoughtless. I should never have agreed to see Peter privately. I should have realised how it might look to someone who…who—'

Ivo finished for her. 'Someone who was not fully aware of the situation between Jossie and myself,' he said smoothly.

'But I still don't perfectly understand why you had to meet Peter in such a clandestine way, Jossie. Though I cannot condone her behaviour, I can see that it was quite natural for Rosalind to come to the wrong conclusion, especially in her present state. What did you think you were doing?'

Jossie gave a wry smile. 'Trying to help an old friend.'

'Peter? How could he ask such a thing of you after—?' She stopped. Then she went on, 'But why does Peter need your help?'

Lady Frances said briskly, 'Perhaps you should ask Peter that. I am sure he would tell you if you asked him. You were always in his confidence, Eleanor. And, as Jossie said last night, their meetings were unwise, but perfectly innocent. To be frank, I really think she ought not to concern herself with the matter any further. Peter and she may have been friends in the past, but no one could suggest that he has any claim on her time now. Talk to Peter yourself, my dear!'

'Of course! Though it may no longer be necessary—
today's news has made us all very happy.'

Sir Thomas came into the room at this point and heard
these last words. 'So you've told them?' he said, rubbing
his hands together.

'Not yet, my dear. Our guests came to enquire after
Rosalind, but I haven't yet given them our news.'

'She's much better,' said Sir Thomas. 'And I'd be
obliged if you'd put the fuss last night out of your minds.
Least said, soonest mended. She's a sweet little thing—
I'm sure she didn't mean any of it. All explained today,
of course.'

Jossie stared at this sudden change of attitude, but the
reason was made clear in his next words.

'My daughter-in-law is in an interesting condition,'
said Sir Thomas proudly. 'I believe that's what you call
it in polite society. She's breeding!' He listened com-
placently as Lady Frances and Jossie exclaimed, and
went on, 'I hope it's a boy, of course. But even if it's a
girl she'll be welcome. And brought up as a girl! Eh,
Jossie?'

'It would be better, certainly,' said Jossie with a
slightly bitter smile.

'Aye. Rosalind'll make a fine mother,' said Sir
Thomas proudly. 'I'll get the Dower House sorted out
for them as soon as we get back to Somerset. If they're
starting a family they'll need a place of their own.' He
chuckled. 'To think that I'll be a grandfather!' Then, as
he beamed at them, he said suddenly, 'But I'm forgetting! We haven't had a chance to congratulate you on
your own good news, Trenchard. You've got as fine a
lass in our Jossie as you'll find anywhere. There was a
time when…' He looked a touch wistfully at Jossie, then
shook his head and carried on, 'But Rosalind's a good

lass, a good lass. A grandfather, eh?' He chuckled again, obviously in high good humour, coming over to shake Ivo's hand. 'You make sure you take good care of Jossie,' he said. 'She deserves the best.'

Ivo took Jossie's hand. He said, 'Jossie will be as happy as I can make her, Sir Thomas. But...' he went on, looking at his aunt, 'I am sure we ought not to take up any more of Lady Radstock's time. She must have a great deal to see to.'

'We'll all be busy! We're off to Brighton in a day or two,' said Sir Thomas. 'I want to make sure Rosalind has plenty of good, fresh, sea air. Exercise, that's the thing!'

'And rest, and amusement,' said Lady Radstock gently.

'What? Oh, yes! Rest. Amusement. Of course, of course! What a girl, eh?'

Lady Frances rose and took her friend by the hand. 'I am so very glad to hear your news. And I'm sure that Brighton will work wonders for Rosalind.'

All three of them took their leave and left the Radstocks to their rejoicing.

As they were walking home, Lady Frances said, 'Well, Peter's problems seem to be sorting themselves out without anyone else's intervention. Except perhaps the difficulty with your stepmother...'

Jossie nodded. 'But he will be much happier now that his wife is accepted fully by his father. Rosalind has done the one thing which was certain to win Sir Thomas's approval.'

Ivo had been listening with growing incredulity to this conversation. 'Do you mean to say that Peter Radstock risked your reputation and his own wife's happiness, in order to ask your advice on his own, trivial, domestic problems? Family tiffs? I thought he must be desperate—I even wondered whether he wanted to declare that his love for you had returned, to ask you to run away with him!'

'I would never have listened to him if that had been the case. You know that, Ivo!'

He regarded her with a smile. 'I should have remembered. Beautiful, rich, witty...and straight as a die. But a jealous man isn't always reasonable.'

Jossie gave a sniff of disbelief. 'Jealous! You! Don't talk rubbish!'

Peregrine paid his visit, and took leave of his father. Lord Veryan, who was not always the most tactful of men, mentioned Arneston and told Perry that Ivo had interceded on his behalf.

'I'm sure my brother is very good,' said Perry coldly. 'I was not aware it was his to dispose of.'

'Of course it isn't, you ungrateful cub! But it would have been his one day! D'you want it or not, Peregrine?'

'Thank you, sir. I accept it with pleasure. It's a beautiful estate.'

'Never liked it very much,' said Lord Veryan. 'Glad to get rid of it. I'll speak to the lawyers. Have a safe journey.'

Seething with resentment Perry next looked for his aunt, or Ivo. On being informed that they were both out, and not expected back for another hour, he sought for and found Jossie sitting by herself in the little parlour.

'You seem pensive, Miss Calverton,' he said after they had exchanged greetings. 'Or is it that I have put myself beyond the pale?'

Jossie gave him a straight look. 'You have certainly caused me some distress, sir, with your over-zealous tongue.'

'I am truly, deeply sorry, ma'am. I never wished to harm or distress anyone. I merely mentioned Madame Rosa to Mrs Radstock and she wormed the rest out of me. I thought it harmless enough, believe me! I had no idea that she would react so violently, otherwise I would have been more discreet. However, I did call on Mrs Radstock this morning, and was pleased to hear that she had suffered no serious effects. I...er...I understand there is a very happy explanation for her nervous state.'

'Yes.' Jossie found herself disarmed by Perry's gentle voice and the frank contrition in his eyes. 'I suppose she did misunderstand you?'

'I assure you that she did! But mine was the fault. Were you very distressed? Surely it proved to be a happy occasion for you?'

'Why?'

'Your engagement.'

'Oh, no! Lord Trenchard ought never to have made such an announcement. An engagement is by no means planned. To tell the truth, I am in something of a quandary!'

'Why is that?'

Disarmed again by his sympathetic look, Jossie explained. 'Lord Trenchard has been a true friend and guide during the past year. He and my godmother have done so much for me! And now he has committed us to each other in front of the better part of Society—merely to save my good name! He would never otherwise think of marrying someone like myself. You know what his taste in women is like, I am sure. Not anyone like me!'

'And you are averse to the thought of marrying him?'

'In the present circumstances, yes!'

'Yet I think you love my brother, Miss Calverton?'

Jossie said after a pause, 'I cannot imagine a worse fate than to be married to someone you love, but who feels only friendly toleration in return. Lord Trenchard needs a more sophisticated wife than I could ever be. However acceptable it may be in Society, I…I know that I could never look with complaisance at my husband's casual amours.'

Peregrine shook his head sadly. 'His reputation would hardly suggest that he would be faithful for long.' He paused, then added, 'And I cannot offer much hope of a change. He has been like this ever since I have been old enough to notice. In fact…'

He paused and put his hand to his eyes. Jossie asked anxiously, 'What is it, Mr Trenchard?'

He sighed and shook his head. 'It is an unhappy story, Miss Calverton, and one I should rather forget,' he said gravely. 'I'm afraid it does no credit to the man you say you love.'

'You may have gathered that I am not altogether unaware of his faults, Mr Trenchard. I think you could tell me.'

He continued to shake his head. 'There are others, beside myself, who are involved.'

'I see. I suppose in that case I must not press you…'

'And yet…I think I will confide in you. I can be sure of your discretion, I know.'

'Of course!'

'You see, Ivo took from me the one woman I ever loved. Took her, and then rejected her.' He looked sorrowfully at Jossie. 'She was the daughter of my father's best friend.'

'But what happened?'

'Charlotte and I were happy until Ivo came home on leave. He can be very charming, Miss Calverton, and before long Charlotte made the mistake of falling in love with him. I do not believe he was ever in love with her. When he and Charlotte were caught, *in flagrante*, in an isolated cottage on the estate, the two fathers demanded that Ivo should marry her. He refused. He and my father were estranged for over a year because of it. But of course Father eventually forgave him—he always did.'

'What happened to the girl?'

'She was in despair, naturally. She was too ashamed even to see me, though I assure you, Miss Calverton, I would have been proud to make her my wife. In the end she was taken away to Bath, and forced to marry a man old enough to be her father! I hear of her now and then. In fact, her father is at present lodged near me. I do not believe Charlotte is happy.'

Jossie was shocked, but protested, 'Mr Trenchard! That is a dreadful story! I can't believe it! I have always found your brother to be an honourable man!'

'He is! In all matters, except in his attitude to women.' He got up. 'I can understand how difficult it is for you to believe me. But would Sir George Gurney's word be enough to convince you?'

Jossie was perplexed. Peregrine had sounded sincere, but she found it quite impossible to believe his story. Ivo had his faults, but she had never heard him accused of the seduction of innocent girls. 'If it would not offend you, I should like to hear what Charlotte's father has to say. Would he talk to me?'

'I'm sure he would, if it meant that his daughter's fate was not repeated by someone else.'

'That is most unlikely as far as I am concerned, but I cannot leave it like this, nevertheless...'

'Will you be at Carlton House this evening? Sir George is certain to be there. I could arrange for you to meet him.'

'Thank you. I shall be there.'

'I shall not see you again after that, Miss Calverton. I am leaving London tomorrow.'

'So soon?'

'I am being sent off to Derbyshire. Ivo is uncomfortable in my presence. And who can blame him? Make my excuses to him if you would. I thought he would be here, but I do not feel like waiting to see him till he chooses to come.'

He collected his hat and cane and went out. Once beyond the corner, however, his demeanour changed. Drooping shoulders straightened, a lagging gait smartened up, and his expression of sorrow bravely borne changed into a complacent grin. Helena Calverton was a fool! She obviously had no idea how deeply his brother was in love with her. Peregrine himself had found it hard to believe at first, but it was certainly so. After years of philandering, Ivo was truly, seriously in love! Perry laughed. It had been a stroke of genius to think of old Gurney. Charlotte's father was still convinced it had been Ivo who had seduced his daughter. And once he had said his piece tonight Miss Calverton would be equally certain. After tonight brother Ivo was not going to find it at all easy to win the girl he loved! He might even fail altogether.

After Peregrine's departure Jossie was left a prey to conflicting doubts. She simply could not believe that Ivo had behaved as badly as Peregrine had claimed, and sincerely hoped that what Sir George said would present it in a better light. There must be some other explanation, there must be!

However, there was no evidence to the contrary in the few facts she had of Ivo's past history. She knew of his long quarrel with his father, had heard the name Charlotte Gurney in connection with it, remembered vaguely that he had been reconciled with his father after it became known that Charlotte Gurney had married in Bath... But it still seemed impossible!

Ivo's reputation was far less in dispute—almost the first thing she had heard about him was that he was the worst flirt in Europe. His attitude to her sex in general was very cynical. How many times had she heard his comments on the women he had known in Brussels and London? She had always assumed they deserved what he said of them, but how could she be sure?

On the other hand, Ivo had always been the soul of honour in his behaviour towards her—but then, as she had said, she was not really Ivo's usual taste in females. He had never flirted with her, nor had he ever regarded her as a possible wife before the previous night. His proposal had merely been an absurd extension of his curious determination to protect her, which had started after Peter's coming of age, and had now become a habit.

The change was in *her*. She had come a long way from the girl she had been then. What she now needed from any man who was to be her husband was not the milk-warm affection of a father figure, but the passion of a lover, the satisfaction of her deepest needs as a woman, a lifetime commitment from someone who would be the other half of herself...

She sighed. She had no desire to be tied to a philandering cynic, a charmer who might well be fond of her, but would betray her without a second thought once the honeymoon was over. No, whatever Sir George might tell her, she *could* not, she *would* not marry Ivo Trenchard!

Chapter Sixteen

Tormented by these and similar thoughts, Jossie found it increasingly hard to stay calm that night, to keep her smile serene and to make the right responses. Everywhere she and Ivo went their friends and acquaintances asked the date of her wedding, what she would wear, where she and Ivo would live after they were married, and a thousand other questions, all equally impossible to answer. Ivo himself was so charmingly attentive to her, so carefully *considerate*, that she felt she might scream. Even Lady Frances, usually a staunch supporter, was talking about their forthcoming marriage as an accepted fact—in private as well as in public. Jossie felt she was being slowly shepherded into a position from which she would find it impossible to escape, borne inexorably to the altar on the back of public opinion.

At Carlton House she was the object of the tabbies' constant interest, an interest which became avid every time Ivo spoke to, or even looked at, any of his former amours. He was as charming as ever to them, though, as was now usual, Jossie was often at his side. Unfortunately several of them made it very obvious, to Jossie at least, that they thought it only a matter of time before

Ivo would be back in their arms. The Prince Regent himself commented on their engagement and jokingly advised them not to make it a long one. 'Don't let him escape, Miss Calverton!' he said with a laugh. 'We all know what he is!'

During the supper interval she saw Peregrine beckoning to her. She slipped across the crowded room. Ivo had gone to collect refreshments, Lady Frances was with a friend—she would be back before either of them returned. Outside on the terrace Peregrine introduced her to Sir George, then bowed and tactfully withdrew. Jossie was at a loss. How on earth could she begin?

But, ignoring her embarrassment, Sir George said abruptly, 'That Trenchard fellow wants me to tell you about my daughter. Is that right?'

Jossie nodded. 'If you think you can, Sir George.'

'Shouldn't be here if I didn't. I don't like any of the Trenchards, and I certainly wouldn't do any favours to them! But it's only right *you* should know. I've seen you with him—the older one, I mean. The soldier. They say you're engaged. Is that right?'

Jossie said uncomfortably, 'I…we are at present, yes.'

'My advice is not to have anything to do with him. Seduced m'daughter, and then the damned fellow wouldn't do the right thing by her. Refused absolutely. I fell out with the lot of 'em over it. Veryan was m'best friend, too. Not now.'

Jossie's heart sank. So it was true. Sir George looked round. 'Is that all? I'd as soon not hang about here. Don't like talking about it much.'

She made a considerable effort and thanked him. 'Your daughter—is she happier now?' she asked hesitantly.

'Good Lord, yes. In Paris at the moment. Havin' the

time of her life. Respectably married. Luckier than she deserves. I suppose you're askin' yourself why I didn't pursue the matter with Trenchard? I wanted to preserve Charlotte's good name, d'y see, and it worked. Only Veryan and his sons know what happened in that cottage at Sudiham—and now you. No one else. The world has no idea, and it must never learn. I know I can count on you.'

Jossie nodded, curtsied and took her leave. She got back to her seat just in time, but after a short while she could bear no more of the laughter and chatter. She pleaded a nervous headache and they left Carlton House early. By the time they got back to Charles Street her headache was real, but she was determined to have no more to do with any engagement.

Ivo had been aware all evening of her growing tension. He would normally have done his best to calm her down, try to make her laugh at some of the absurd things people had said, but on this evening he was himself equally angry and disappointed. Jossie seemed to be slipping further away from him with every day that passed. Ever since their engagement, she had been on her guard against him, and the thought was surprisingly hurtful. The trusting directness which had so enchanted him had vanished, the real Jossie becoming more and more elusive. Yet he knew that the real Jossie was the girl he must find again if he was ever to persuade her to love him as he wanted. As the days passed it seemed less and less likely that he would ever succeed. Tonight, for no reason that he could see, Jossie had appeared to be more determined than ever to keep him at a distance.

When they got back to Charles Street, Jossie turned to face Ivo. 'I'd like to talk to you in the library for a moment.'

Lady Frances looked at her stormy face. 'Sleep on it, Jossie. I don't know what you want to say, but I'm sure it's better said after a night's consideration.'

'It can't wait. I need to speak to Ivo. I…I can't go on like this!'

Lady Frances looked from one to the other, then shrugged her shoulders. 'Very well. I'll be in my room if you want someone to pick up the pieces. Good night.'

Ivo saw her to the stairs, then returned to the library. Jossie was facing him. She said abruptly, 'Ivo, this has to stop. I have no intention of marrying you, and I hate the deception. It's time I went back to Somerset.'

Ivo was silent for a moment. Then, in a harsh voice quite unlike his normal deep drawl, he asked, 'And where do you propose to stay? With your father? I doubt his wife would agree. Or do you wish to take my aunt with you, away from all her friends? Aren't you being just a touch ungrateful? Or are you too selfish to see how much she's enjoying herself?'

Strangely enough, Jossie had been too preoccupied with her début to give any real thought to what she would do when the season ended. This was a rude awakening. What *would* she do? To go back to her father was out of the question. Lady Frances, Lord Veryan and…and yes, Ivo himself, had become her family during the past year. There was no one else. Suddenly there was a frightening hole in front of her. If she left London now, where could she possibly go? If Lady Frances grew tired of her, where would she live in future? She stared at Ivo, unable to think of a reply.

He went on with an unpleasant grin, 'Perhaps you could join your friends, the Radstocks, in Brighton? I daresay Peter has one or two other problems you could sort out for him. Is that what you want? To end your days as a kind of spinster companion to a spineless dolt?'

Jossie went white. 'Ivo!' she said sharply. 'Don't talk like that! Why are you saying such things? You are not usually cruel!'

'Aren't I?' Ivo's temper was getting the better of him. 'You surprise me! I thought there must be something truly awful about me! You've nowhere of your own to live, you're not apparently in love with anyone else, yet you wouldn't consider marriage to me, dear me, no! You can't even bear to stay engaged to me, not even for a few short weeks. Not even to save both our faces—' He broke off and turned to face the fire. After a moment he turned back to her. 'What have I ever done to make you dislike me so? Announced our engagement without consulting you? Is that it?'

'N-not exactly, but…'

'I can't think what else it might be! God knows, it's not as if I had claimed any of the privileges of an engaged man!'

'W-What do you mean?'

'What happened to the trust you had in me, Jossie? Do you remember how you *asked* me to teach you how to kiss? Why is it different now? Why do you stiffen every time I come near you? Do you think I haven't noticed? You're good, you're very good! You hide it well. I doubt the eyes of the curious see anything wrong. But I do! I *feel* you flinch if I pull you too close, feel your hand pull against mine if I hold it too long. Why is that? I thought we were friends as well as—' He broke off again. After a moment he asked abruptly, 'Did I frighten you the last time I kissed you? Is that it?'

'No! Yes. I don't know!'

He came across and put his arms around her. 'You

used to like my kisses, Jossie,' he said. His voice was soft, but the dark blue eyes were determined.

'Yes. Yes, I did. But please, don't do this, Ivo! Please!'

'Why not? Don't I deserve a little kindness?' His face was near her face, his lips almost touching hers.

His nearness was undermining her resolve. Thought of Charlotte Gurney faded into the background, banished by the familiar stream of excitement running through her veins, the remembered desire to be closer which only Ivo could evoke… It would be so easy to forget, she thought. To give in, just for a short while…just once.

'Jossie?' His voice was tender now and deeper than ever.

With a sob she put her arms round his neck. His eyes darkened, then he groaned and pulled her tight against him. For a moment they were still, gazing into each other's eyes. Then he murmured her name again and bent to kiss her.

Fireworks at Vauxhall, scintillating flashes of light from the crystal chandelier at Carlton House, the flames of a thousand candles…an explosion of light and power… The two figures in the library were lost in a dazzling, intoxicating swirl of feeling, never before experienced by either. The kiss this time was no lesson, no pretence, offered little comfort and certainly no safety. It was harsh, primitive, wild, quite simply a man demanding and receiving a passionate response from the woman of his choice.

They were both completely transported, and when the kiss finally came to an end they stared at each other in bewilderment and shock.

'Jossie!'

For a moment Jossie clung to Ivo as she slowly came back to earth. She would have fallen otherwise.

Ivo rocked her in his arms. 'Oh God, Jossie! Oh, my love! My life!'

Jossie swallowed. Shame was beginning to overwhelm her. How could she have been so abandoned? Ivo could have taken whatever he wanted from her during those wild moments, and she would have done nothing to stop him. Even now he was covering her face with little kisses, caressing her throat with trembling fingers, pulling her to him again... Oh heavens, the temptation was so great, but she must resist this madness, it mustn't go any further! She forced herself to be calm, to use her mind to quell her unruly emotions. Whatever he might say in the heat of the moment, Ivo was not in love with her. This was the great lover at work, the worst flirt in Europe... Remember that, Jossie! His touch was expert, but then it would have to be. He would never change, that's what Peregrine had said. Was this how Ivo delighted his other women? How he had delighted Charlotte Gurney? Was he now using his expertise to seduce *her* into doing as he wanted?

'No!' she cried, pushing him violently away from her. 'No, I will not be used!'

Ivo was suddenly still. He stood for a moment then said quietly, 'Used? How "used"? I thought we were unbelievably close, Jossie, but I don't understand you. What do you mean?'

Jossie was sobbing as she cried, 'I won't let you persuade me to marry you. You don't love me, you just want a complaisant wife, someone who is grateful enough to put up with your ways!'

Ivo laughed in relief. 'Jossie, my darling, my only

love, this is arrant rubbish! You are not yourself, you can't mean this!'

'Oh, yes, I can! I've seen you at work, I've heard what you say. You expect women to be as faithless as you are yourself! Marriage doesn't mean anything to you. You have no respect for women, married or single. I know about Charlotte Gurney, too!'

All laughter vanished from Ivo's face. 'Charlotte Gurney?' he exclaimed sharply. 'What do you know of Charlotte Gurney? Who told you about Charlotte Gurney?'

'Peregrine told me all about it! How you were caught with her and refused to marry her.'

'Peregrine!' The loathing in Ivo's voice appalled her. 'You'd listen to *him*?'

'It wasn't only your brother. Charlotte's father said so, too! Oh, Ivo, that poor girl! How could you?'

'I didn't seduce Charlotte Gurney, Jossie,' he said, his face white, his voice devoid of expression.

'I want to believe you, but how can I? Perry says you did, Sir George says you did! You and your father quarrelled when you refused to marry her. Isn't that so?'

Ivo looked as if he had just received a body blow. He turned away and put his hand on the mantelpiece. 'And I thought we were close…' he murmured. 'I thought you knew me, trusted me…' After a moment he turned to face her again. 'You seem very sure of my guilt,' he said coldly.

Jossie was trembling with distress. 'I don't wish to believe it, Ivo! Help me! Explain it!'

Ivo considered her in silence. 'No,' he said at last. 'I don't think I want to. How strange that that episode has twice ruined a relationship I thought important…' He gave her a smile as remote and as cold as the Arctic.

'I'm sorry, my dear. You'll have to ask Peregrine if you want to know any more. Meanwhile, you may safely stay in London as long as you wish. I shan't be asking you to pretend anything any further. Tell my aunt that I have moved out of Charles Street. I shall stay at my club for the present. I leave you to say what you like about our engagement.' He bowed and went swiftly out of the room.

Jossie sank to the floor and sobbed. She felt as if her heart had been torn from her body, had left with Ivo. The pain was intense. When a hand touched her shoulder she looked up wildly, thinking that he had come back, willing to talk, willing to explain. She would have thrown herself on him, begged to be forgiven for doubting him. But the hand wasn't Ivo's.

'My dear!' said Lady Frances. 'Jossie! Don't! You'll tear yourself apart! What has happened? What has Ivo done?'

Jossie could only shake her head at first, but then as the fit of sobbing abated she managed to say, 'He h-hasn't done any...anything. H-he's gone aw-away.'

'But why? What happened?'

'I s-said I c-couldn't m-marry him. Or b-be eng-engaged to h-him any...any m-more. He...he's so an-gry.' She lapsed into silence, as tears rolled down her cheeks.

Lady Frances looked grave. 'I rather thought that was what you wanted to tell him,' she said. 'It's not surprising he's angry. I wish you had waited as I suggested, Jossie. You were neither of you in form tonight. To-morrow you might have been able to discuss the situation more calmly.'

Jossie said wearily, 'It wouldn't have made any difference. I won't marry him!'

'That is your decision, of course. But tell me why you are so set against the idea.'

Jossie shook her head. Badly though she wanted to confide in her godmother, she could not tell her of the business with Charlotte Gurney. That secret was not hers to tell. In any case, there was another, greater bar to marrying Ivo.

'He doesn't really love me,' she said. 'Not the way I want.'

Lady Frances shook her head. 'Well. I don't know what you want, Jossie, but I would have said that Ivo loves you as deeply, as seriously as any man could.'

'That's not so! He still thinks of me as a child, someone to protect! You've seen the way he acts.'

'Of course he wishes to protect you! It's what a man, a real man, regards as his first responsibility towards the woman he loves! But that's just the beginning.' Lady Frances leaned forward and said with great seriousness, 'I've known Ivo a long time and I have never seen him in love like this before. He loves you now in every way there is, my dear. Every way. You may take my word on that.'

Jossie gazed at Lady Frances as if she could somehow find an answer in her godmother's face. 'Why haven't you said anything before? I didn't know…' Her voice grew stronger. 'In fact, I still don't believe… He has never given the slightest indication…at least—' She stopped and coloured painfully as the memory of Ivo's last kiss returned. 'Why did you never say anything?' she whispered.

'He forbade me to.'

'But *why*?'

'Try to understand, Jossie! For years Ivo has skimmed over the surface of life, seeking and taking pleasure wherever he found it. It wasn't at all difficult. He is handsome, rich, immensely charming... Women have pursued him ever since he entered society. It was perfectly understandable that he should become somewhat blasé in his attitude towards them. He has never before felt uncertain, or inadequate, or cautious—he has never had to.' She paused, then went on, 'Then, when he is almost thirty he finds himself attracted to a naïve seventeen-year-old, as far removed from his usual world as she could possibly be. Of course he fought it! Of course he refused to acknowledge it, even to himself! And then, when he realised it was not going to go away, he was afraid. He had rescued you, given you your success— what if you married him out of a feeling of obligation? What he wanted was your love.' She smiled ironically. 'Ivo doesn't want your gratitude, my love, any more than you want to give it!'

Jossie put her face in her hands. 'Oh, my God! What have I done?' A great sob escaped her. 'What have I done?'

'What *have* you done?'

'I...I can't tell you. But I've lost Ivo forever.' Jossie was rocking herself to and fro in growing distress. Seriously worried, Lady Frances abandoned any further talk and rang for one of the servants. In a short time Jossie was in her bed, sipping a warm drink into which her godmother had put a sleeping draught. Before long she had fallen asleep. But her sleep was uneasy, broken with nightmares and an unbearable sense of loss.

Lady Frances had not really believed matters were as serious as Jossie had said. She even persuaded Jossie to stay till the end of the week in London, in the hope that matters could be mended. But the next few days proved her mistaken. Ivo did not return to the house, but stayed at his club. He acknowledged his aunt and Jossie courteously at the soirée they attended the next night, but made no effort to join them, and spent the evening with his former associates, flirting outrageously with the ladies. Society watched, nodded, and said they were not surprised. Miss Calverton was very beautiful, but holding the attention of one of London's acknowledged flirts was clearly beyond her. Jossie held her head high, and parried all enquiries with a serenity which amazed Lady Frances, who knew how much of Kendrick's skill had been needed to hide the ravages of her mistress's distress.

And so it continued. No announcement was needed. London soon assumed that Miss Calverton's short-lived engagement to Lord Trenchard was at an end, since the parties apparently never spent more than a few minutes in each other's company. Ivo's conduct only confirmed Jossie's doubts. If he had truly loved her, she told herself, loved her in the all-consuming way she wanted, he could not now appear to be so unaffected by her presence in the same room, laughing, dancing, talking with everyone, it seemed, but her. But he was if anything more carefree, more devil-may-care, more outrageously flirtatious than ever. Her godmother was wrong, very wrong. Soon the strain began to tell and she decided that she must leave London as soon as possible.

This was easier to accomplish than she had feared. Lord Veryan was tired of London. He had come to see Jossie's success, and that he had done. He had hoped to see her engaged to his son, and that had also come to pass—but not for long. Now he was tired and jaded. He wanted to be back in his own home, breathing his own fresh air.

Lady Frances, too, was ready to go. As far as she could see, there was little point in staying any longer. She had tried to talk to her nephew about his quarrel with Jossie, but he had proved so impenetrably courteous that she had finally had to give up. Though she suspected that behind it lay something more than Jossie's refusal to marry him, she had no idea what it might be. Whatever it was it had gone deep. In spite of his apparent enjoyment of life, Ivo was hurting every bit as much as Jossie, she was sure. But he remained charmingly, and adamantly, uncommunicative. At the end of the week all three of them, Lady Frances, her brother and her goddaughter, were more than ready to leave the noise and dust of London behind them for good.

They reached Lyne St Michael when the countryside was looking its best. Flowers lined the hedgerows and filled the pastures. The trees were in full foliage, but still freshly green, and the fields were lush with growing crops. The air was full of the scents of early summer.

'Ah! This is better!' Lord Veryan exclaimed as they descended from the carriage at Danby Lodge. 'Much, much better! Isn't that so, Jossie?'

Jossie looked round. Little had changed. The lodge had been well looked after during their absence, and it looked much as it had done almost a year before, when Ivo and her godmother had brought her here after Peter's coming of age. She swallowed. When would her heart stop giving that little twist of pain whenever she thought of Ivo? She smiled at Lord Veryan. 'Much better,' she said.

He frowned at her. 'Hmm. You might at least get some colour in your cheeks down here! You look like a ghost, girl!'

* * *

Later that evening the three of them walked round the garden. 'This place is very pleasant,' said Lord Veryan. 'Very pleasant indeed, Frances. But I must confess that I'll be glad to see Sudiham again. I'll be off tomorrow.'

'I thought Ivo was coming down to collect you and accompany you home,' exclaimed Lady Frances.

'Er…no. He said he will join me at Sudiham at the end of next week. He has some business in London to attend to first. No, I'm afraid you won't see him this time, my dear.' The two older people carefully avoided looking at Jossie.

'We must make some plans,' said Lady Frances brightly. 'The Radstocks are in Brighton for the rest of the summer, but there are some other neighbours to visit. Later on we could perhaps do a little travelling.'

'Will you be calling on the Morleys?' asked Lord Veryan drily.

'I should like to,' said Jossie. 'I don't expect to enjoy it, but I ought at least to call on my father and stepmama.'

'Quite right! We shall do so,' said Lady Frances with approval. She chuckled. 'I don't suppose, however, that they will enjoy it any more than we shall! Gerard Morley is not likely to have forgiven me for ensuring that his daughter was such a success. His wife even less likely! Never mind! What else shall we do?'

'If you don't mind, Lady Frances, I should like to do some exploring for myself. I could ask my father if I could borrow one of the horses. I could perhaps even have Star again.'

'Is that…wise?'

'I need to lay a few ghosts.'

Lady Frances nodded. 'If you are sure, my dear.'

* * *

Lord Veryan left for Sudiham the next day. 'I shall miss you, Jossie,' he said as he was getting into the carriage. 'Come over when you can.'

'I shall. But not—'

'I know, I know,' he said testily. 'Not when that son of mine is there. I shall never understand it, never! I would have thought you two were ideally suited. What happened? Can't you tell me? I'm pretty sure you're in love with him even now. And I know how fond he was of you.'

Jossie looked at him sadly. 'I didn't believe he loved me. And I told him I didn't trust him.'

Lord Veryan leaned out of the carriage. 'You *what*? Good God, girl, what made you say a thing like that?'

'Peregrine told me something about him. Something horrible. Ivo refused to explain. He…he hasn't spoken to me properly since.'

Lord Veryan got out of the carriage again and ushered her back into the house. He took her into the small parlour and shut the door. 'Now. Peregrine told you something. What did he tell you?'

'I…I can't say. The secret isn't mine. But it was confirmed by someone else.'

'Jossie, I know Peregrine is my son, but I wouldn't believe what he said about Ivo if it was confirmed by fourteen bishops with prayer books in their hands! He's a malicious liar! For God's sake, don't you fall into the same trap that I once did! I nearly lost Ivo over it!'

'You did?'

'Ivo's proud, d'you see? He has this devil-may-care manner, but if he loves someone it matters a lot to him what they think of him. I hurt him badly when I didn't believe what he said once.'

Jossie looked down. 'I hurt him badly, too. I can see that now. I think I may well have lost him.' She sniffed.

'Damn Peregrine and his machinations! There's always been something wrong with that boy! He seems to hate Ivo for trying to do him good!' He looked at Jossie's downcast face. 'I'll do my best with Ivo when he comes. I'll try to persuade him to come over. If I manage it, the rest will be up to you.'

Jossie visited her father. Considering the problems, she felt it passed off very well. Mrs Morley was gracious, the Major even went so far as to say that he occasionally missed his daughter. Lady Frances watched the Morleys doing their best to make as little of Jossie's success as possible, and gained her own amusement from that. Jossie found Star in the stables, and was allowed to take him away with her. She was even offered her old riding clothes, the ones she had worn as a boy. But these she refused.

'Thank you, Father, but they belong to the past. I can never go back. Thank you for Star. I've missed him.'

They left with a vague promise to see one other again. The Major watched them rather wistfully as they went down the drive. Life had been happier for him during that past which Jossie now so firmly rejected.

Jossie did as she had said she would. She visited all the haunts that she and Peter had frequented in those old, carelessly happy days—Heversham Beacon, the valleys to the west, the farms and villages round about. Knowing that the Radstocks were safely away in Brighton, she even rode round the grounds of Radstock Court. She sighed, she laughed, she reminisced, and she rid

herself of any last remnants of bitterness. Peter's ghost
was easily laid to rest.

But she did not go to the valley that had meant so
much to her. The memories there no longer had anything
to do with Peter, and were still too painful.

As time went on, any hopes she had entertained that
Lord Veryan would prevail on Ivo to come to Lyne
slowly faded. She would have to accept that Ivo had
gone forever. So she resolved to go at last to the valley,
see the waterfall, rehearse in her mind what he had said
to her there, relive the dramatic scenes of their early
acquaintance. And then she would do her best to forget
them.

She tethered Star to that same tree not far from the
stream, and wandered down the valley. She stood by the
waterfall, seeing herself at seventeen, unaware, bewildered, unprepared for the demands being made on her
by life. Others might have laughed at her, even taken
advantage, but Ivo had been so understanding, so patient.
What was it she had said to him?

*'Perhaps all those years pretending to be a boy
have...damaged me? I shall never enjoy being kissed.'*

Ivo had given a shout of laughter, then he had pulled
her round and hugged her. *'My sweet, darling Jossie!
No one with as kissable a mouth as yours could possibly
not enjoy being kissed sooner or later.'*

*'Well, that's what I wanted to ask you, Ivo. I wondered
if you could teach me how to respond.'*

She had been so naïve, so innocent, making that absurd request without a second thought. And he had been
scrupulous. An honourable man, Ivo Trenchard. How
could she have thought him otherwise?

'*Are you sure you're being sensible? You must have heard what they say of me.*'

'*Lady Frances said once you were the worst flirt in the county before you went into the Army, and she didn't suppose you had changed.*'

'*How very kind of her! Doesn't that put you off?*'

'*Of course not—it's what I want! It's no use asking someone who doesn't know what they're doing to help me in this. I need an expert.*'

And what an expert Ivo had been! It was here, right on this spot, that she had first experienced the wonder, the rapture of Ivo's kisses. Too stupid to realise that it was Ivo himself who made the difference, she had thought the feelings transferable! Well, she knew now. The magic, the chemistry, lay between Ivo and herself. No one else would ever rouse in her that strange mixture of passion and compassion, the explosive combination of overwhelming tenderness and the demon of desire.

Jossie shivered even though the day was warm. It was all over. The desire, the tenderness, the love—all gone. She would not go under, as she had thought she might on the night of Peter's ball—that had been here, too. She would lead as contented a life as she could. But happiness was a different matter.

Sighing, she turned back up the valley. And stopped. In a strange echo of that first time Ivo was coming down the slope towards the stream, eyeing Star. Her heart gave a great leap, and she had to wait till she had enough breath. Then she cried joyously, 'You leave him alone, do you hear? Move away from my horse!'

Ivo looked over to where she stood. 'Jossie?'

She ran to him, tripping and stumbling in her hurry, sobbing his name. 'Ivo, oh, Ivo!' His arms went round her, his head was resting on hers.

'Pull yourself together, girl! You should be threatening me with a gun, not watering my jacket!'

'You came!' She looked at him with shining eyes. 'I'm so glad you came! Ivo, I'm sorry! No, no, don't stop me! I must say this. I should have known better. I don't care if forty bishops each with forty prayer books tell me that Peregrine's story is true, I still wouldn't believe him! You were right, I *do* know you! You would never do anything of the sort. Tell me you forgive me!'

'I love you, Jossie. Never, ever doubt that. With every breath of my being. There's no need for forgiveness between us. I was hurt and angry, I should have told you the truth at the time, but I was too proud. These past weeks have been torture, but I've come to my senses now.'

They gazed at each other in a happy daze. Then slowly, deliberately, Lord Trenchard drew his future bride, his love, to him and kissed her. Tenderness, protection, instruction, comfort, and a leaping passion— they all were there, but, most of all, this kiss was a pledge made to each other, a pledge of lifetime commitment, enduring loyalty, infinite love.

Lord Trenchard had made his choice.

They made their way back to the village, wrapped in a world of their own. When they reached Danby Lodge they found Lady Frances and her brother waiting for them in the drive. One look was enough to tell anyone that Ivo and Jossie had found each other, and Lord Veryan was practically dancing with pleasure.

'You told her?' he asked.

'Told me what?'

'The truth about Charlotte Gurney.'

'I didn't have to, Father. Jossie fell on my neck before I could get a word out!'

'Oh, how ungallant, sir!' said Jossie, laughing.

'It was the best moment of my life,' Ivo said, pulling her to him. 'To know that you had faith in me, loved me after all…'

'Really, Ivo! You mustn't kiss her on the drive in full view of anyone who cares to look! It isn't decent! You're not even engaged!' said Lady Frances.

'What do you mean? Of course we are!'

'In *my* day, it was considered necessary to consult the girl's father before asking her to marry you. Dare I hope that you have already talked to the Major?' said Lady Frances with mock severity.

'Aunt Frances, you are a delight! But not up to the mark every time. Yes, I called on the Major a few hours ago, and he has given a reluctant consent. Only because he couldn't think of a reasonable objection, I'm sure. The wedding will take place as soon as Jossie has her bride clothes.'

'Well, *you* may not care whether Jossie knows the truth or not, but *I* do! Come inside, both of you. We have a lot to discuss,' said Lord Veryan.

As they turned to go inside Jossie whispered, 'Ivo, how soon can the banns be called? I have enough dresses to last a lifetime. Or—couldn't we elope?'

'It wouldn't be difficult to get a special licence—not when the Great Duke himself is one of your admirers. But I wouldn't dream of eloping, Jossie. From now on the Trenchards are going to be the epitome of respectability! No more *affaires*, no more flirting. The only married woman in my life will be Lady Trenchard. And any siren looks will be for my sole pleasure. Understand?'

'Yes, my lord,' said Jossie. And gave him the best one in her repertoire.

After the first rejoicings were over, and the happy couple toasted, Lady Frances said, 'But tell us, Ivo. If you haven't yet been to Sudiham, what persuaded you to come here after all?'

'My Colonel. Who, it turns out, is the new Marquess of Coverdale—I wonder if Adam knows? Anyway, the Colonel is going north any day now, and I went to take my leave of him. He told me I was a fool to risk losing Jossie. And I found I agreed with him. So here I am!' He started to laugh.

'What is so amusing?'

'Colonel Ancroft was just leaving to keep an appointment when I called, so I walked along with him and left him at his lawyer's door.' He paused, then said, 'It's no use. I'll have to tell you the whole! You see, the Colonel has agreed to escort an elderly widow of a nervous disposition on his way north. He doesn't know her—he was to meet her for the first time that day at his lawyer's. Apparently she is taking her husband's ashes back to his birthplace—'

'There's nothing amusing about that!' said Jossie.

'No. But wait! I happened to see this elderly lady of a nervous disposition. She was getting out of her carriage as I turned to go back to Charles Street. She was just as I would have expected—rather stout, and dressed from head to toe in deepest black, including a large veil. But two things were wrong. As she stepped out of the carriage I saw the prettiest pair of ankles I've seen in a long time. They certainly didn't match the rest of her appearance. And the other was—'

'Well?' asked Lady Frances impatiently.

'A sudden gust of wind blew the veil into the air, and she was annoyed. Her voice was attractive, and the accent refined. But the word she uttered is one more commonly used in the back streets of Marseilles!'

'What was it?' demanded Jossie.

'Oh, no, my love. I'm not going to tell you—you might repeat it! But take my word for it—it shocked me! She saw me staring and before she lowered her veil she laughed and gave me a look out of the wickedest pair of green eyes I think I have ever seen.'

'Ivo! What did you do? Did you tell Colonel Ancroft?'

'I thought of it. But then I decided not to. John Ancroft is a sensible, experienced man. He won't be taken in for long. Besides, he is looking for something to take his mind off his problems. This widow of his might turn out to be just what he needs...'

* * * * *

Look for Colonel Ancroft's story.
Coming soon.

Modern Romance™
...seduction and
passion guaranteed

Tender Romance™
...love affairs that
last a lifetime

Sensual Romance™
...sassy, sexy and
seductive

Blaze Romance™
...the temperature's
rising

Medical Romance™
...medical drama on
the pulse

Historical Romance™
...rich, vivid and
passionate

27 new titles every month.

*With all kinds of Romance for
every kind of mood...*

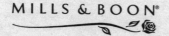

MILLS & BOON®

the

Mother's Day

collection

Margaret Way Kate Hoffmann Helen Dickson

Money Off Voucher

see inside for details

Available from 21st February 2003

Available at most branches of WH Smith, Tesco, Martins, Borders, Eason, Sainsbury's and all good paperback bookshops.

0303/024/MB65

Become a Panel Member

If YOU are a regular United Kingdom buyer of Mills & Boon® Historical Romance™ you might like to tell us your opinion of the books we publish to help us in publishing the books *you* like.

Mills & Boon have a Reader Panel of Historical Romance™ readers. Each person on the panel receives a short questionnaire (taking about five minutes to complete) every third month asking for opinions of the past month's Historical Romances. All people who send in their replies have a chance of winning a FREE year's supply of Historical Romances.

If YOU would like to be considered for inclusion on the panel please fill in and return the following survey. We can't guarantee that everyone will be on the panel but first come will be first considered.

Where did you buy this novel?

❑ WH Smith
❑ Tesco
❑ Borders
❑ Sainsbury's
❑ Direct by mail
❑ Other (please state) _____

What themes do you enjoy most in the Mills and Boon® novels that you read? (Choose all that apply.)

❑ Amnesia
❑ Family drama (including babies/young children)
❑ Hidden/Mistaken identity
❑ Marriage of convenience
❑ Medieval
❑ Regency
❑ Elizabethan England
❑ Forced proximity
❑ Mock engagement or marriage
❑ Revenge

- [ ] Sheikh
- [ ] Shared pasts
- [ ] Western

On average, how many Mills & Boon® novels do you read every month? _____

Please provide us with your name and address:

Name: _____

Address: _____

_____

_____

_____

What is your occupation?
(OPTIONAL)
_____

In which of the following age groups do you belong?
(OPTIONAL)

- [ ] 18 to 24
- [ ] 25 to 34
- [ ] 35 to 49
- [ ] 50 to 64
- [ ] 65 or older

Thank you for your help!
Your feedback is important in helping us offer
quality products you value.

The Reader Service
Reader Panel Questionnaire
FREEPOST CN81
Croydon CR9 3WZ

HISTRD502

FREE!

2 Books
and a surprise gift!

We would like to take this opportunity to thank you for reading this Mills & Boon® book by offering you the chance to take TWO more specially selected titles from the Historical Romance™ series absolutely FREE! We're also making this offer to introduce you to the benefits of the Reader Service™ —

- ★ FREE home delivery
- ★ FREE gifts and competitions
- ★ FREE monthly Newsletter
- ★ Books available before they're in the shops
- ★ Exclusive Reader Service discount

Accepting these FREE books and gift places you under no obligation to buy; you may cancel at any time, even after receiving your free shipment. Simply complete your details below and return the entire page to the address below. *You don't even need a stamp!*

YES! Please send me 2 free Historical Romance books and a surprise gift. I understand that unless you hear from me, I will receive 4 superb new titles every month for just £3.49 each, postage and packing free. I am under no obligation to purchase any books and may cancel my subscription at any time. The free books and gift will be mine to keep in any case.

H3ZEB

Ms/Mrs/Miss/Mr ....Initials................................
BLOCK CAPITALS PLEASE

Surname..

Address..

....

....Postcode ....

Send this whole page to:
UK: The Reader Service, FREEPOST CN81, Croydon, CR9 3WZ
EIRE: The Reader Service, PO Box 4546, Kilcock, County Kildare (stamp required)